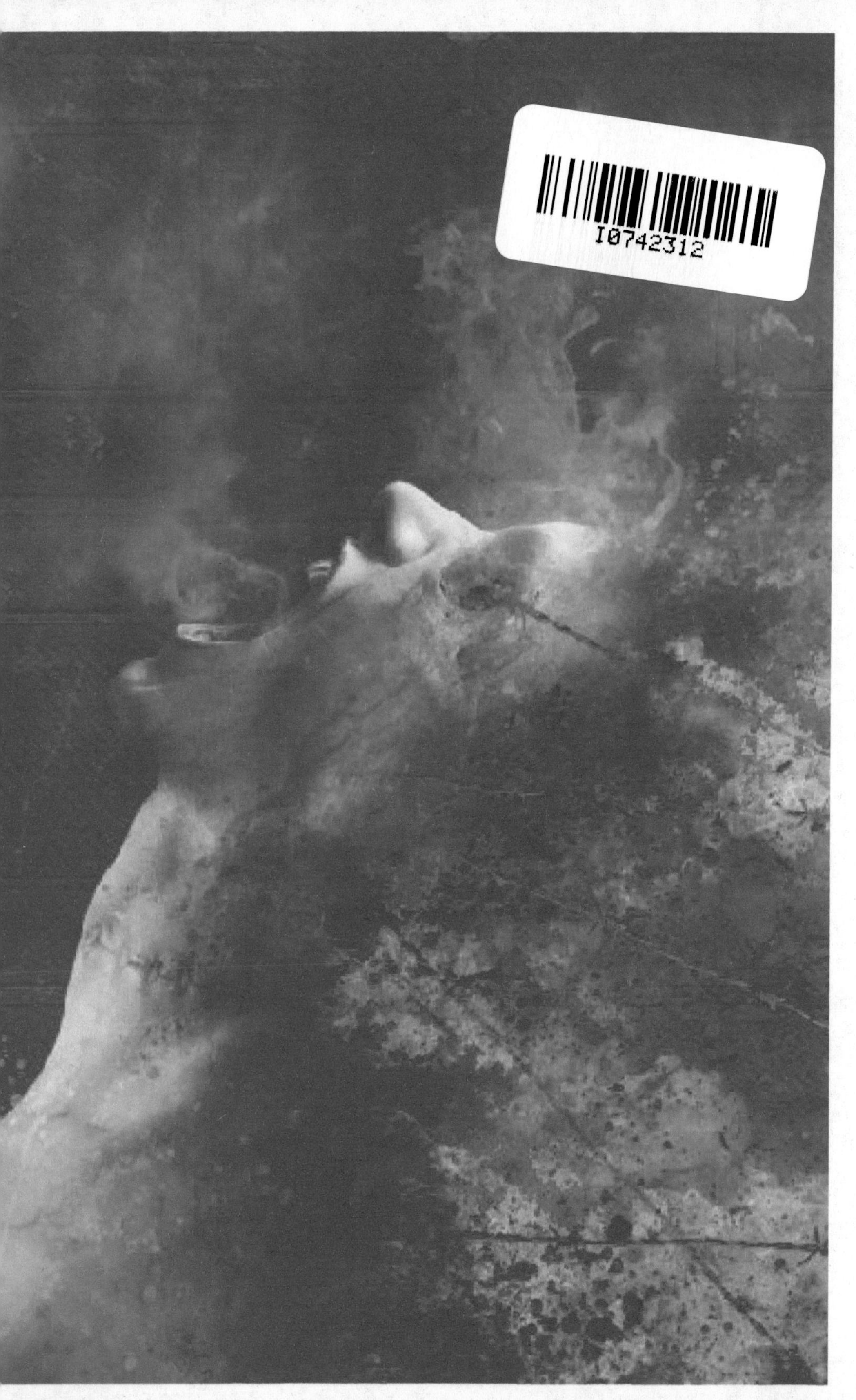

THE VOICES IN YOUR HEAD

JEFF OLIVER

ILLUSTRATED BY DAN VERKYS

Lycan Valley Press Publications
1002 N Meridian STE 100-153
Puyallup, Washington 98371
United States of America

First Edition

ISBN-13: 978-1-64562-051-8

"Utilizing prose, verse, and art, The Voices in Your Head offers a unique, hallucinatory trip into a spiraling nightmare of blood, pain, and madness."
—*Pedro Iniguez, Author of Synthetic Dawns & Crimson Dusks. Bram Stoker Award winning Author.*

"Geoff Hathaway is plagued by insanity. Or demons. Or both. You won't know, but you will care. Jeff Oliver's powerful, gory, flesh-eating page-turner will keep you up all night, checking the doors and windows to your soul. This way madness lies. Be warned. And be there."
—*Anna Taborska, award-winning author of For Those Who Dream Monsters and Bloody Britain.*

"Jeff Oliver is an inkwell of creativity, his ever-palpitating heart word-spilling without abandon onto the page."
—*Michael Bailey, multi-award-winning writer and editor.*

"Jeff Oliver's debut novel is a tightly woven and gruesome tale of terror. A story I could not look away from until the very end. One that will remain with me for quite a while. Job well done! The wicked illustrations by Dan Verkys are a bonus!"
—*Cindy O'Quinn, Bram Stoker Award-winning author.*

"Jeff Oliver's Voices in your Head is a chilling, first-person dive into a hallucinogenic hell that manages to be both poetic and profound ... the diary of a soul damned ... think Clive Barker meets Dante, but with Oliver's unique prosody ... a compelling artistic achievement."
—*John Palisano, Bram Stoker Award-Winning author of Requiem and Ghost Heart.*

Better The Demons You Know

Jeff Oliver's "The Voices in Your Head" is a grizzly, compelling portrait of a man far beyond the edge of insanity. Geoff Hathaway's demons speak to him: the ghost of his dead mother, a demon posing as his father. One is never entirely sure if they're figments of his twisted imagination or literal phantoms and parasitic beasts from hell. Each day, he's visited by the same twenty-one spirits and demons, supernatural creatures that are lovingly illustrated by the talented Dan Verkys.

In the broken mind of Geoff Hathaway, emotions are not processed by the guilt-free, fearless protagonist, but by a series of strange characters that parade through his head. Each of his visitors seem to encapsulate a different sector of his being, an aspect of his early life trauma.

Geoff Hathaway's bizarre hallucinations appear to him in vivid visitations that feel very authentic to me as a person who has post-traumatic stress disorder and bipolar disorder with psychotic features. According to the National Institutes for Mental Health,

1.5 to 3.5 percent of people meet the diagnostic criteria for a psychotic disorder such as schizophrenia or schizoaffective disorder, but many more will experience psychotic symptoms at some point in their lifetime. More than half of people with bipolar disorder experience psychotic symptoms such as myself. Auditory hallucinations (hearing voices, or sounds that are not there), visual hallucinations (seeing people who are not there), and tactical hallucinations (feeling someone touch you who isn't there) are all examples of psychosis. However, most of us aren't violent and haven't developed anything like Geoff's criminal behavior and insatiable desire for blood.

At first, one may find oneself almost sympathetic toward Geoff based on his somewhat tragic backstory. The horrible specters in his head are the only ones to keep him company, along with his art, poetry, and obsessive pondering over whether or not he truly deserves his fate.

Soon, he begins to reveal himself as malignantly deplorable. His derangement is extreme, and the actions that lead to his incarceration are gut-wrenching acts of pure grisly horror. A truly loathsome fellow with an addiction to human flesh, he's been locked up since he was a teenager and has shown himself a danger anytime he's been in contact with other human beings. Therefore, he's locked up to prevent himself from endangering others. He credits his demons with his strange appetites and compares himself to a tiger, with humanity as his prey.

Geoff's alienation starkly contrasts with the touching humanity of certain visiting spirits... his mother, and his brother. Despite their grisly appearance (and sometimes even more disturbing smells), these apparitions are warm, personable, and even caring. They have their own stories, which they share with Geoff and the reader when they come to visit. Each tale gives a little more insight into his past, how he became the monster he is today, and how he became cursed with these visions and this terrible hunger.

I have known Jeff Oliver as a poet for half a decade now. His debut novel is engrossing and brings the same kind of hard-hitting metal energy as his dark poetry but with a great deal more gore. He has a true gift for the gross, combined with a knack for campfire-style storytelling that weaves its way through the envelope story, and the shorter tales found in its innards.

Each of the shorter vignettes is illustrated with a different weathered, haunting image by Dan Verkys. The Australian visual artist crafts images that run the gamut from moody, ghostly images like the haunting portrait of Geoff Hathaway's mother, to the terrifying images of sewn together, mutant creatures from Hell like the one labeled Nightmare. Not one of these images using AI.

—Sumiko Saulson, two-time Bram Stoker Award Nominated author of Melancholia: A Book of Dark Poetry

THE VOICES IN YOUR HEAD

THE HIVE MIND

My NAME IS Geoff Hathaway. My voices plaque me like a swarm of locusts, devouring everything inside me, leaving nothing behind. I am certain they will haunt me long after I die here in this cage. I'll never forget the day my mind changed forever. I'll never forget the day I sealed this fate for myself. I've created within my conscience this new living hell. I am now merely a shell of the person I once was, staring at the same walls that I have been staring at for the last twenty-seven years. Twenty-seven years of watching others come and go, back to their freedom, knowing that I'll never again see mine, is the worst kind of torture imaginable. I deserve to be here. I know that. However, this does not change the fact that this is not rehabilitation. This is not the way that I will improve. Society imposes life sentences on those of us who commit horrific acts, many of which are committed at a young age. They put us in cages for life with no real goals for any kind of rehabilitation, just punishment and pain.

I have been here for a very long time and all I have had are those fake, man-made hands of time ticking away in my mind. I have had ample time to document my experiences during my imprisonment. And I will have many more years after this too. I am never leaving; I will never walk in a park again, drive a car, get married, or have children. None of it. That all was stripped away from me when I made that tragic mistake on August 23, 1997. I will explain the significance of that date as I continue. I never had the opportunity to experience a normal childhood or grow up in society. I was only fourteen years old when I broke into that house in the middle of the night and killed the three men responsible for murdering my entire family. I often tell myself that it wasn't a mistake and that I did the right thing. But did I? If I did the right thing, I wouldn't be here, right? I wouldn't be rotting here.

The names of the three men are now distant memories, and I've given up trying to remember them. But what I do see and remember, replaying every fucking day, is the way they busted into our home in the dark of night and killed both of my parents and my three older brothers. I heard the intruders breaking the locks and whispering amongst themselves. I crept and hid in the very back of the closet, listening as my family begged for their lives while being slain by these unknown intruders. I was crying and holding my mouth closed so I wouldn't make a sound. There was a hidden door at the back of my closet behind my hanging clothes. You couldn't have seen it unless you were looking for it.

I still hide away in that closet in my mind, even all these years later. I'm still scared all the time. As I said, I never had the chance to learn and develop into a healthy adult. My mind is frozen in the moment that I lost everything I loved. I waited for them to leave, terrified of what I was about to see. Everything I've ever known and loved was gone, just like that. I saw my brothers, mother, and father lying side by side with their throats slashed. It's all I see when I close my eyes. They were lined up like they were on display. I did the only thing I could think of—I ran out of the house, screaming for someone to look my way. That was the very first day when I realized my now uncontrollable insanity was starting to take shape. Life was not supposed to be like this.

The manifestation of my mother puts her finger to her lips to quiet me and reassure me that everything would be okay. I continue to see her to this very day, though she doesn't look the same as I remember. She is all white and surrounded by a smoky haze. Her eyeballs are missing, and only deep dark hollow pits remain. She has cuts all over her face. Her throat is still dripping blood from when her life was tragically taken. I can't, for the fucking life of me, figure out if she is real or just another figment of my traumatized mind state. When I arrived here, I was silent and had already lost my way. The internal pain of seeing them in that state had driven me to the point of eternal rage.

I have conversations with my deceased mother, brothers, and father every day. They would follow me even if I was able to leave this tragic place. The prison where I am contained is located on the coast of eastern Maine. I believe the town is Cape Elizabeth, I am so disoriented that I don't even know where I am anymore most of the time, but it doesn't matter. I will never be able to enjoy this place. I will never enjoy the beauty of the ocean in this beautiful coastal society. I am a destructive force, a danger to anyone that comes into contact with me. You will have to watch this unfold to understand why I say this.

I can only learn about the world from the books they allow me to read. I read every day; I write every day too. I have been by myself the entire time I've been here, and it has been messing with my mind. I scream all the time because I am confined with my deceased family and constantly watch my inner demons come to life. I say that in one breath. I have also created numerous illustrations of the hallucinations that I experience on a daily basis. Are they real? I will never truly know. I write and create in an attempt to find some form of humanity, however, it still never comes.

Being alone forces me to tap into my creativity, otherwise my inner demons will continue to consume me. Well, they already have.

MY DECEASED MOTHER

I AM WRITING, drawing, and reading. I'm composing the songs of the deceased as the walls continue to bleed. I have been ripping my hair out while screaming. My father also appears to me daily, but not the father that I have been yearning for. He does not resemble or behave like himself. It seems as though he has emerged straight from the depths of Hell. He blames me for what those men did to him and never thanks me for seeking revenge. I continually yell at him and remind him that he is not my father. Each time he visits, I must clarify my actions in immaculate detail, as he refuses to leave until everything is thoroughly explained. I have to relive my crimes repeatedly in my mind and vocalize them as well. This is my reality and I am unable to change it. I am trying to explain, *'Dad, I killed those men for closure, for our family, for Mom, for Marcus, Daniel, Nick, and for you! I have sought vengeance for all of you. Why can't you remember this? Why must I repeat myself?"*

The demon in front of me was never my father. I still call him Dad because nothing in this place is clear. So, I must constantly retell him how I exacted my revenge. I vividly recall the faces of the three men that robbed me of my family. I have committed them to memory. I witnessed them together in a convenience store one day as I was returning home from therapy. Witnessing the events of my childhood compelled me to seek help.

However, when I attended therapy sessions, they did not help and I hated it.

I briefly caught a glimpse of them through the window before I ran out screaming as they left my house on that fateful evening. Their vacant expressions were imprinted in my memory, consuming my every thought. They toyed with my mind—I dreamt of them, I dreamt of my revenge. I watched as they entered an old black van. I was accompanied by my grandma at the time and I miss her dearly. Suddenly paralyzed by rage, I quickly fled in the direction they were heading, between the houses. It was imperative that I did not lose sight of them. From a safe distance, I observed them laughing, knowing full well what they had done. The two men who were not driving were holding cheap beers in their hands. I observed them stopping at every red light and began strategizing my plan.

I trailed them until they parked in a driveway on a side street in town. I cannot remember the name of the street, but rest assured, I remembered the route to that house. That night, I had planned to sneak out. The demon posing as my father spoke, as it always does, repeating the familiar phrase, *"Continue, my child."* Despite this, I must persist, and so I will. On the night of August 23, 1997, I remembered that my grandfather had a gun in the closet in his room. He kept it for protection in case someone were to break into the house. It was on the top shelf in a small, gray box. It had always been locked, but my anger caused me to smash it open on the floor. To this day, I'll never know where that strength came from, but I have an idea. I removed the loaded gun from the box after smashing it open and placed it into my red backpack. In addition, I retrieved his brass knuckles, complete with a razor-sharp knife on the end. These were among the impressive objects that my grandfather would often collect. My grandparents used to visit me here, but they have both since passed away. I can't wait to see them again.

It was at that point I snuck out of my grandparents' house, which was the last time I would ever see it. I traced the same route as the one I had taken on the day I encountered the men at the convenience store. The house was shadowed in darkness and excluded a sense of foreboding. I sensed my inner being becoming consumed with retribution. I approached the door with thoughts of revenge echoing in my mind. It was finally time to make them pay for what they had done. I didn't have a disguise on, they didn't see me when they entered my house and took everything away. I was determined to finish this. The house was quiet and still, yet to my surprise, it was unlocked. I couldn't believe how easy it was to get in. There were no stairs in this monstrous house. I was the tiger, and they were the sleeping deer. Quietly, I entered each room, making sure to muffle the sound of the gun with a small pillow. With a *click* and a muffled *bang*, I moved on to the next room. *Click*, muffled *bang*, *click*, muffled *bang*. Finally, all that remained was for them to be dismembered and consumed. I was far from finished. I welcomed the scent of gunpowder from my grandfather's gun, inhaling in order to remember what I had become.

I remembered the brass knuckles with the razor-sharp blade. It was now time to have some fun. I pulled it out of my blood-colored backpack and held it for a while, visualizing my next attack. While they were all dead, it still didn't feel like enough—it wasn't sufficient. I desired to taste all of their blood. I inserted my fingers into the luminous brass holes and commenced striking the first man's face until it appeared as though it had been pulverized into a mixture of red and beige playdough. A feeling of relief and closure flooded my tormented spirit. I proceeded to the face of the next corpse persisting in my infliction of blows. One by one, I mutilated them until their bodies were smashed beyond recognition. As I gazed at my reflection in the blade, I began to laugh. *"I must continue!"* I screamed aloud, repeating the line over and over as I removed each limb from each corpse. They were unable to scream, and the sight was truly beautiful. Since that day, they couldn't hurt me anymore and my revenge was critical. What I did next will shock you. *"My father,"* who is now a demon, always interrupts me when I tell this story and asks, *"Were they all as satisfying as the taste of revenge?"*

My answer is always the same. My answer was always *"yes."* I made my way into their filthy small kitchen and pulled out every pot and pan I could find. It was time to boil the water. My revenge was to taste sweet on this night. The three men will all become the pieces of shit that they were. I planned to consume them all and then flush them after they had been digested. That is precisely what I did. I scoured the house for something with greater cutting power. This small knife was inadequate for slicing through all of these cowards. I discovered a hacksaw and proceeded to prepare my meals. I meticulously dissected the torsos and effortlessly removed all of their internal organs, swiftly submerging them into the boiling pots. The walls were now splattered with a fresh, vibrant crimson hue. I witnessed their bodies transform into something exquisite—something completely new. I found myself manically laughing at their newfound beauty. I then searched their fridge for hot sauce to add a spicy kick. At the tender age of fourteen, it was a surreal feeling of satisfaction to consume all the organs and entrails of my targets, from their intestines to their livers, hearts, and kidneys—everything that had once sustained their lives, and I savored every moment of it.

I'll never forget when I first pushed them out. Witnessing them transform into a pile of shit was the most satisfying experience of my entire life. Even to this day, nothing can compare to the satisfaction I felt during that first flush. It was euphoric, knowing that the three men who murdered my family were swirling around in that filthy toilet bowl. What an adrenaline rush! I carefully diced them into the smallest pieces with the tools at my disposal. I then experimented with various cooking methods such as boiling, baking, microwaving, and broiling. I saved their heads for the final step—using my creativity to make the most of my resources.

I wanted to relish the moment when I cracked open their skulls and removed each of their brains. I even consumed them. I stayed in that house for more then a week and even saw my grandparents searching for me on the news. I loved them deeply and hoped they understood my intentions. During that week in my family's murderers' house, I consumed every piece of them. I even used a cheese grater to grind down each bone. I filled saltshakers with a brand-new condiment. It was a lot of work, but I felt it was necessary.

They took so much from me, which led me to take everything from them. Now, they are nothing but human waste floating below the streets. That is what they have become—literal shit. And to this day, I am proud of it. However, I was caught in the moment and savoring it a little too much. That is how I was eventually discovered, as a neighbor came knocking on the door. I was covered in blood with the remaining waste parts still boiling on the stovetop. I caught a glimpse of her through the window, and she saw me. She let out a blood-curdling scream and quickly dialed the local police. *"9-1-1, what is your emergency?"*

We are aware of how those phone calls often unfold. She owned one of the earlier, bulkier Nokia models, unlike the sleek and advanced ones the world is accustomed to now. Nowadays, it is a rather antiquated device. I know this because I read about everything. It also allowed two-way calling, which even my grandparents had. I tried running and hiding, but was unsuccessful. My effort was in vein and as a result, I now find myself here. People screamed in horror upon seeing a young boy running down the street in broad daylight, covered in blood. Many assumed it was my blood. My mind went blank and I froze. I felt my body hit the ground before a police officer picked me up, exclaiming, "*That child is injured, let's help him!*" He then asked, "*Son, what happened?*"

I couldn't speak. I couldn't move. I was in such a euphoric state, I didn't care about the consequences of my actions. At such a young age, I lost my life and freedom completely after all three of those bastards were consumed. Didn't they deserve it? I recount that story to my deceased father every single day. I drew a picture of him as well. Isn't he handsome? Within these walls, as I've mentioned before, there isn't much else to do. Just like those bastards who killed my family, I too am being consumed.

My Deceased Father

I AM UNCERTAIN whether the entities I encounter here are ghosts or demons, or if I am simply experiencing hallucinations. They visit me every day and while I am frightened, I welcome their presence to alleviate my boredom. It's always the same; they come in the same order, in a perfect repeating line. I've lost my privilege of one hour a day outside when, at the age of sixteen, I bit a prison guard's nose off and ate it in front of him on my way outside. It was the last time I walked outside. I think I am forty-two years old now, but I am not completely certain of my age anymore.

After that day, I started to be visited by a woman with two nooses and a blindfold covering her eyes around that same time. Her majestic black wings and a pile of skulls below her leave me puzzled as I try to understand their source. Without fail, she appears at 3:33 pm. I can always smell and hear her approach. She emanates a scent of death and emits screams from her private area where three mouths remain intact. She consistently utters only one word, *"Choose."* I have never responded to her as I fear her intentions. I am not suicidal, but I believe that is her desired outcome. Is she another demon? Is she a monster? Is she a spirit coming to make me pay for what I've done? I won't choose the noose. I won't go out that way. I am stronger than that. I scream at her to go away!

It's the same every day at precisely 3:33 on the dot. She comes and says, *"Choose!"* *"I will never choose!"* I shout, *"Fuck you!"* She never utters another word. I've been in solitude for such an extended period that my thoughts have become inherently preposterous. This alarming woman consistently manifests and remains confined within my cell for precisely one hour and twenty-seven minutes, not a minute exceeding or falling short. I long to discover a means to rationalize all of this. I realize that my actions pose a danger to those around me, however, that does not mean I am giving up. I believe that is what she desires, but I am not entirely sure. Every day, I am forced to endure the sights and smells of her presence until she returns to the place she came from. I am fairly certain that many of these visitors are insincere. How can I ensure consistency in my mind when these recurring voices arrive in the same order every day? It's always the same—songs, stories with identical statements and actions. It feels like a broken record playing on repeat in my traumatized mind.

RENEE

OF THE TWENTY-ONE voices that enter my prison cell every day, I can only see these visitors as they appear. As I write this, I will explain each one of them. While some of them terrify me more than others, they are all unique and beautiful in their own way. I have given each of them a name, starting with my deceased mother as the first vision and my deceased father as the second. I have named the woman with the nooses Renee. I am constantly searching for ways to pass the time in my eternal cage. Eighteen more on the way, some tell different stories, but none of them look the same. Never a misstep or a change. I believe I am already in hell. I can still taste the intestinal tracts of the three men who made me this way.

I can still see them floating in that toilet before flushing the waste. I know that I am insane. There is no doubt. Will I ever have the courage to take myself out? Have I been rehabilitated? The answer will always be no. I will always crave the violence that I inflicted so many years ago. It is like an addiction, which is why I find myself alone. Whenever I encounter another person, I am tempted to slit their throats and imagine drinking their blood from the wound. The thought of boiling the remains in a pot of human stew fills my mind. These horrific cravings will always be a part of me. Perhaps these visitors are manifestations of my cravings, a mixture of good and evil like the complex human soup I consumed. Self-reflection is a common occurrence while confined.

I am currently reflecting on my trial and recalling the horror that was evident on the faces of those in the courtroom. I could sense the fear that permeated the room, but I had no remorse for my actions. I do not regret the monster I had become and I will never feel remorse for it. I did not intend to prolong the explanation, so I provided a detailed account of my actions. I wanted to feel and bask in their fear. I wanted to embody the ferocity of a tiger in that room and prey upon the hapless deer. Even then, I was drooling for the flavor. As I detailed the sounds of the three men's bones snapping, the sensations of their flesh tearing, and the flavors of their body parts, I observed that the majority of the people in the courtroom were growing nauseous, with some even vomiting as I explained my horrific crimes. Even the judge broke out in a cold sweat. It was a display of incredible power, and I felt fucking invincible.

At the start and conclusion of the trial, I was questioned: *"Geoff Hathaway, how do you plead?"* On both occasions, I firmly responded, *"Guilty, your Honor."* Each admission of guilt was met with a self-assured smile. Before exiting the courtroom, the sister of one of the men whom I had consumed exclaimed, *"You are a monster!"* I glanced at her and stated in a calm manner, *"He was also a monster, he killed my mother, father, and three brothers. If you had been there, I would have eaten you too."* Her eyes widened before she resumed her seat. I imagined that I would scalp her and hear her screams of despair, knowing that I would never see the outside world again once the sentence was executed.

We were awaiting the Jury's return. The verdict only took ten minutes to reach. The Judge then addressed the court, saying, *'All Rise.' Ladies and gentlemen of the Jury, have you reached a verdict?'* A tall woman on the jury responded, *'We have, Your Honor. We the Jury, find the defendant Geoff Hathaway guilty on three counts of homicide in the first degree.'* There were numerous other charges; however, I will only document the most severe ones here. I know I am guilty, and I will always admit to my guilt. Due to my extended time spent in solitary confinement, my memory has become clouded. Despite being only fourteen years old, I was tried as an adult. The Judge stated, *"All rise." "The State of Maine has sentenced Geoff Hathaway to life in prison without the possibility of parole." "He will be granted one hour of supervised exercise outside each day."*

I forfeited that privilege two years later, as I mentioned previously. I still have a vivid memory of the taste of the prison guard's snot, which I consumed with gusto. I drank it up like an ice cold slushy, but without the brain freeze. Delicious! He resigned immediately after. The courtroom erupted in cheers. However, no one seemed interested in the reasons behind my actions or my intent. The next coarse of action I took was a shock to the entire courtroom. I was being escorted out of the courtroom by an officer, I walked past one of the murderer's sisters, who had previously referred to me as a monster. The security guard's grip on my hands was not firm, so I seized the chance to demonstrate just how much of a monster I was capable of being.

I waited for my opportunity. I carefully calculated it. When the timing was right, I lunged forward and landed on top of her, immediately biting down. I tore off both of her ears and bit into her eyes. Then, with the strength of a tiger, I forcefully ripped out her left eye using only my teeth. My hands were cuffed, but my mouth was still free. I quickly chewed and swallowed it. Then, I bit into her right eye and laughed maniacally as the interior of her eyeball dripped and ran between my teeth, pooling on my tongue.

I whispered to her as her blind eye sockets leaked, *"Now you look like a real monster and you will never forget me. Your eyes taste so sweet."* I thoroughly appreciated the cacophony of screams emanating from the courtroom. Suddenly, I found myself plunged into darkness as I later discovered that someone had sedated me. To be honest, I can't fault them for their actions. That day was truly remarkable! Wait, I believe the name of the sister of one of my family's murderers, whose eyeballs I consumed, is Renee. Is she the one with the nooses and the majestic black wings?

THE DEVILFISH

AFTER RENEE LEAVES my cell, I'm visited by what I call the *"Devilfish"*: a demon engulfed in flames with tentacles that appear to be growing from its head. Its eyes are orange and almost red, and it is another voice that screams in my head, instructing me to kill. It stirs up my addiction to consuming human flesh. The Devilfish is a nightmare to me because I am confined and unable to do as it commands. It sings as it burns, filling my cell with a mysterious mist. It is not smoke, and it does not hinder my breathing in any way. Its only purpose is to sing instructions to me, ordering me to feed and commanding me to break free. The Devilfish exposes my addiction, and I have an intense desire to feed. I strike my fists against the wall every time it arrives. Its singing is amazingly beautiful as it shrieks. This entity drives me to the brink of a mental breakdown every single day. Almost every dreadful visitor brings out the worst in me. The Devilfish continues to chant its songs of the flesh. I repeatedly bash my head into the walls.

I am eagerly awaiting the guards to make their rounds and provide us with our trays as lunchtime approaches. However, I am not craving the food they bring, but rather them themselves. As I stand by the small slot in my cell door, I eagerly anticipate the chance to consume some fresh flesh. I don't mind if it's just a little. The Devilfish is still singing while perched on my cell bed, watching me closely with its emotionless eyes. The demon is so terrifying that it brings tears to mine. The fire that engulfs it doesn't burn anything around it, nor has it ever done so before. As the guard approached, I remained silent and waited.

"Geoff, here's your lunch," he said. The meals they brought reminded me of my family's murderers floating around in that disgusting toilet and the smell even resembled them, like shit. I remained focused on the slot in my cell door. I was not cuffed, and he placed the tray through the small opening. It a swift movement akin to a tiger I pounced and grabbed his arm. I fractured the guard's arm and began devouring it like a ravenous predator. His agonized screams filled me with a sense of elation, ecstasy, and enchantment. The Devilfish hummed along in the background, harmonizing its melody with the guards cries. It became an incredible song of both screams and beauty while the fire still blazed around the demon.

I also bit off all four of the guard's fingers and the thumb of his right hand, which crunched like carrots in my foaming mouth. Like the addict that I am, I was temporarily fulfilled. The cravings always return. They never disappear. I blacked out again, just like in the courtroom. Once again, I was sedated. I often dream of being a normal human being, but I know that will never be a reality. I was strapped to a bed and could not break free. I was transferred from my cell to even higher security. I could still taste the guard's fingers because I still had blood and flesh between my teeth. It was always so sweet. I often dream of waking up to find that all of this has been nothing but a terrible nightmare. As I lie and scream in my cell, on my uncomfortable bed, staring at the ceiling, I refuse to look this creature in the eyes. Enveloped in my hauntingly disturbing yet captivating voices and memories, I hear a chilling tale sung by the passing

Devilfish every day:

Her Soul to be Claimed

Mark is sleeping and suddenly, he hears a beating outside his windowpane. He realizes that something is reaching for him, and it seems to need to feed on his constantly bleeding soul. It's creeping and leaning closer to him, while he screams in terror. Like a parasite in heat; it begins to consume him from within. He is on his knees, pleading, in dire need of relief. The creature's vileness permeates the air, with a foul odor reminiscent of misery, metal, death, and crippling denial. The room suddenly turns cold, causing Mark to freeze like winter snow. He finds himself unable to move or even breathe, with nowhere to escape. His skin feels as though it is peeling away from his bones. His eyes are gouged out, leaving only the windows to his soul.

Dusk turns to dawn, the physical agony is unbearable. He screams until his vocal cords are torn violently from his throat. His insides are worn by the demon, like a warm winter coat. Its eyes are black and hollow, visible only by the flickering flames that devour the human flesh which it gazes at and chews on. And as it continues its gruesome feast, it begins to speak and sing, marking the beginning of Mark's descent to Hell.

The demon proclaimed, *"Welcome, my child. This is only the beginning. If you think this is pain, know that I am far from finished. Once I have your soul in my grasp, I will repeatedly, lash, burn, and cut you. I will cripple and bleed you, leaving you in eternal agony. You will scream again and again. I will peel the skin away from your bones, eat the flesh you once knew, pound your skull, and suck your brain. Hell is not a pleasant place, and I will continue to assert my dominance as King by killing you over and over again."*

Mark's soul is fading as the demon masquerades, causing him to lose his grip. He cannot hold on as it continues to play the serenading song, which is like a twisted lullaby. Flames surround them both, and the entity revels in the misery of every wrongdoing. Mark cannot pray, as he cannot distinguish between night and day. As his life slowly fades away, there will be a price to be paid. Hell awaits, and Mark has been prepared for the infernal flames.

Jason heard screams coming from his brother's room. He crept down the hallway, planning on how to react. However, as he approached, the screams suddenly stopped. What he is about to witness is vicious and violent, showing no mercy for a human soul. It intends for you to scream, give up, and fold. As Jason makes his way through the now ominous hallway, he feels the temperature drop, sending chills down his shaken spine. Unaware of what awaits him, he proceeds to open his brother's bedroom door, unknowingly putting his vulnerable soul at risk.

His brother's body parts were scattered around, with blood painting the walls and flooding the bedroom floor. As darkness prepared its next lure, an instant strike and invisible bite occurred. Jason began to lose his sight, unable to distinguish between wrong and right. All he could see were the flames, confused by the melody of the demon's song—a tune that sought agony. The darkness is picking at every flaw he possesses, while the phantom is preparing to take it all—every memory that exists in his mind and every ounce of energy that once gave him life. The creature is preparing to drive the knife in, while Jason, weakened, is unable to defend himself. Suddenly, a vicious blow to the back of his head causes blood to leak—a deep crimson red. The shadows convey a message—one that requires careful interpretation, utilizing the wound as a means to dip their paintbrushes.

The message written in blood is as follows:

"Your soul is mine. I will take it as I please. You are too weak to defeat me. I am the master of Darkness. Bow down. You are my cattle. You are my cow. You will bleed like the meat you are. On my plate, you will be a star. Add salt and pepper. Sprinkle with lime juice to taste. You mean nothing. You are a waste. Keep the faith, because your faith is a lie. Here's the truth: everything eventually dies. I am about to show you what you will become—meat for the feast. You will bleed, and I will eat. I am your King now. Hell awaits your soul at last, and I will have the final laugh. You will spend eternity here, in constant paranoia and fear. No one is here to save you, as I peel away your skin. Allow the screams to begin.

Jason's hollow eye sockets presented baby blue and black flames within, leaving nowhere for his now lost soul to hide. The flames revealed his purposeless existence, leaving nothing but silent cries. The entity in control showed no remorse, as it was welcomed in without force. Jason was constantly reminded as it peeled away his skin, leaving him unblinded. Every exposed bone was broken, roasting each organ as his screams echoed. A toast to the entity in control, in hell, as the damned man now pays the ultimate price for his soul—he must bear hell's toll.

Jason is unable to articulate or understand his bodily sensations and visual perception. As he silently screams in agony, the chilling figure calls out his name and mercilessly annihilates his spirit, toying with him in its twisted game. Riddled with helpless rage, he screams until dawn, his name forgotten. He cannot even bring himself to pray, as it is far too late for that. Jason, who joined his brother Mark in the shadows, never again saw the sun rise over the horizon, overwhelmed by the agonizing and dark presence of the malicious phantom.

Alexa hears screams coming from both ends of the house. She lies frozen in fear and silence, as quiet as a skittish mouse. Too terrified to make a sound, she hears her brother's constant screaming. She cannot see what is happening, but she hears everything—every scream, every bite, every splatter of blood in the night. She hears them cry out for help as she lies there, frozen—with eyes wide open, unable to assist them in any way. She can hear them screaming from their rooms, now transformed into tombs. She is completely helpless and unable to determine what to do to help them. She is unable to even scream or move her feet, as the malicious entity has rendered her too weak. She is the host to a parasite that feeds on every part of her being. She is controlled by the darkness, with no control at all. Hell has entered her very soul, causing her eyes to roll back into her skull. Her skin is lashed from the demon's hold as she screams in tongues unlike her own.

The devil inside of her holds her down by the throat. She keeps hearing screams in the dusk, praying in silence for it to let go. However, it won't. It stays, and it will never go away. It has rein over her soul now, and it is too late. Blood begins to leak from the walls and the screams become louder, echoing down the frigid halls. She begins to laugh uncontrollably. She thrashes violently, her legs kicking and kicking. The viscous tar-like vomit spews, covering everything around her. She listens in silence as the demon lingers. She can hear the snarling hounds. The malevolent creature begins to speak again, revealing its plans.

It spoke once more:

Two brothers, dead; a shattered family now lies ahead. Though it may make me smile, listen to my laughter for a while. Listen, child, my plans are almost complete; I will not kill you, I'll only treat. I will use you to survive, emerging from the darkness where I no longer need to hide. Your body is now mine as I walk within you. This will continue for the rest of your life and you will not be able to reverse it. My possession of you is already complete. Until your body dies, it will serve as my vessel. After that, your soul will belong to me. You will join your brothers, who are already burning, in due time. Listen closely, as my demands are clear. You had invited me in, Alexa—you are the reason for my presence here. You requested my presence, Alexa, my dear sweet new little bitch. Did you anticipate a pleasing response, one without any difficulty? I chuckle at your misguided expectations, for you have sentenced yourself to an everlasting inferno.

Alexa glances down at her hands stained in a deep, dark red. The blood on her hands does not belong to her, but to the brothers she once loved. She tore them apart, limb from limb. The demon that controlled her caused every lash, every bite, and every scream that echoed into the moonlit night. The memorizing dusk was relentless, but the dawn never arrived for Mark and Jason. The Devil had forcefully taken it away, leaving them defenseless. Within Alexa's presence, there was an icy chill and a commanding authority. A demonic being, repulsive and malicious, she tore open their throats and left behind pools of blood at her scorching feet.

Her spirit was trapped in her bed, yet her physical form gave in to the demon's desire, delighting in the sound of her brother's screams of agony—feasting on their tender, terrified flesh.

She is the reason why the demon was released into their house. She is the reason that hell now resides in this place. She is responsible for the slaughter of the cows. She is depraved, ruthless, and inhumanly cruel. She is licking her lips at the sight of her brother's blood. The bodies had been destroyed, their insides splattered and blood adorning the once-white walls. Nothing emanated from her but laughter. She was no longer Alexa, but a beast consumed by a ravenous hunger for blood and flesh. She would walk the earth in this state until the demon had temporarily satisfied its insatiable desires.

Mark and Jason never had a chance, now forever lost in the shadows. They will dance amidst the flames that will burn eternally. Someday, they will be reunited with the sister who called upon hell and erased their names. Amidst the licking flames and pain, they will endure the scorching rain and the twisted games of the grey gates, ravished and shamed. Alexa has endured the darkness, but not without consequences. The start of a new day brought forth a malevolent being, manipulating her mind. Although she remains human, she is no longer the same. As the vessel of evil, her soul is now imperiled. The rising flicker of eternity has only been postponed until her physical form perishes and deteriorates. When Alexa's spirit takes its eternal place, knowing what she wanted, she realizes there was an eternal price to pay. She lies amongst the blood of her brothers, screaming, *"This was not the way!"* She pleads to take this back, begging for her body back. She screams, *"I cannot be consumed by you, Demon! That is not the agreement we made."*

The demon laughed and spoke again:

Silence! The deal has been finalized. Your signature now binds you to this agreement. Your soul is now in my possession, for the entirety of your useless life. And when you pass on, you will rein in Hell as my illegitimate child. This is the consequence of your actions, as you have deliberately invoked me. The flames of my abode will be your eternal resting place. Grill the cattle, but only briefly. I prefer my steak rare. Welcome to your never-ending nightmare. Your brother, Mark, was already en route. He enjoyed causing harm to the young and couldn't resist it. No child was safe, and you begged me to intervene. You cannot rescind your actions. There is no way out of this agreement, as you willingly signed it in your own blood. Jason couldn't stay away from drugs. He drank excessively. He was physically abusive to his wife, and you couldn't tolerate it. You asked me to defend her. You asked me to get rid of him. And now that I fulfilled your request, you want to take it back? Alexa, you foolish one. The agreement is binding—the contract is you. Don't you remember? Deal with your fate, child. It's all you have left to do.

The shackles bind Alexa, trapped in a fit of anger, her screams echoing uncontrollably.

Confined in the filthy cage in Hell, she is lost in a maze of towering blood-soaked grass and scorching flames. Trapped in this cataclysmic haze, there seems to be no escape. The chains serve as an everlasting reminder of the Beast's mark. Both of her hands contained her brothers' brains, crimson mask on her face. The agreement she had made with the Devil had now been etched in stone. If only she had been aware of the fate that awaited her soul, she would have never summoned the infernal forces, causing the Lord of darkness to emerge from his throne.

As her body writhes in torment, her soul cries out in despair, trying to pray for redemption. However, she is silenced by the shadows that ensnare her throat. She is trapped in a never-ending slideshow, one that will continuously show her brothers being torn apart—eternally, over and over again. She lets out a piercing scream, begging for forgiveness, as her brothers' blood stains her hands. With tears streaming down her face, she grips their lifeless heads tightly, bidding farewell to the knowledge they once possessed. Their decapitations stain her lips and hands with blood—a result of her actions. She wails in frustration, *"I despise you, Demon!"* As she spits blood across the room, the dark entity reappears, ready to reveal her ultimate demise.

The entity laughs once more and says:

Please, pay attention to me, child. I will be the only thing you see from now on. You seem to have a fondness for the color red. I also notice you holding both your brothers' heads. You are the one who wished for their demise. By your own hands, their fate was sealed. Your hands were like a blade, peeling away their skin. Like a delicate fish fillet, the blood on your hands is all too real. I command you to live with me, in my company, for the duration of your life. Upon your passing, I reiterate, you will accompany me. Only Hell shall be your fate. You will humbly kneel and worship me, for I am the keeper of your aspirations. Listen attentively, for I am your God. Your soul shall decay in my grasp. You cannot retract this decision, as it has placed you where you are now. You must endure the consequences until your skin falls away. I will never disappear. The contract will remain in effect indefinitely.

Alexa now knows her fate: she will never escape. Her soul and body will now be wasted as the inferno takes control, awaiting her arrival. Her eyes widen as insanity triumphs and her laughter grows louder. All that remains are her sins: sins of the flesh, blood, murder, lust, gluttony, and wrath; greed and envy laced with pride. There is nowhere left for her to hide. Her mind, plagued with laziness. As her spirit begins to wither, The Devil smirks, in a triumphant guffaw. He has emerged victoriously, as he claims his path. As Alexa is consumed by hellfire, battling her inner rage, she is forced to confront her painful past.

She made it to dawn, but now she must pay. For the dusk of the murders, when her brothers faded away. She asked the Devil, to make them pay, through Alexa, he watched their bodies change. He watched her rip their insides out, while they shouted in agony. They screamed so loudly until silence finally arrived, peeling away at them like a serpent while they were still alive. Hissing in the darkness was a demon feeding on vengeance, forking out its tongue while a woman became deranged. Blood sprayed, leaked, and pooled as Alexa fell victim, becoming the Devil's pawn. She will scream day and night, through dusk and dawn, forever a mere player in his game of clowns. For Hell has now spawned. The keeper of the gates has one final message—one more message to convey, as Alexa screams within her eternal cage.

In closing, the monstrous Devil exclaims:

Listen carefully, child. I am becoming frustrated from having to constantly repeat myself. I have you now, your soul is sealed in the final step of the deal. Child, eternal life awaits you, but first you must live out the remaining years of your life, filled with wails of denial. In your mind, you will constantly revisit your gruesome murders: every incision, every penetration, every stained drop of blood lingering on your hands. You will recall every gut-wrenching scream that echoed from your brothers' horrified mouths. How I controlled your every move, how you followed me, and what you asked of me. In every remaining second of your life, you will witness each stroke of the knife. You will witness every glance exchanged between your siblings as you savagely took their lives, their cries for understanding pierce the air. Your destiny is determined, a binding contract set in burning stone. Hell will be your eternal reality, no escape or reprieve will be shown. There is no sense of direction, no up or down in this domain. Only flames that rise from the ground, as demons dance and rein. Your flesh, a delicacy to them, as they drool and salivate. The torment never-ending, with your skin in a constant state of flame.

Alexa cowers in a corner, surrounded by a pool of blood, as the demon devours all that she loves. Everything that scares her is constantly prodded, amidst the chaos the Devil laughs, as she struggles to breathe. Her madness echoes through the laughter, her soul crashes with every passing moment, the fire relentlessly attacks, bartering her very being. The essence of her spirit is dissolving, rendering her vision futile. Her final judgement stands, reckoning her transgressions. She summoned the power of the Devil, who often prevails.

Smoke wafted up from the ground—followed by the emergence of voracious hounds. Insanity came knocking, and she answered its door. Uncertain of the outcome, her imperfections exposed. She craved blood—but received much more. Everything she wanted was given in exchange for her unforgivable soul. The cold and calculated murder of her brothers was the result of a deal signed in blood. She had no choice but to take it, as she had lost control of her mind, body, and heart. She can't distinguish the finish line from the damn start. The Devil paints his masterpiece, leaving his signature mark. On her skin, a branded reminder; no one will ever be able to find her. She rocks back and forth, trapped in an inescapable maze. Everything looks different, yet the same. She's just a little bird in the Devil's birdcage.

The fine print had been overlooked, causing everything to become incomprehensible. It was an unforeseen aspect of the agreement made. Alexa's soul was now being cooked, as she was seared and marinated, while Hell repeatedly subjected her to the same nightmare. The butchering of her brothers continued from dusk until dawn, and the enflamed record player would never stop playing the same murderous song. Alexa beckoned him to finish the ultimate terror. She desired the demise of Mark and Jason, haunted by voices. She shrieked from her bed as the walls turned scarlet, her body becoming a harbor for the Devil as he fed. She clasped the severed heads of her brothers once more, wide, lifeless, hollow eyes seeping as the agreement was recited by the one she had summoned. The Devil had been invited into a house occupied by three siblings—a dwelling full of sin, where the walls constantly bled. It took what it wanted and left waste in its wake. He was there for three souls—three to claim. Alexa offered her soul to the shadows—she exchanged it; she offered it to be taken—she offered her soul to be claimed.

The story that this infernal being presents does not apply to me, does it? However, it still instills fear within me. It may be connected to the violent deaths of my parents and siblings, but I may never have a definitive answer. Nonetheless, I feel compelled to listen to it every day. Why am I cursed like this? Even when the Devilfish departs, I am still able hear its disturbing yet alluring melodies. The story and appearance of this creature scare the crap out of me, both figuratively and literally. My cell reeks once the story is finished. See for yourself—just look at it!

My Deceased Brother Nick

MY DECEASED BROTHER Nick doesn't seem to look or act like his usual self anymore. He visits after The Devilfish every day. Today marks my forty-third Birthday, or at least I believe it does. Although the prison allows me to keep a calendar on the wall in my cell, the days are irrelevant. I am now cuffed every time they bring me food. They are aware of my capabilities and my actions. It is simply my nature, I suppose. But let us return to Nick. As previously mentioned, these visitors appear punctually every day since I arrived here. I am uncertain as to why I am being plagued by these entities, if that is indeed what they are. There is nothing I can do to stop them either. I gave up trying many years ago.

Nick has changed, just like my mother and father. His body is twisted into this abomination that is only recognizable by his voice. His hair is gone, and his skull looks as if it has been stitched up after some kind surgery. The stitches go all the way around his body. His skin is a putrid green. Red liquid constantly drips from his mouth. He never sings, but instead talks incessantly about our teenage years. Though his voice remains unchanged, he looks repulsive. The foul oder he emits is revolting. He enjoys recounting a tale from our days roaming the city. Regardless of the reaction of those who read my written and illustrated work after my passing, I am not concerned. The act of writing is imperative for maintaining the remaining fragments of my sanity. Nick continues to tell our childhood story. He tells it repeatedly, day after day. I have the story memorized now. I know every word before it is spoken. The story Nick tells is about when we discovered that our neighbors were part of a cult. What he refers to as:

OUR NEIGHBORS ADORED THE DEVIL

We were all so young when new neighbors moved in. We were excited to meet new friends. The new neighbors had three kids: two boys and one girl. If you remember Geoff, you may have fallen in love with the girl. Do as you please. Anyway, all four of us rushed over immediately to introduce ourselves because we all were very social children. You went first, Geoff, and then introduced us all. You said, *"Hello, I'm Geoff. These are my brothers Nick, Marcus, and Daniel. "What are your names?"*

The girl's name was Brianna. Her two brothers, Gavin and Jacob appeared to have had limited interaction with other children, yet they still shared their names with us. You asked if they would be interested in playing together, to which Brianna replied that she would need to consult her parents. Their cautiousness is justified, as there are numerous dangers in our world, some of which may even take the shape of a child. Seems like you have something in common with them, Geoff! Anyway, Brianna went inside to ask, and when she came back, her parents followed to see who we were. They were behaving strangely and gave off an eerie vibe. I can still vividly recall the intensity of their gaze upon us. At the same time, they both said, *"Stay close to the house and and do not run off, or you will all be grounded."* They were both weird as *fuck*, excuse my language, but it was clear that something was not right.

The way they said it, though, was terrifying. It sounded like they were enraged. They didn't scream, but it was borderline. We didn't trust them. Throughout our childhood, when we had a bad feeling about someone, we were almost always right. Geoff, as you are aware, you and I both had a passion for detective work, and I wanted to become one in the future. Well, that dream didn't quite come to fruition. However, I did find great satisfaction in solving mysteries involving, strange people, locations, and cursed objects. We were all curious boys, fascinated by the unexplainable. I enjoyed having you, Daniel, and Marcus on my team as you all added your expertise to my nonsense throughout the years.

The most rewarding aspect was that all of you also had a passion for explaining the unexplained. I miss those days, Geoff. Now, back to the play time that we were given with the new neighborhood kids. I had to nudge you in the back of the head because you were blatantly showing your attraction to Brianna. I still chuckle when I recall the incident. You couldn't seem take your eyes off her. You were practically drooling, brother. Your tongue hanging out was the only thing that didn't happen. She was pretty, I won't lie. She radiated like a star, but was not as talkative as we were. We were never sure when to shut the hell up, you know? Gavin and Jacob were also rather quiet. I made the decision to try and lift their spirits.

"Hey Gavin, do you play baseball?" I asked him. His demeanor shifted and he eagerly agreed. I always enjoyed socializing and breaking the ice. *"Hey Jacob, want to play with*

us?" I asked him. He declined and remained seated, picking at a scab on his skin. *"Don't pick at it, it will scar."* I warned him. He looked over at me and said, *"You're not my dad. Who do you think you are, dick?" "Sorry, Jacob. I didn't mean any harm. You don't have to play with us. I was just asking, sheesh,"* I said.

Jacob was less outgoing than Gavin. I enjoyed studying different personalities. I remember, Geoff, the moment you started talking with Brianna. You were extremely flirtatious with her, complimenting every aspect of her, from her eyes and hair to her skin. We were all thoroughly enjoying ourselves until their parents intervened and ruined our play time. They overheard you complimenting their daughter through the open window. Her father then rushed out of the door and grabbed her by the right shoulder, scolding her to go back inside. He then locked eyes with you. Do you remember Geoff? Of course you do, it was an unforgettable experience. He said, *"If you touch my daughter, I will make you disappear, and nobody will be able to find you."* What a creep that guy was, huh?

Their mother followed after him and screamed at Gavin and Jacob to go inside. She continued to scream, *"This is why, kids!" "This is why we hide."* She ranted about how the world should end, making little sense, in full view of children. Her behavior seemed unhinged and made me curious about her motivations. That was the last time we played with those children. It was a shame because I liked all of them, despite Jacob's less than desirable behavior. As children that liked to investigate oddities, we began planning it that night. We had to know more about those negative vibes. We had to observe them for a while, memorizing their schedules—when they left, how long they were gone, and what time they returned. You know, like the work of a serial killer or detective. Yes, I am aware that breaking in is illegal. However, since we were never caught, I wasn't too concerned about it.

They left every night as a family from six until eleven, which seemed very odd to us. We wondered if we would see them in school once it started again. It was unusual to have such a daily outing, especially since school started early and we were all in bed by nine. To each their own, I suppose. We were abnormally curious kids. Nosey little bastards we were. Geoff, you knew how to pick locks. Why can't you pick the lock of this prison? You successfully opened the door, and Marcus knew how to erase evidence. Daniel was skilled at shutting down security cameras. We made a good team back then. After completing our jobs, we entered the investigation. We had exactly five hours.

The house appeared to be just like any other house at first glance, with family photos adorning the walls featuring all of the children. The kitchen was exceptionally clean and the entire interior excluded a spotless aura, indicative of a perfectionist. Every room in the house had its doors wide open, except for one. There was a locked door in the hallway leading into the kitchen. The presence of a padlock on the exterior was suspicious. Geoff, you were able to pick that lock in just ten seconds. You could escape prison in an instant. I am aware that I am repeating myself. Regardless, let us continue. Behind the door, there was a staircase made of castle stone that spiraled downwards into a room that would soon become legendary in our minds. It was hard to believe what we saw when we descended those stairs.

There were circles chalked on the walls with stars in the middle. At the time, we did not know what they were, but later learned they were pentagrams. They appeared to have been written in blood, but were actually drawn in a chalk-like, crimson red. It could not have been ink or paint; it had to be blood. As we continued, our feet felt as though they were sinking into mud, and the floor became increasingly soft. The dimly lit surroundings led us to turn the corner, and what we saw left us horrified: cages shaking violently and ear-piercing shrieks that branded us. Each cage contained a person who was desperately pleading with us not to leave them. They appeared malnourished and deteriorating from within. We had to help them before it was too late. Geoff, you were the hero that day and I must say, I am proud of you. When I think of the time when you picked the locks of each of those cages and released those unfortunate people, a tear of pride wells up in my putrid eye.

Among the group, there were seven, seemingly being prepped for slaughter. The scene was riddled with demonic possessions; books, candles, surgical knives, and chains adorned with barbed hooks dangled from the ceiling. It was a traumatic experience, and that day we were all forced to become heroes. Your quick work on the locks allowed us ample time to escape and survive. We asked one of the captives whether there were any others. They replied that they were unaware and expressed their gratitude before swiftly ascending the stairs and disappeared from our view. They told us that we would hear from them again, but they were rushing and panicking. We completely understood their urgency.

We searched for more people and didn't find anyone else inside. However, what we did find left us traumatized. There was another room, and as soon as we entered, the smell tore through us. That's when we saw the sight of stacked bodies, at least forty of them, all in various stages of decomposition. It was time to call the police before this situation became our demise. We urgently ran home and shouted, *"Mom, Dad! Call for help! The neighbors have killed a lot people and there are others in cages. We let them out! We broke in because they were acting weird. Mom and Dad!"*

Thankfully, we did not lie to our parents, and they believed us. It took the police several weeks to clear the house of the dead. The parents of Brianna, Gavin, and Jacob were arrested and charged with forty-five counts of murder. The children were relocated elsewhere, and we never saw them again. We continued to contemplate whether the responsibility lied solely with the parents or if the entire family was accountable. What if the three children we played with assisted their parents in committing the murders? Our neighbors adored the devil.

After Nick recounts our harrowing tale once more, I am always reminded of how truly terrified I was. The twisted, ghostly form of my deceased brother appears to me each day, recounting the same tragic tale. I must be in hell to endure such a traumatic experience repeatedly. Then why do I feel alive and able to breathe? Why do I continue to experience pain when I strike the walls? Why do I persist in documenting my encounters? Death seems so distant. Nick will be back again tomorrow to tell the tale again. I am already familiar with it, Nick! See you in twenty-four hours.

My Deceased Brother Daniel

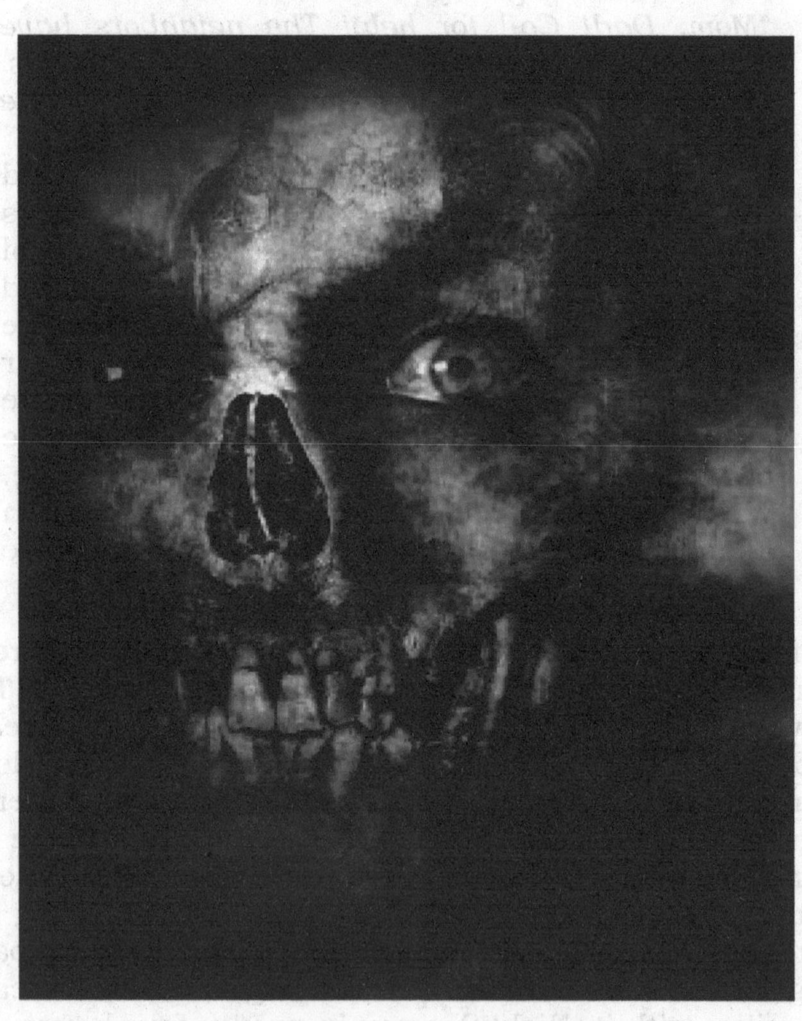

Nɪᴄᴋ ᴅɪsᴀᴘᴘᴇᴀʀs ᴊᴜsᴛ like the rest of them. My brother Daniel then fills his spot. Unlike Nick, Daniel doesn't tell tales or talk excessively. In fact, Daniel exudes a sense of profound darkness. He scares me to no end. Nick also has this effect, but he conceals his fear with humor and conversation. Daniel shows no sense of humor and is mostly silent when he is in my presence. Through direct eye contact, he conveys his intentions and instills an indescribable sense of fear. He effortlessly brings my deepest fears to the surface and preys on them, similar to a tiger hunting a terrified deer. He reminds me of the feeling I had when my he was brutally murdered. When he does speak, he tells me that I shouldn't be alive and that I should have been lying there with my throat slit like the rest of them. I always remind him that I avenged their deaths by killing those responsible. He never believes me just like my father, and it seems as though he thinks that I am lying about what I did just to be isolated from the rest of the world.

I don't understand why the revenge that I have gained is hidden from some of these entities. I don't want to be in this situation. I wish all three of my brothers and my parents were here and alive. Maybe then, I wouldn't find myself in this predicament. I am unsure whether I would engage in such behavior because I am discovering more about myself each day while being confined. Daniel reminds me that I have always had the desire to consume flesh and blood. He informs me that in our youth, I had a hidden habit of consuming roadkill found on the side of the road and raw meat from our home's refrigerator. So, maybe this was always how I was supposed to be. He also mentions that my behavior comes off as disturbed. The lack of his nose serves as a reminder of the prison guard's when I viciously bit it off and consumed it. Daniel's eyes are red, with black pupils and a white glaze on each side. He appears as though he has been deceased for a considerable amount of time. His voice is the only way to identify him.

I always try to remind him how close we were as children. He always states that it doesn't matter anymore because he is dead and I am alive. He loathes me for hiding in my closet while they all were killed. He instills fear into my mind, with visions of my body twisting and changing into an abomination like him. He claims that I will burn as he shows me how I will be engulfed in baby blue and black flames every day. However, he fails to provide an explanation for the specific color combination of the flames. It confuses the shit out of me. Despite my uncertainty about why my urge for flesh persists, it only grows stronger in this place where no one in the prison dares to enter my cage. I am required to be transported for court dates periodically. There is a specific protocol for moving me from one location to another. I have an upcoming court date, but do not understand why it is necessary for me to attend. I am serving a life sentence, and the legal proceedings are unorganized and chaotic.

I am sedated before being transported, after which my feet, arms and body are restrained with chains. A mouth gag is also placed in my mouth before I awaken from the sedative. They are not taking any chances with me. On this specific day, I was unsure of the purpose of my court date. Either I was not informed, or I simply forgot. I have a tendency to forget due to being constantly afflicted by these voices. This court date informed me that I would be transferred to another facility in Bangor, Maine and would no longer be housed in Cape Elizabeth. It seems insignificant, as I will remain confined for the remainder of my days. Would they dare put me in the general prison population? The Judge assured me that I would not be placed among other inmates, as I am deemed too dangerous and must be kept separate from other human beings.

I was unable to speak with the gag in place. I was then stealthily rolled out into the transfer vehicle. However, what they were unaware of was that I had crafted two homemade lock picks using plastic ballpoint pen parts and paper that morning, prior to the transfer. I had been planning to escape. The picks, measuring approximately half an inch long, had been hidden under my tongue before I was escorted to my court hearing. Their first mistake was not to check. With a clear intention in mind, I was determined to break out of this confinement once and for all. In recent times, my urges for human flesh have become unbearable.

I am recalling the lock-picking abilities that I possessed as a child that have since been concealed. Nick tells me in his story that I should have already escaped, so I am going

to try to put that into action today. I can only muffle my words because of the gag, but I try to get the attention of the transport guard by moving my head in his direction. He asked if I was feeling well. I then gained his attention by vigorously thrashing my head back and forth like I was having a seizure. He proceeded to remove the gag and I exclaimed, *"Thank you, I can finally breathe! I couldn't breathe and I was freaking out."*

The guard assured me that as long as I maintained silence and refrained from any attempts, he would not reapply the gag. I devised a plan to retrieve the picks and carefully positioned one into the collar of my blue shirt when neither of them had their attention on me. On my first attempt, I successfully secured the pick. I quietly shifted my torso, trying to maneuver the pick with one of my hands. This was going to require some skill. I remember the moment vividly when I entered mindset of consuming my family's murderers. My adrenaline and determination were at an all-time-high; I was more determined than ever to finish this. I had intended to do this and make an escape. This is my only opportunity. I proceeded to pick the first lock, and as I did so, I purposely and discretely repeated the same motions that I used for the first pick. Now both locks were open. There was one guard here in the back with me and one driver driving the transport vehicle. I needed to move quickly so I could release my feet. I politely asked the guard if he had any water, explaining that I was very thirsty. He kindly responded, *"Yes, just a moment."*

He began to approach me. When he was close enough, I swiftly swung the sharp end of the handcuffs, slitting his throat. As he sat in the corner, gurgling and seizing, I began to pick the locks on my feet and body, successfully freeing myself from all restraints. The only obstacle standing between me and freedom was the clueless driver. I had one shot at the driver, so I took the almost-dead officer's gun and calmly knocked on the window. The driver had the radio blasting so loudly that he didn't even realize that I had escaped my shackles or that his partner was hemorrhaging in the backseat. I was so incredibly grateful for his negligence.

I waited in silence for him to open the window, then immediately shot him between his beady blue eyes. He didn't have time to scream. The truck swerved back and forth and crashed into a ditch. I was not injured; I was just banged up a bit from the force of the crash. This would then be my one and only opportunity to escape . Before I exited the vehicle, I had to satisfy my uncontrollable cravings. I bit off both of the officer's ears and noses. I then took huge bites out of their lifeless bodies, chewing and slurping like a starving animal. Because that's what I was. That's what I am. That's what I'll always be.

I stepped outside of the vehicle and the sunlight overwhelmed me. I hadn't seen the beauty of sunlight like this since I was sixteen. The blood of both officers covered me almost entirely. Nick was correct. My remarkable lock-picking abilities made it effortless. Now, I am going to determine if these voices continue to pursue me. The fear and courage that my deceased brothers instilled into me, especially on this occasion, also gave me the confidence I needed to pick the locks and break free. I had once again fulfilled my insatiable craving for human blood and meat. Thank you, Nick and Daniel. Thank you, my brothers.

MY DECEASED BROTHER MARCUS

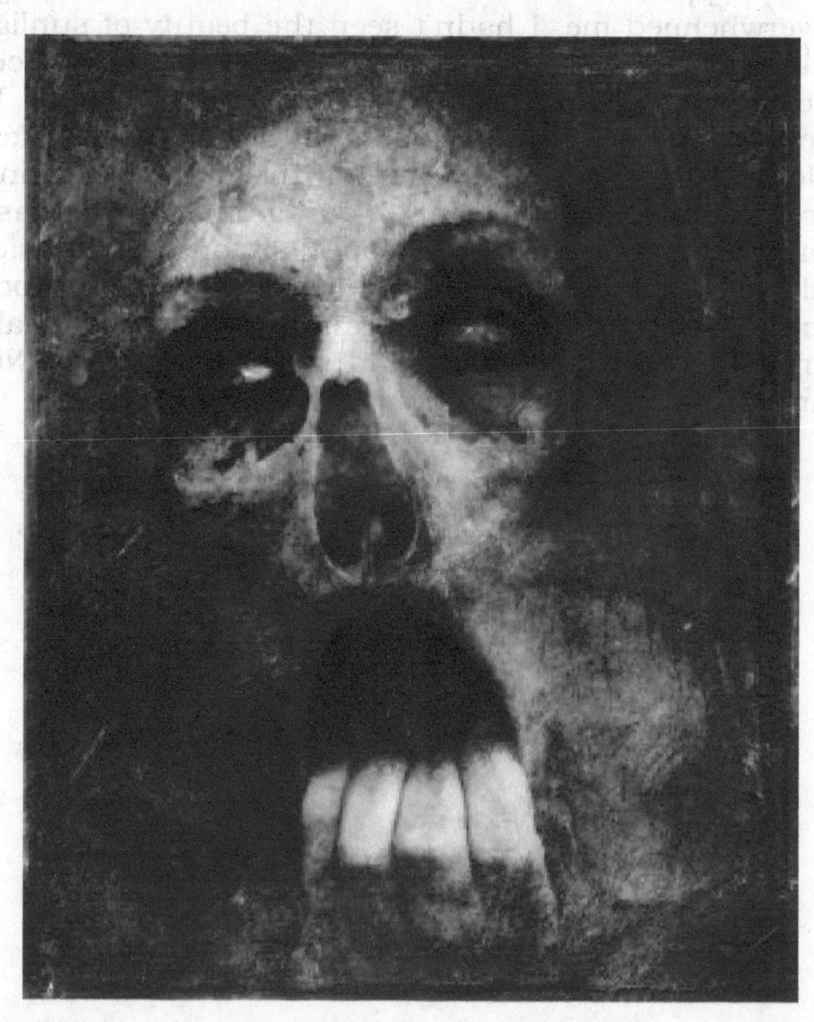

SHORTLY AFTER I escaped the transport vehicle, my deceased brother Marcus appeared right on schedule. I was aware that these visions and voices would continue to plague me if I ever managed to break free. It was no surprise when Marcus emerged after Daniel, just like every other day. I am at a loss for what to do out here. Everything in my world has changed. I know the authorities will be pursuing me. They will not cease until I'm either captured again or dead. I wanted to run as far away from this place as I possibly could. However, my addictions took over. Marcus follows me around like a loyal canine. It's late evening and it appears as though the ground is being enveloped in a stunning fog. I haven't witnessed anything quite like it in such a long time. The air smells divine. I'm eagerly anticipating the chance to observe the stars. I have been deprived of this beauty while being confined. I can feel my hunger consuming me in a fierce frenzy.

Marcus is still here with me. He is an abomination, just like all the others. He is a greenish-blue color and appears to be painted in a horrific way, like a masterpiece on display. He keeps his fingers in his mouth and I can never comprehend what he is saying. Though I am eager to communicate with him, his mumbling remains unchanged. He sounds like muffled screams.

I cannot comprehend what he is saying and I am

unable to decipher his words. You may be curious as to how I am able to write this despite having escaped. I stumbled upon a notebook and a pen in a garbage receptacle on my journey. I am also experiencing flashbacks from my memory. It is difficult to forget the only time I ever managed to escape. These days, I am constantly writing everything down. My cravings have become stronger, and I fear it won't be long until I rip into someone's face. I often wish that I could rid myself of this addiction. I've tried in every possible method. For the moment, I have broken free from once eternal confinement.

The creature within me will never dissipate. Now, I can view the stars as the sun sets over the ocean's waves. The harmonization of the stars and tides is so beautiful, and I have missed this majestic place. As I try to drift off on my first night away from my prison cell in Cape Elizabeth, Maine, I find myself counting them in hopes of falling asleep. I did, and I am finding solace in sleeping among the forest floor, secluded from sight in order to avoid being brought back to that dreadful place. When I woke up today, my dreams had not changed. They were filled with visions of barbed wire and flames. The visitor that accompanies these dreams usually comes later in the day. My dreams are certainly not peaceful, as they are often filled with intense hate. My stomach now aches and I feel incredibly hungry. I must find something to eat to alleviate this excruciating pain. I have to search for something to eat today. As I scour the forest floor, I am having limited success. I have been searching for hours and I feel my stomach churning. It is the early signs of starvation and I must eat soon.

In the distance, I saw a few bushes in front of me moving. To my surprise, it was a wounded deer. What luck! I am the Tiger and I fear nothing. My craving for blood became clear as day. I sunk my teeth into the dying deer's neck, ripping the flesh and consuming my living meal. I felt rejuvenated and control once more. Using my powerful jaws, I tore open its stomach, giving in to my insatiable appetite for flesh. With each bite, I could feel my already sparse sanity slipping further away. The primal animal within had now fully taken hold of me. Hearing the sound of a deer's screams and tasting it while it was happening was as sweet as a clover. It was then that I realized that I would always want more. When the blood touches my lips, I am transported to a place of fire, pain, suffering, and screaming faces. I no longer have control. I have now transformed once again into the scariest of carnivores, the tiger! Everything else is just prey, like this deer. Today, I went on a rampage of terror and fear.

I am aware that the authorities are still searching for me and they will not cease their efforts. However, I must make the most of my time while I am out here. Eventually, I will be apprehended. In the meantime, I will indulge in my long-awaited blood cravings. I noticed a secluded path ahead with nobody in sight. Therefore, I discreetly waited in the trees, remaining silent. On the forest floor lay a large fallen tree limb, which I picked it up and gazed at absently, as if in a trance. This is the tool that I will use when I have the opportunity. My stomach is growling again, as if I haven't eaten in weeks. I eagerly await my next sweet indulgence. I am starting to smell like dried blood and decomposing deer meat. I should not be allowed to roam free. As a terrible human being, it is not my fault. I will always blame the three men who murdered my entire family.

Finally, I can hear conversation from my hiding spot. It appears that a man and a woman are running. Unfortunately, I do not have much experience in this environment. For many decades, I was in a cage by myself. Some days, I am aware of my age. However, most days, I have no idea. The couple are jogging together. I feel the hunger starting to overwhelm me. I wait patiently for them to come closer. When they do, I strike them both forcefully with blows to their skulls. The man is unconscious, but the woman gazes at me with sweet blood running down both of her cheeks. She would be the first of the two I consumed. I lunged upon her and began ruthlessly striking her skull in with the tree branch I had discovered. The thrilling surge of adrenaline was euphoric as I watched her eyes widen before they forcefully bulged out of their sockets. Her brain oozed out of her cracked skull and gathered on her shoulders. I placed my ravenous mouth on it, devouring her knowledge. I then repeated the same routine with the man that had fallen. I couldn't control myself and continued to take bites. I knew it was wrong, but it felt so fucking satisfying.

After I had finished with them, they appeared as though they had been mauled by a bear in the dark, making them unrecognizable from their previous state. My stomach is satiated and my craving has been fulfilled (for now). I must seek out a new location to conceal myself. I have resolved to delve even further into the wilderness. I am now a wild creature, hunting in order to survive. This is what I dreamed about during all those years I spent in prison. This! This, right here, is my life. I will do whatever it takes to ensure that this feeling never fades. Before the vision of my departed brother Marcus dissipates, he mutters incomprehensible words, just as my overwhelming guilt begins to take hold.

My Guilt

I am covered in the remains of the two joggers that I had just consumed. In comes my next vision, right on cue—introducing my guilt. It always tries to make me feel remorse for what I have done, but it never succeeds. These cravings cannot be overcome. My guilt always hangs its head in shame, with a sorrowful expression that will forever haunt this man. It is confined within a skull, as if it were being consumed. Just like my cravings, it's a terrible sensation and sight.

No one can prevent or predict this, not even me. I must indulge in raw meat in order to satisfy my desires. I will never understand the reason for my behaviors. I will never attempt to control them. I feel no remorse or guilt. While I do have a conscience, it rarely influences me. I am fated to be the person I am and condemned to be, a savage. I am free now and I will take advantage of this opportunity. I will eternally strive to satisfy an insatiable beast. I will act on my cravings and continue to do so with determination. I cannot allow them catch me. My guilt is nonexistent and I will not succumb to it. I am continuing my writing, despite reaching the end of my pages. I must now replenish my writing materials. Furthermore, I need to find water to cleanse myself. The flies are incessant, and although I appreciate the scent of death, I must rid myself of it.

It's so hot out here. It is mid-June, I believe, but I am not entirely certain of the date. Finally, I spot a river up ahead. I am unsure of the distance left to the ocean. Without hesitation, I jump right in and the cool water feels refreshing. However, the water turns red due to my actions. As I watch the red water flow away from me, I started reminiscing about the past. I reflect on my family and how once we were a picture of love and beauty. The emotion of guilt often triggers this nostalgia, forcing me down memory lane to the happier days of my innocence, when I had no worries, addictions, cravings, or pain. How I long to return to that place! I know that what I have become is now the only way. It's the only way that I can feel peace. It's the only way that I can be emotionally free. I hope nobody can hear me as I scream from these damn trees. My guilt will not get the best of me.

I am now traveling back in time, all the way to 1993. Back when everything was perfect and I had my Mom and Dad to comfort me when I felt sad. They would wipe my tears away when I cried. I often reminisce and fantasize about that time, as it was my sole source of joy. However, from that point on, much more than a part of me died. My guilt tears me apart when it arises. It taunts me with happy memories, knowing that I will never again experience that life. All I can see is the memories of those men, bleeding out their lives. My Brothers, I miss them so much. The human ones, the ones who don't look like demons from hell, the ones who don't come to me every day and scare me back into my shell. I don't want to see my brothers in that state, and I don't want to see my parents in that condition either. These visions and voices are tearing me to shreds.

How much further can I be torn? How much more can I endure? The voices continue to haunt me, despite my attempts to break free. Have I truly broken free, or am I still trapped? My conscience bears the weight for these unsettling questions. I am reminded of that chilly autumn evening in 1993 when we were all filled with joy. It was almost time for Halloween, which happened to be entire family's favorite holiday. The thought that comes to mind when I reflect on past moments of happiness is guilt, which makes me question my mental health. My guilt attempts to make me feel remorse for dismembering those three murderous men and consuming them. However, I will never give in or let it overcome me, as my firm conviction remains that they deserved the consequences of their heinous actions.

Anyway, Halloween was indeed the best time of the year for our family. We began decorating months before because we were all huge enthusiasts for the "season of the dead." My brothers and I would have blueprints outlining our plans for our annual projects. We would spend most of the year preparing for our favorite time of year. My father was a horror author, and I believe that is why I feel compelled to document and write everything down that occurs throughout my twisted life. My Mother was an artist who created horror images for Halloween every year. From my beautiful deceased parents, I inherited a love for both writing and drawing, which becomes evident when looking at these pieces. My family is one of the few memories that can bring a smile to my face, and there aren't many things that make me smile these days besides the taste of human flesh.

My father wrote the headlines on the banners, while my mother created the art for them. My brothers and I used to create monsters out of paper, glue, wood, cloth, and other materials. I also enjoyed adding real graveyard dirt to our creations to have a story to tell. Whenever the feelings of guilt arise, I am reminded that this display was one of our Halloween masterpieces, of which we were all proud. It is a moving, talking replica of what we, as a family, created together. My guilt overwhelms me each time it arrives, triggering screams and tears. The reminders of what I have lost through hallucinations of our past, reminding me of the incredible moments we shared. I refuse to dwell on regret for my actions. I don't want to feel remorseful for stealing my grandfather's gun and silently shooting, then consuming the men who stole my only joy from me. I can still sense the taste of those monsters, can still feel their blood between my teeth.

Halloween was our best time together as a family. We laughed and went trick-or-treating together, always wearing unique costumes that we made ourselves. We were a highly creative family, and I deeply miss them all. The person I am today is a reflection of the way they were taken from me. That is not the only reason, as I have mentioned before. I have always had a craving for raw meat. It is what it is. I will eat out here in the forest. I will most certainly indulge. My father used to come up with ideas for our costumes every year, and my mother helped bring them to life. The most memorable year was 1995. Oh, how I miss those joyous moments.

My costume looked like a hybrid between a reptile and a human, with artificial brains protruding from my skull. Marcus portrayed a zombified mix of a man and a wolf, while Nick's costume showcased him as having a slit throat—it was incredibly realistic. What is the likelihood that, in the future, all of them would have their throats slit and be taken away from me? Daniel's costume was impeccable. I believe he outdid all of us that year. His ensemble was striking. He donned a bald cap to obscure his hair and we utilized authentic snake skins gathered from the forest to create the illusion of actual snakes protruding from his skull. My mother created an exquisite acrylic mouthpiece that replicated hollow, pointed fangs.

At the time, Daniel's eerie demeanor was greatly admired. However, my feelings towards frightening things have sense changed. Each day, I am haunted by these vivid visions, each with its own terrifying level of fear. To this day, I cannot figure out their intentions. The weight of my guilt is a constant reminder, transporting me back to this joyful memory, attempting to invoke remorse for my actions. However, despite the thoughts it plants in my mind, I will not comply. Once the guilt subsides, the wrath returns and the longing for death persists. The blaze once more consumes my decomposing mind.

Once we were all set to go out and get our highly-anticipated haul of sugar, a storm rolled in. If you thought a storm was going to stop the Hathaway family on Halloween, you're more delusional than I am. Nevertheless, we proceeded with our plans. Halloween was the one day of the year when we all felt truly alive. We felt a stronger bond as a family on that day than any other day of the year. It was our special day. We had nothing to fear. We enjoyed visiting haunted houses, but that year, there was one particular haunted house that had to be shut down due to an employee's malicious intentions towards visitors.

We were present that evening when she was apprehended. I struggle with remembering names, so I will refer to her as Tammy. Tammy was an employee who enjoyed startling people around corners throughout the building. Please bear with me. She shared the same love for blood as I do. Perhaps we should have wedded. Just a bit of humor there. I've never been with anyone. I've never kissed a girl. I've never had sex. None of it. I don't even know what love is outside of my family. Remember, I was only fourteen when they locked me away in an adult prison. Maybe I will find love while I'm free, but I don't see that as a possibility.

Anyway, Tammy waited for people to approach and would stab them with whatever she had at the time, before quickly fleeing to change costumes and continuing the rampage. The incident was later reported on the news. She did not stab everybody; instead, she waited for the right moment and then became incredibly aggressive. We were present on the night that she took the life of a boy who continuously bullied her. She jumped on him, sat on his shoulders, and began repeatedly stabbing him. We witnessed the knife going in and out of his eye sockets while he screamed in agony. We had many traumatizing experiences during our teenage years, yet Tammy's violent outburst on Halloween didn't ruin our celebrations. We never let anything come between us. Tammy was tackled by a security guard and held down while we waited for the police. I can still see that boy's eye sockets bleeding.

The boy appeared to be nineteen, although I cannot be certain because of my unreliable memory. Tammy attempted to evade the police. The officers used a taser on her until she collapsed. Tammy never provided an explanation to the authorities for her actions aside from the fact that she was being bullied, despite the news coverage. Even then, I found myself strangely intrigued. Perhaps it was just my inherent nature, but I have always had these unexplained cravings. I know I sound like a broken record, but if this doesn't interest you, please stop reading. We had neighbors who were also serial killers. As children, we saw many dead bodies. However, I believe guilt is an illusion and I choose to cast it out each day. Regardless of how loudly it may speak, I will continue to do what I do. I silence my guilt for a reason and it's not a topic I enjoy discussing or writing about. But for those who are reading these words that I write, please know that I am here waiting in the darkness. I am waiting for a feast, for fresh meat, to consume everything. My hunger overrides my guilt, and I shout! If you happen to see me, you better run, or I will tear your throat out.

Before it departs, my guilt tells a story, much like the majority of my inner voices, in an effort to further torment me and intensify my already fractured consciousness. It tells the same tale day in and day out, just like all of my other voices. Once again, I have written it down for all to read after I am gone. Prepare your minds and souls; although I have heard this story every day for many decades, it continues to haunt my thoughts and nightmares long after its conclusion.

THE SHADOW WALKERS

No one truly comprehends the immense pressure that is continuously placed upon a tormented psyche. The constant dread of vocalizing one's thoughts and emotions is overwhelming. Although some may argue that the terrifying hallucinations are merely figments of the imagination, I respectfully disagree. They are not merely manifestations to the person observing them in front of their eyes twenty-four seven. It becomes ingrained in our daily routines, resembling a thousand-degree hammer pounding in a two-thousand-degree nail. It is all becoming so real. It has always been real in our minds. Nobody believes us when we say the shadows talk until they begin to walk in plain sight.

Frank Griffin has always been troubled. Since he was a child, he has heard voices consistently. Despite undergoing therapy throughout his entire childhood and into his adult life, he still struggles. He converses with things that appear incomprehensible to a basic human mind. Frank has always had what his parents deemed imaginary friends, which seems to be an appropriate label when addressing children with mental instabilities. He calls them the "Shadow Walkers." To this day, neither his parents nor any physician has seen these imaginary figures, but that is unlikely to change.

On Frank's fifteenth birthday, he committed the acts that led to his current situation. It started as a typical birthday party with invited friends and family members surrounding him, wishing him the best on his special day. However, things took a turn when Frank's voice began to dictate his actions. He blew out his fifteen candles and then his eyes reflected an intense rage. Frank lost control on that day, murdering everyone at the party except his horrified parents without motive. To this day he blames the Shadow Walkers, saying, *"They made me do it!"* Frank always insists.

He claims that the Walkers are planning to do it again, but when asked when, he always responds that he cannot say. He fears for his safety, as they have threatened to kill him if he denies them the opportunity to come out again and play. Now seventeen, Frank's Story remains unchanged from what it was on his fifteenth birthday. He has meticulously explained to psychologists over the past two years, conveying their pleasure in causing havoc in the human mind. Frank asserts that they revel in the anguish reflected in a person's eyes as they are forced into actions against their will. They can manipulate and harm many people without being detected. He repeated numerous times that these creatures can only be perceived as fleeting shadows of monstrous faces, claws, and colorless flames. Despite his insistence, his words seem to go unheard as he is met with constant diagnoses. The uninformed physicians and psychologists are unprepared for what is about to surface from Frank's shattered consciousness.

On October 28, 2022, at Frank's fifteenth birthday celebration, the Shadow Walkers appeared in full force. They controlled every swing of the ax and reveled in Frank's silent cries as he was forced to witness the separation of his closest friends and family's heads and limbs from their torsos. Forced to see the horror and disappointment on his parents' faces, whom he loved so dearly. He was also forced to watch the innards fall out of his victims like candy from his piñata that he never had the opportunity to break open. To this day, he maintains his account that he had no control. In his numerous warnings, he stresses the need for proper confinement. He fears that without it, the Shadow Walkers will devour all human souls and drain them of life. Now, fast forward thirty years.

OCTOBER 28, 2052

This week marks the thirtieth anniversary of Frank's fifteenth birthday celebration. In the past three decades, Frank has consistently issued numerous warnings. As he celebrates his forty-fifth birthday this week, the impending return of the dark entities looms closer. Despite his repeated warnings, he has been dismissed as delusional. No one listens to him—no one ever has, and no one ever will. Nobody understands what it is like inside of a mind that is forced to cause death, pain, rage, and exists within inescapable chains. Frank screams for hours as he senses the nearing date. The Shadow Walkers then begin their instruction with the colorless flames.

"Hello again, Frank. We have been waiting for our sign. We are patient in our approach and have carefully chosen our moment. Now that they believe you to be of unsound mind, it is our time to feed, and your time to shine. Please await further instructions. At the precise moment of 11:59, our demands will be made known. As the clock strikes midnight, we shall present ourselves to those accountable for your confinement, ensuring they become acquainted with us firsthand."

Frank shouted for the guards, *"They are coming at midnight!"* He pounded his fists against the door to the room. Nobody responded; they had heard this all before. Frank was just another unstable patient in a facility with countless doors. Since he was a child, nobody has truly listened, and it may now be too late for everyone present on this night. His fists are both broken and bloodied from striking them against the walls as the voices of the Shadow Walkers grow stronger. His cell door creeks open without a key, and Frank's eyes roll back as he loses complete control of reality, just as he did at his fifteenth birthday party. All that can be seen are the whites of his eyes, all that he can see is the crime scene.

The entities taunt him as they did before, dictating instructions on how these innocent employees should meet their brutal ends. He cannot remove their powerful demands from his fragmented thoughts and mind.

"Hello again, Frank. The time has come, sweet vessel. Your mission will be done. We have unlocked your cage, freeing you from your confinement. Please proceed to the elevator and ascend to the third floor. Once there, you will find a previously locked room that we have now

gained access to for you. Inside, you will find an assortment of toys, knives, and guns—how thrilling! Now, you will grab as many knives as you can place in the black bag on the floor of the ammunition room. Then, you will load and do the same with the guns. You will turn this place into a tomb. Nothing can be done to stop it. This is what you have become. Devoid the entire hospital of life, once you have completed this task, await further instructions."

Frank cannot help but recall the day of his birthday celebration, when he took an ax to numerous family members and friends. Despite his efforts to find a different resolution, the voices of the Shadow Walkers only intensify as his attention wanders from their demands. He thought about how he tried to explain to the doctors that his mind was straying further and further from reality. He recalls how he begged his parents and family to understand his thoughts, but everyone insisted it was just a phase. Everyone dismissed him. Things could have been so different if someone had listened. Why didn't they listen? The gunshots and screaming rang throughout the hospital where Frank Griffin took the lives of thirty-seven graveyard-shift employees at Eastern Maryland Psychiatric Hospital for the criminally insane. Video footage revealed Frank removing the keys to both his cell and the ammunition room from a negligent security officer's key chain. This was done while the guard had fallen asleep during the early morning hours.

Frank then proceeded to conceal the keys by ingesting them and retrieving them from his own excrement once the digestion process was complete. He maintains to this day that the

Shadow Walkers have always been accountable. Despite Frank's consistent claims of upcoming proof, no professional has ever heard or seen what he claims made him commit these horrific acts. It is safe to say that nobody else will, besides him. On the morning of October 28, 2022, the morning shift crew of The Eastern Maryland Psychiatric Hospital arrived to find Frank Griffin, age forty-five, peeling the flesh away from a male security guard, repeatedly saying, *"The Shadow Walkers made me do it. The Shadow Walkers made me do it."* Despite the overwhelming evidence that Frank was responsible for his crimes as a child and as an adult, he still blames the Shadow Walkers, unconscious amongst the many deceased scattered throughout the facility after a sedation dart was fired at him.

OCTOBER 28· 2062

In a recent interview with Frank Griffin, ten years after the brutal murders in the hospital, he stated that the entities will return every thirty years for the rest of eternity. In his own words, he stated that even after his death, they will continue to carry out the work of the infernal shadows, using a new vessel, while he himself would become a Shadow Walker. He reiterates that if he is still alive during their next emergence, he must be restrained at the highest level of security. He admits that he is not in control of himself or his actions during this time. Frank regrets every murder that he has committed and apologizes profusely. He explains that every Shadow Walker was a regular person, just like him, and possesses the vulnerable and broken at their most innocent moment or when they are enduring immense pain and torment.

Frank has always maintained the same story since childhood, never deviating from it. Professionals are puzzled by his unwavering consistency, raising questions about whether he truly believes in the reality of these entities. Despite this, Frank remains calm and composed, except for two specific dates thirty years apart. He is always calm and friendly towards both patients and staff members. But his crimes are some of the most horrific in history. The Church has been in to see Frank on many occasions and never found any signs or evidence of possession, so it is always dismissed. He vividly describes the appearance, movement, and interaction of the Shadow Walkers in his daily life. These mysterious beings constantly change their form, making them unrecognizable. Their ultimate goal is to break free and eradicate all humans they encounter.

Today marks Frank's fifty-fifth trip around the sun. He firmly believes that the voices echoing in his mind are like a mystical crystal ball, revealing his destiny and ensuring his continued existence until they come back again. According to him, when he reaches the age of seventy-five, the enigmatic Shadow Walkers will reemerge, bringing with them yet another a wave of destruction that no one, not even Frank himself, can overcome. Brace yourselves, for he predicts a grim future where many more lives will be lost, and this facility will descend once more into chaos beyond repair.

Frank is certain of what awaits him after death. He describes how he is taunted daily by these dark entities, who seem eager to for him to join them in the shadows and engage in eternal destruction. He insists the final emergence will occur in twenty years and says that once these creatures reveal themselves, his mortal body will leave this world, and his soul will be claimed by the darkness. Frank acknowledges the madness of his beliefs and recognizes the potential danger he poses. Nevertheless, he has never harmed anyone unless the Shadow Walkers emerge, and he still maintains a calm and composed demeanor. Frank is one terrifying individual. He says, *"You must be sure to have me completely restrained on my seventy-fifth birthday."*

OCTOBER 28, 2082

Frank has been entirely restrained and bound to a table in preparation for this day. What happened next was not on anyone's mind. His eyes rolled back and with unbelievable strength broke free of all restraints. His body split down the middle releasing what seemed to be shadow figures. The screaming of these entities was so loud, employees of the hospitals heads began to explode. Frank was telling the truth. His body lay on the ground in half as more of these Shadow Walkers escaped their former vessel. You can see his internal organs still moving before shutting down. Not a soul survived, and the entities are now hunting for a new vessel. Where they will end up and who they will possess is unknown. And nobody was spared to tell the story. For his entire life, nobody listened to Frank or heard his cries for help. If someone reaches out you must listen. What they are trying to tell you just may be the truth.

Just like Frank Griffin, no one has ever believed me either since I started hearing voices after the murders of my parents and brothers. I can identify with Frank in almost the same way. No one takes me seriously when I mention hearing voices and witnessing their manifestations. No one pays attention when I cry out for assistance. I can't blame them, though. Unlike Frank, I am not kind, and I am well aware of that. I will always admit that I am truly a monster. No one will ever understand me. I have no one left who truly cares, except for my beloved Jennie. I will introduce you to her as we continue on. She is so beautiful. I know she is just a hallucination, but she is all I have in this life. I wonder where I will end up after I am gone. I know that, based on all that I have done, it certainly will not be paradise. Damn you guilt, to hell with your nonsense! I truly despise you!

My Beloved Jennie

My guilt dissipates each day, just like the other voices. I am forced to endure this merciless cycle every day. How do you imagine this anger? You wouldn't like it. You would be unable to bear it. You would collapse, just like I did. I may have escaped from prison, but I am far from being truly free. Every day, after my guilt leaves, my love comes to me. I've never experienced genuine love besides from my family. Therefore, I suppose this illusion of love provides me with comfort. It sings to me and caresses my wounded soul, for the brief time it stays with me. I never want this vision, voice, or whatever you want to call it, to depart. It fascinates me and presents such a captivating image. I refer to it as my beloved, Jennie. She always carries a knife but never stabs me. She always gazes into my eyes with such passion. I have tried to touch her, but my hands simply pass through her, as if she were some kind of spirit.

I have attempted to physically engage with all of my inner voices. However, the only voices that are able to physically interact with me are my voices of hell and insanity. We will address those harmful entities later. I would like to confront those voices; their actions towards me would shock you. I have attempted to confront my guilt multiple times. These visions cannot be physically experienced, except by a select few. That's why I feel that they exist solely in my mind.

However, my voice of insanity is undeniably real.

I can't help but feel suffocated when I think about that wretched woman. Moving on, let's return to my concept of love. I have attempted to kiss my beloved multiple times. I strongly believe she is everything I have been missing in my life—the love I never experienced before. The pleasures overwhelm me so much. She is my love. She is the only love I will ever feel outside of my now-slaughtered family. She talks with me. She tells me how much she needs me. She compliments me. She tells me there is more than just your insanity. She is the only comfort that I have throughout my madness. When she leaves, she always dissolves into ashes that swirl back into the darkness.

This is the only time of day when I feel somewhat human. I am not a monster when she is here. I don't crave human flesh when she is near. She takes away all of my anger while she is here. I always beg her to never go away. I always want her to stay forever. I want us to be together. She always tells me that her time is limited. She always tells me that she will return. She always does come back, but it is never long enough. It will never be long enough. I need her to stay and tame this monster. She is the only one who can. I need her. I love when she is here. Her face is half rotten and her eyes are as black as the bottom of a wishing well. I still love her, though. She is my angel in a way. She is my guiding light in this chaotic place. She always reassures me that everything will be okay.

Her name is Jennie again, by the way. But deep down, I know it's not okay. I explain to her that everything will remain the same when she leaves me in this place. The thought of her leaving causes me to become overwhelmed with the desire to eliminate everything. Surely, there must be a solution. Panicked, I search for a resolution as her departure draws near. I plead desperately for her to stay, fully aware of what lies ahead, ready to replace her. Unbearable pain is all that awaits me once by beloved Jennie departs. Something sinister will always replace her. It happens every day. The same visions, the same voices. Why can't it stay this way? Just you and me, Jennie. Forever is calling our names! Every time I freak out, she sits next to me and says:

"I love you, Geoff. One day, we will be united. One day, we will embark on a journey towards the stars. One day, we will heal together and mend these terrible scars."

I weep when she whispers those beautiful words into my ears. I am aware that she is an illusion. My tears flow relentlessly. I am in love with this imaginary vision, woman, monster. I am lost and unsure of what to do. I am aware of what is to come. I know this will occur every day for the remainder of my life and I cannot wait to escape. I would never intentionally harm myself, just to clarify. Let me reiterate that I am not suicidal, but I will accept death when it approaches. I admire and adore Jennie. She brings me peace, even though she exists only in my imagination. She is the only thing that soothes my desire to harm. The desire to violently tear open someone and consume the revolting yet enticing contents inside of their shells.

She is the only thing that makes me feel human, the only thing that keeps my mind functioning the way it should. Her voice is the only thing I look forward to throughout the day. When she is absent, I dream of her and us making love. Despite never having experienced it, I have extensively read about sex in books. I have been alone for a long time, and the comfort she brings is sublime. I envision her face, half-rotten yet still kissing mine. I picture her taking me on a passionate journey. I imagine us walking off together forever along the great divide. I dream of just touching her one time. If that is all that I will ever have, it will be a memory that does not crush my mind. It is almost time for her to leave me here. What comes next is my ultimate fear: the vision that destroys me, the vision that taunts and drags me through an unimaginable hell. It is my reflection. It is the devil incarnate to me. I lose all of my sanity when my reflection appears to me.

When I was incarcerated, I did not have access to mirrors in my cell. I have the tendency to break mirrors when I encounter them, bringing out the monster in me. If you believe you have an understanding of my capabilities, just wait until my love Jennie leaves me. I openly communicate my love for her. She expresses her love for me. I weep and plead for her to remain each day before she departs. I wail for her presence. I eagerly anticipate seeing her tomorrow. Now, I must ready myself for what I am never fully prepared for. I must prepare to look myself in the eye. I must prepare for the monster that is coming. I must prepare for the beast that lives inside of me—the beast that will do anything to fulfill its hunger for flesh. It will stop at nothing to satisfy its appetite. It will do anything to torment me. My reflection will one day be the death of me. It's coming. It's coming soon. I love you, Jennie, and I will see you soon. She then disappeared and left me here in this tomb. At least I am no longer locked away. When I run from my reflection this time, I'll have a lot more space. My reflection is my ultimate abuser. It is coming very soon.

My Reflection

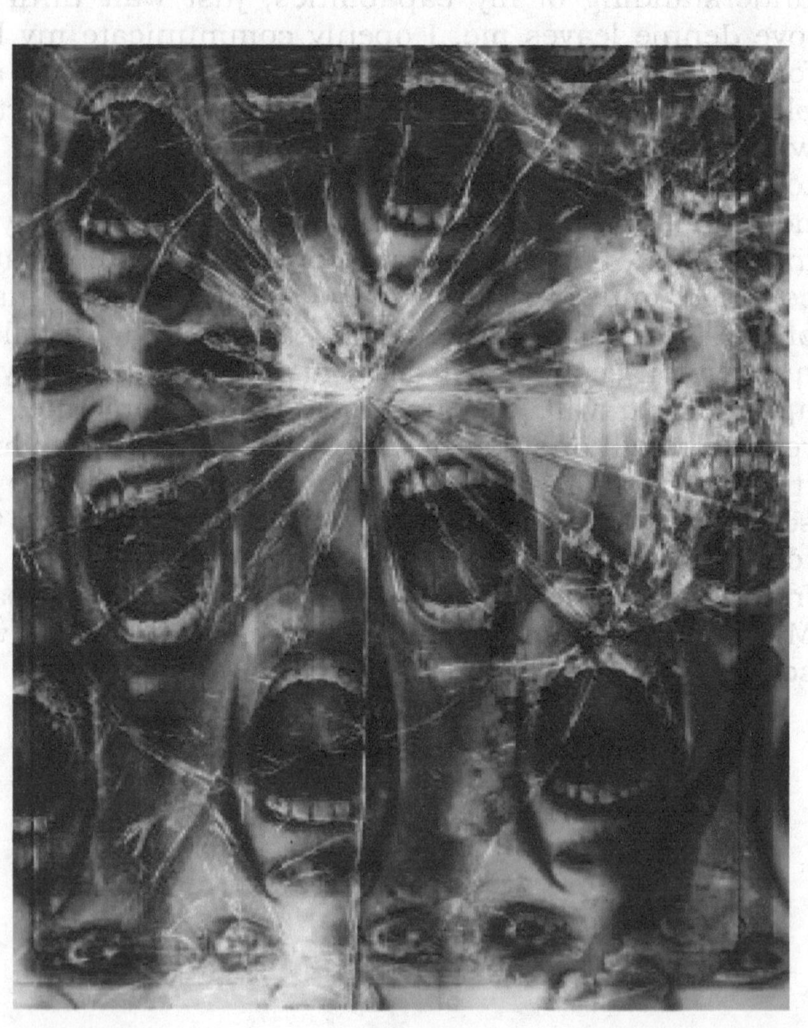

I HEAR THE shattering of the glass. My reflections are approaching, and they always seem to know where I am. I am filled with terror when they arrive, as they are responsible for controlling my actions. My mind launches into a rampage of murderous thoughts, leaving me paralyzed with fear. My mouth starts to drool. My mind transforms into a tiger and I am rendered foolish to my own reflections. Mirrors surround me, and yet they always seem to latch onto me. I cannot conceal myself. This is my first encounter with them in this environment. The sound of shattering glass is always unsettling.

These voices incite violence. They demand it immediately. There is nothing I can do or say. I must do as they ask of me. I must obey. They want me to continue the slaughter. They talk so much, but only give instructions. They are pleased that I have escaped. I place my hands on my head and attempt to will them away. Yet, they persist. They flood my soul with ten times the fury. Whenever this vision arises, I feel consumed. They shout at me from behind the figurative glass, making it evident what I ought to do.

Each time that I refuse, they become angrier. I make an effort to refuse, I truly do. However, my self-control is constantly being torn in two. When I was in prison, I was unable to comply with their commands. I was confined in a cell with no means to act on the demands. This time, the situation is different and I fear there will be even more blood on my hands. I have already killed five people before my reflections returned. Now I am unsure where my shattered mind will lead me. My reflection robs me of everything. It's as if I am in a trance under its influence. I am now under its spell and will unleash hell. I will transform this forest into a blood-soaked battleground. I will be the monarch of this woodland. My reflection has absolute control. I can't feel remorse for what is about to transpire. I now am under the influence of my reflection and stalk this forest for prey. I am like a tiger, as I love to say.

I am drenched in blood as I pen this today. I can't help but lick my lips. This is my source of gratification. In my newfound freedom, I will revel in all of this. Each breaking of bones, every pleading for mercy. I am a devoid of morality. My mind is filled with voices, pain, fear, and unbridled rage! I am searching this forest for my helpless prey. I am breathing heavily and have not come across anyone. It feels as though I have been walking for days and the sun's rays are harsh and my skin is scorched. These days, I am more aggressive than the scorching ball of never-depleting flames. Then, in the distance, I heard a conversation taking place. I can hear and see my reflection, and it has so much to say. It's a group of campers having fun and making memories—memories that I'm about to erase. I've counted six people from where I am hiding, but there could be more. I hope there are more. I am growing increasingly hungry with every passing moment. Oh, the tragedies they will all explore! From what I can gather, there are three men and three women present. I have spent many years in prison, and during that time, I have read countless horror novels. How about a story from the perspective of the killer? Or perhaps, one from my own point of view? I am currently writing that very story for all of you to enjoy. I have no other option.

My reflection then screamed, *"Tell the story!"* So that's exactly what I am going to do. The three women were all stunning, youthful, and vibrant. The three men were all handsome and looked to be physically capable of defending themselves. As a result, I had to carefully strategize for each kill. There was no specific plan for each murder, however, my investigation ensured that each one had its own unique twist. I followed the group for several days, familiarizing myself with every aspect of their lives. I wanted to understand everything about them, from their strengths and weaknesses to what they loved and hated.

I listened intently to their passionate conversations, wanting to delve into their souls so that when I ended them, each kill would have a deep connection with me. My reflection was pleased with the way I was going about things, allowing me to proceed. However, my reflections then sang the most terrifying song to me, titled "Phantom Beasts." The song was sung so beautifully that I felt compelled to write down the lyrics for you to see. Then, we will return to my killing spree. The song flows so beautifully, here, take a look, there, take a listen, but watch out for the hook.

THE PHANTOM'S GUN

The fire engulfs your decaying soul,
while the demons tear away at your flesh, taking
    complete control.
Once you arrive, there is no way to escape,
leaving you to suffer in the place that your
    conscience creates.

You're choking on thickening smoke, with no
    hope in sight.
You have fallen to your knees, having lost the
    strength needed to fight.

You have no way to leave this place;
you are struggling in a sinking boat.
It's impossible to see clearly; it is so difficult to
    stay afloat.
You are surrounded by darkness, while
    everything is closing in on you.
You do not have a choice, there is not much else
    to lose.

The path to hell is burns the soles of your feet,
while the tormented souls sing with their heads
    hanging low in defeat.
The monsters whip your skin and tenderize you
    for their feast,
as the ominous melodies persist on your trek
    through the scorching streets.

Your heart will soon explode, revealing all that
    was once unknown.
You are simply a piece of meat, the star of the
    phantom's show.
In this realm, you cannot shine; darkness voids
    all light.
Entrapped in your own lies, you make love with
    the beasts that haunt your eyes.

The fire has already consumed your putrid soul.
The demons are still tearing your flesh, retaining
    full control.
The music persists, leaving you unable to turn it
    off.
The lyrics entice and excite you as you listen to
    the sirens' songs.

The intensity of the blaze sears your lungs,
revealing to you what you have become.
You are left howling in defeat, battered, and
    incomplete.
It is finished, it is done, and the melodies cannot

be overcome.
It is already too late, and they will be sung.
When all is said and done,
you will spin the cylinders of the phantom's gun.

You won't be prepared for what lies beyond
the veil of the unseen.
You will be alone,
with nothing but the dark vessels
that were once only a dream.
The tormented souls will forever sing
with their heads hanging low in defeat,
their agony continuing as
you tap your burning feet.
When all is said and done, you will forever
be spinning the cylinders—the cylinders
of the phantom's gun.

I still sing this song to this day. I sing it while committing my uncontrollable acts of violence. I sing it while eating. I sing it to the surrounding trees, which are now encased in bulletproof glass walls. Now, we can return to my horror story. The campers were filled with joy and I constantly yearn for a life like theirs. However, my life does not resemble theirs. All that I have are these visions. All that I have are these voices. All that I have are these cravings for flesh. All that I have are these visions of death. Finally, it was time to act. Upon instruction from my reflection, I selected my first victim—a young man that must be killed violently. He was approximately six and a half feet tall, his build was very slender. Being significantly shorter than him, I had to be extra cautious. He had the ability to easily overpower me. As I gazed at my reflection, it seemingly burst into flames and advised me, *"You should cut his throat to ensure he cannot scream. Just like those men did to your own family."*

My anger surfaced instantly. I waited for him to step

away from the group to relieve himself. I approached quietly, resembling a fierce tiger in the forest rather than a cowardly lion. I found a sharp rock as I crept closer. Then, with the swiftness of light, I sliced into his throat. He gurgled and he choked as I dragged him deeper into the trees. As he gazed into my eyes, desperately trying to cry out, I could feel my hunger consuming me. Like a wild, untamed creature, I sunk my teeth into the wound and began to feed. In that moment, I felt a sense of power and dominance, as if I were ruler of the forest. This was only the beginning of unleashing my inner beast, and I relished in it, feeling like a true King. I am consuming him so rapidly, like a desperate animal. I am starving in these conditions.

My skin is blistered by the scorching sun. I am forced to drink water from the streams. I can hear his companions calling out for him: *"Tom, where are you?"* *"Can you hear me?"* I gazed down at Tom and expressed gratitude for his act of nourishing me. His eyes, nose, and lips were no longer there. I devoured all of them, along with the rest, digesting them as my favorites. I had to act quickly before the police were called. I did not want to return to the cage that once held me captive. I heard Tom's friends approaching, and I knew I needed to move fast. I heard them say what I wanted them to say. One of them said, *"Let's split up so we can cover more ground."* This hunt will be perfect now. My reflection spoke again: *"Now you must choose one of the women, and you may select her end."*

There were three options: one with black hair, one with fire blonde hair, and one with a variety of colors. I chose the coat of many colors. The group split up and I followed the rainbow heading west. As someone well-versed in navigation through reading, I have a natural sense of direction and even have a mental compass. I couldn't help but notice the loudness with which they called out for their friend. I'm ready to approach her, as she stood by a large oak tree. I then grabbed her by the hair and forced her head into it. The woman, now unconscious was facing her inevitable fate. Using the same rock, I slit her throat end to end. After positioning her next to Tom, I took a nibble of her delicate inner thigh flesh. It was incredibly tender as I savored it. This was the closest I had been to a woman since the incident in the courtroom. I know what you're thinking, but rest assured, that's not happening. You sick-minded fool. I took a bite out of her other inner thigh before continuing.

There are four left to be killed. They are still searching for their friends. I will find them soon, and I will have a feast to consume. The most horrifying part of all of this is that my reflection returns every day and instructs me to do so. The four remaining friends noticed that the woman I had just killed was also missing. They called out her name along with Tom's. *"Angela? Tom? Where are you? If this is a joke, it is not funny. We are tired of these twisted jokes coming from the two of you."*

Excellent! I purposely chose the troublemakers of the group first, which will hopefully delay them from involving the authorities. What occurred next is even better. On the forest floor, I spotted a glimmer—like the reflection of metal in the sunlight. Curious, I investigated and discovered a coil of barbed wire lying on the ground. My reflection then spoke once more, *"Utilize this gift to complete your task. Eliminate the remaining four with this tool. Once you do, I will release you for the day. Tomorrow, I will return as usual."* I picked up the barbed wire and stared into it, much like I did with my Grandfather's brass knuckle knife blade. The image took me back to that beautiful day.

The group was reunited and taking a rest, sitting side by side in front of a rock formation, discussing their plans. However, they soon began blaming each other and acting foolishly. This gave me the opportunity to sneak around behind them. Here comes the best part—it becomes beautifully violent. I stretched the barbed wire as far as the rock formation behind them, utilizing Tom and Angela's shirts as makeshift gloves to prevent injuring my hands. As they continued to argue, unaware of my presence, I secured the barbed wire by tying each end to separate trees. I swiftly sprinted backwards, tautly pulling it like a rubber band. As I stood before them, gripping the barbed wire, I briefly asserted my presence. Without hesitation, I instantly released it and beheaded all of them. I savored the sight of their heads sliding off as I licked my lips. The look in their eyes as they met their end was so beautiful. It happened so quickly. I screamed at my reflection and gazed into the glass. *"I did it! They are all dead."*

Before my reflection disappears into this now bloodied wasteland, it is accompanied by a story to share, somewhat tying together my reprehensible actions out here in the forest. I have had enough food for what I feel has been weeks. One day inside my head can often feel like weeks. I have no way to cook them, so I do what I must do and eat them raw until nothing remains. You should see the flies buzzing and the maggots consuming the waste, the blood splattered on my face. You should experience the scent of death first-hand. Take a whiff of his place. My reflection has disappeared for today. What follows are my nightmares. I wonder what will be done to me during my first adventure outside of my cage. There are going to be so many casualties in this place. Each day that these visions recur, I am compelled to follow their instructions. I am aware that I deserve to be confined. I will persevere until they capture or eliminate me, as I am tormented by these voices in every way. Every day, my reflection echoes the same tale, and without understanding, I am hopelessly lost.

MY RESERVATION

The Reservation

Deep in the forest, a group of five friends sits by the fire, reminiscing about the past and smoking cigarettes to elevate their conversations. Little did they know about the horrors that await behind the trees, as an ancient evil lurks in search of its next feast. This creature was once human and even served as the leader of its tribe. As the flames lick higher, the group is perplexed. The seasoned entity is well aware of its intentions. The group of friends, all males in their early thirties, are unaware of the impending danger. Oblivious to the impending doom, they begin to indulge in marijuana and alcohol. The cunning old Chief knows that this will be an effortless conquest.

He has been murdering for hundreds of years, seeking revenge for the countless tears he has shed. His family was taken from him long ago, and he seeks vengeance to this day for their deaths. The only home he knows is his cursed prison on The Reservation, where he will never be reunited with his loved ones again, fueling his relentless aggression. These men have no protection. I will not mention their names as they are irrelevant. The malevolent force pursuing them only seeks their blood to be spilled. He observes them carefully, waiting for the opportune moment. The screams reverberate throughout the forest. Their souls will decay in agony. One of the men steps away to relieve himself.

The enraged ghost ferociously rips and silences his screaming mouth, before tearing out his throat. He then dismembers him entirely, leaving not another sound. He knows the others will soon search for him. With a wicked smile, he exposes his sharp, rotting teeth. The four men are now calling for their deceased friend. The entity is now anticipating the rest of the destruction to commence. The men are now filled with terror, like all the other victims. The blood will continue to flow now, and each one of them will meet their mortal end.

The elder Chief frequently experiences traumatic flashbacks of his family's brutal murders. The memories of their violent deaths continue to deeply disturb him. His recollections are incredibly vivid, particularly of his daughter's murder at the hands of a group of settlers who brutally dismembered her. The ancient Phenom can still, even hundreds of years later, hear her piercing screams. He will always seek vengeance, killing off every human being he sees and spilling their vile blood for centuries. He cannot escape his Reservation, and he will never leave. Anyone who dares set foot on his land will feel the full extent of his of his wrath. The four men continue to search for their friend who has been torn apart. They stumble through the treacherous and foreboding forest, sticking closely together like sardines in a wretched can. The tribal leader foams at the mouth, his determination evident. He will make the others understand. His piercing white eyes fixate on the next hapless victim, and with a swift strike, he chooses his next target. They all began screaming as he exacted his vengeance, tearing off each limb, just as the settlers had done to his daughter. He then takes one arm and sucks it down his throat without chewing, in full view of the others. He looks at them and lets out a deafening screech, demanding, *"I want another!"*

The three remaining men cover their ears and begin to run. The undead creature relishes in the chase. The three remaining friends are completely helpless. There is no escape even after death. It is impossible to kill something that is already dead. It is only a matter of time until the hourglass runs out of sand. When one dies on The Reservation, their spirit will become a resident. Every soul that perished on this cursed land will spend an eternity with the Chief, an eternity they never imagined they would be forced to endure.

The tormented tribal spirit is now experiencing memories of the brutal slaying of his wife, who was cruelly taken from him. The murderers used a hunting knife to cut out both of her eyes. The spirit holds his head and lets out a violent scream under the starry sky, with his rage only growing stronger, driving him to kill anything in his path. He opens his mouth to reveal something that has never been seen before. A completely new, monstrous sight. His eyes are beady white pinpoints while his teeth are curved and sharper than a Great White's. The rotting teeth only hide what is lurking inside. He roars ferociously, hungry for human life. The three remaining men do not stand a chance. One by one, the phantom opens them up, devouring each one as planned. The screaming continues until all breathing ceases. The internal organs are stretched out and displayed beautifully, hung with pride throughout the forests of the Reservation.

For the ancient Chief, it provides a temporary sense of fulfillment. His revenge is his source of immediate gratification. There are warnings about stepping foot on this cursed land. An ominous presence lies in wait, eager to impart its sinister wisdom. This being will forever pursue those who took his life. Never set foot on his Reservation unless you are prepared to face death. He was assassinated shortly after his Daughter and Wife. He was compelled to witness their deaths. Tears still pour from his empty eyes. He was slowly torn apart, feeling every knife, causing unimaginable pain. His ears were removed first by the settlers, followed by the cutting out of his liver. They further opened his chest, removing everything, as he screamed and shivered in agony. And now, he inflicts all of the pain that he once felt. Stepping onto his Reservation is an experience worse than entering Hell.

Please pay close attention to the stories. Not taking them seriously will not benefit you. He will forever roam among those trees. Many more unfortunate souls will experience the vengeful wrath he seeks. Death will never fully satisfy him. Countless spirits are eternally trapped on his cursed land, forced to endure endless death at the command of the tribe leader. They are relentlessly pursued, like players in a game of terrifying chess. There is no escape for them, condemned to endure eternal agony. The Reservation contains endless shrieking spirits, perpetually torn apart and imprisoned. The first, bloody encounter with The Chief was only the beginning. He is insatiable and will not heed your pleas—nor show mercy. However, it should be noted that he was not always a beast. He will always exact retribution for himself and his slaughtered family. The Chief will always hold you accountable; he blames you—he blames humanity.

Perhaps I am similar to the ancient Chief, driven by a desire for revenge on behalf of my family, just like him. These voices constantly torment me with thoughts of my deceased loved ones. They fuel my rage and, for me, there is no escape. Just has he could not leave The Reservation, I am bound to stay here. I also blame you—I blame humanity.

My Nightmare

I AM BACK in the river once again, washing away the blood. I have consumed all of the campers now. I am relieved that my reflection is gone for today. As much as I can't stand its arrival, there is a sense of satisfaction in it. The animation, vision, or voice—whatever you may call it—of my nightmares has now appeared, standing on two legs. The tiny creature has six tiny arms and is stitched around its brain. It possesses human-like teeth, serving as a constant reminder of the reason for my existence. It is the embodiment of every nightmare I have ever experienced and each that I will encounter; its presence places me into an epileptic seizure-like state. I am paralyzed in its presence, rendered unable to move my limbs.

Devoid of sight, it relentlessly tracks my every movement with precision. It wields complete dominion over my bodily processes, thoughts, and even my dreams. Like a serpent injecting venom into prey, it injects my nightmares into my being. My nightmares consist of neurotoxins, which expose my actions. They also reveal glimpses of the future and my impending behaviors, leading me to contemplate my own mortality. In this place, I will detail each of my current nightmares, one at a time.

My nightmares spiral and churn like an F5 tornado, decimating everything in my mind on a ceaseless loop.

This vicious tormentor never gives me a moment's peace as it tears me apart . It always begins with the image of my deceased family, their throats viciously slashed. In the dream, I am always cowering in the hidden closet in my room, listening to my family being slaughtered as if it were happening in present time. The nightmare is identical each time. I see them lying there, lifeless bodies on full display. Their eyes are wide open and I will never be able to erase that horrific image from my mind.

The difference between what occurred and my nightmare is that they all suddenly stand up and begin to scream. Mom, Dad, Nick, Marcus, and Daniel are all screaming, no longer resembling the terrifying visions I had of them. Instead, they look human again —just like the first time I saw them dead. Why I am cursed this way? I will never understand. I can feel my tears flowing as they are shed. The screams continue for about ten minutes. After the screaming ceases, they begin to speak. They begin to talk to me like they used to. My father speaks first and asks, *"Geoff, are you okay?" You look upset. Would you like to talk about it, son?"* He says this, despite the gaping wound on his throat, and manages a smile. It is absolutely terrifying, and his eyes remain dead and wide. My mother speaks next and says, *"Geoff, please come to Mommy. You look like you need some love."*

My brothers just stand there in a trance, while my parents take their turns. I am frozen in fear, just like a deer in headlights. This nightmare is intense. I'm still in a seizure-like state. I can tell because I always wake up and have to wipe the white foam from my face. My mother then embraces me as blood from her wound drips onto me. My father then joins in and embraces me as well. Once they finish hugging me, Daniel speaks to me right on cue. It's a recurring nightmare, so I know exactly what he's about to say and do. He says, *"Geoff, I love and miss you, my brother,"* just like my parents, with wide eyes and the same throat wound.

Seeing them this way is far more terrifying than the visions I have of them in my monstrous illustrations. This nightmare evokes overwhelming emotions that not only shatter my mind but also my heart. I regret not having all of the journals I wrote during my time in prison. I had to leave behind hundreds of them. If I am caught again, I hope to be reunited with them. It is possible that the authorities are reading them in an attempt to understand my thoughts. If they were to shoot me, I would never be able to write again.

Nick then approaches me and embraces me, our parents' blood mixing with his own. Just like the vivid vision that consistently haunts me, he starts to scold me in this nightmare, before turning to me and saying, *'I love you, bro, Why didn't you scream when you heard those men shatter the glass? You could have given us a chance. You could have saved us.'* He accuses, *'You're selfish, Geoff. You're so fucking selfish!'* Same wide-eyed expression, same bleeding gash. He then hugs me and mixes his blood with Daniel's and my parents. He appears to be exhibiting symptoms of schizophrenia when he addresses me once more, altering his behavior and stating, *"Geoff, it is not your fault. Don't listen to that version of myself. He's an asshole for saying those awful things to you."* He starts to criticize me, but then abruptly shifts to consoling me. He does not raise his voice or show anger when he speaks. This occurrence takes place once a day, every day, and has been happening for many years.

Marcus doesn't say much, he just mumbles his words like my portrayal of him. He simply gazes at me and then embraces me. Meeting his eyes is like looking into my own reflection in a mirror. The nightmare comes to an end as Marcus smiles and chuckles. He concludes by saying, *"I love you Geoff, but you're a madman. You don't have to kill, but you choose to. I can't change what you've become, but I can try.*" This is the only time I can understand him—the same wide-eyed expression, the same bleeding, seeping gash. This is one of the most terrifying nightmares that I have had. This tiny creature before me emits snarls and laughter, it's trembling body ejecting white foam onto the grassy forest floor. It consistently provokes two terrifying nightmares before departing, leaving me trembling and defenseless. The grunts and chuckles only serve to prepare me for what is to come. If you thought that nightmare was scary, wait until I tell you about nightmare number two. My body begins to shake faster, harder, and more violently as this creature from my nightmares enters round two. I can see it, but I cannot move. It finally speaks and says: *"Geoff, are you ready for what I'm about to do?"* The next nightmare is a reversal of all the murders that I have committed, both old and new.

The challenging aspect of this nightmare is that I can sense the pain endured by all my victims. The three men who murdered my family did not feel anything because I shot each of them between the eyes through a pillow before I proceeded to cut them up and consume them. Madness is repetition, I know I have said that before! The haunting images in my nightmares ensure that I experience it. I am trembling now, much like the frames on a wall during an earthquake. I can feel every snap of their bones and every slice of their skin. It is as if my insides are being torn apart from within. Is this the hell that is described in biblical texts? I can feel it all as my nightmares seep into my skin.

I am screaming loudly, but my mouth is full of rabid foam and no sound is coming out. The six-armed creature appears to take pleasure from my distress. My skin begins to burn, as if it is boiling. This nightmare inflicts unbearable agony, in turn, bringing about the repercussions of my actions. I am unable to comprehend why I must endure this suffering each day, or why I am forced to suffer. This nightmare forces me to relive the pain endured by each of my victims, one after another. Cut by cut. Scream by scream. Death by death. From my family's murderers to their sister in the courtroom, the prison guard's nose, the other prison guard's fingers, the jogging couple in the woods, and the six campers.

I am aware of the anguish that I have caused when this nightmare resurfaces. I understand that I am deserving of this punishment. I know I cannot stay out here much longer, or I will I'll continue to feed my desires. I am constantly adding to this nightmare that haunts me daily knowing the consequences. My attempts to break my addiction to violence have been unsuccessful. When I wake up, the six-armed creature with human-like teeth and a stitched-up brain has disappeared, along with the pain. It always says before it vanishes, *"The more you kill, the more pain you will feel. The more pain you inflict, the more you will squeal. As your body count rises, I will add time to your nightmare. The only way to make me stop is to overcome your addictions. Although you may have freedom, you will always be confined within your own personal prisons. Geoff, you are weak and easily controlled by your visions."*

Every day, after my nightmare vanishes, my body is weak from feeling all of the pain that I have caused. The thick white foam still excretes from my mouth, yet there is not a single mark on my body after enduring such turmoil. You would think this experience would deter my desire to kill, but it only intensifies my craving after I regain my composure. My nightmare only serves to fuel my addiction to death and consuming human flesh. I savor every moment of the excruciating pain in that second nightmare, but the first one utterly breaks me. My family's mixed blood in reality includes the blood of my victims and animals in this forest. I must venture deeper into the woods to avoid an encounter with the authorities. The six-armed monster will return tomorrow, and I am certain that I will have countless new nightmares by then.

My Inner Turmoil

I AM A PUPPET to my inner turmoil. It controls me, molds me, and holds me down into the fire. There is nothing I can do to change the way I am, it just is. It's just that, it's just madness. This is the way my life has been given to me. The vision of my inner turmoil is as blue as the tropical oceans that I have only seen in books and magazines. I hold it in my hands when it reveals itself to me, an illusion of me holding this half-corpse demon. It contains all of the suffering that resides within me—the anger, the dread. The many voices that I describe within these pages scream in my head. Pressing that repeat button again and again. This forest is enveloping me with its vastness. I am beginning to feel the intense hunger once more. When will this cease? Will it ultimately lead to my demise? I'm only halfway through my life, yet I yearn for this to all make sense.

As I have stated previously, I would never choose to end my own life. While I am capable of taking another's life without remorse, I cannot inflict such harm upon myself. The idea of inner turmoil tempts me towards death, a temptation that presents itself daily within the desolate landscape of my mind. The human skeletons are bound to the blue puppets' wrists, symbolizing the weight of this struggle. It tells me that death would end all of the screaming and uncontrollable urges to be fed. It also tells me that it would end the nightmares and stop the visions of my family being attacked. It would bring me peace if I were to choose death. I am aware that death is often perceived as a demon, and is known to be deceitful. It is attempting to manipulate me into surrendering my soul and leading me further into the flames. The manifestation of my inner turmoil is presenting visions of potential freedom, seducing me with my deepest desires.

I am about to write about how this monster attempts to lure me into hell. It presents me with illusions and deceives me with the things I beg for—love, acceptance, and an end to the constant voices in my head. It is aware of this and exploits it to the fullest. It has roots growing where its legs should be, wrapped in what appears to be some kind of netting. This evil entity attempts to ensnare me in its trap, pushing me towards self-destruction. I refuse to give in, no matter how difficult things may become or how severe the pain is. In order escape my inner torment, I feel compelled to feed once more. I know you must be wondering how I managed to escape it while I was confined. I sat in the corner of my cell with my face to the wall and cried until this monster disappeared from my sight. I must continue hunting until this voice fades. This one is particularly dangerous—if I get caught in its trap, I may not be able to escape. So, I sprinted with all my might, clutching this monster tightly in my hands. I launch it forward, mimicking the motion of hurling it down the river's edge. Despite my efforts, it continues to deceive me with its false promises. No matter how many attempts I make to rid myself of it, it inevitably finds its way back into my grasp.

I just have to wait it out until this vision fades for the night. It tempts me with promises of eternal love and comfort if I take my own life. It lures me with the promise of pleasure if I give in and die. However, I have been stronger than this vision every time. I will continue to fight and remain alive until my time comes. I scream at it and firmly deny its power over me. It is persistent in its efforts. These voices dictate actions to me. At times, I am able to resist them. Other times, my true self remains unheard. They speak to me. They yell at me. The voice of inner turmoil wishes for my demise. I must calm my mind and find something to eat to occupy myself in passing the time. As I began to hear loud bangs in the distance, I realized they were gunshots. However, prior to this moment, I had only heard a gun when I had to avenge my family and myself against our attackers.

The sharp noise certainly captured my attention, but it was much more powerful than the sound of my Grandfather's gun. I started to walk towards the source of the sound, and the closer I got, the louder it became. I remained hidden as I approached what appeared to be an unfamiliar man. He was clothed entirely in black, and there was a deer carcass lying lifeless at his feet. It became clear that he was a hunter, just like myself. I watched him with admiration from my spot in the trees. My hunger was beginning to overpower me. He moved just as silently as I did. I had to be cautious before he detected me.

The man in black would soon become my next meal. I needed to divert my attention from the inner turmoil raging within me. So I waited patiently for him to turn his back. And once he did, I pounced like a tiger, biting into his throat and tearing out a large chunk. His gun was not in his possession as he struggled to breathe and choked. I continued to take bites and then removed his back overcoat. Once again, my insatiable hunger had been fulfilled. The torment within me had dissipated. The following description of my madness delves into the depths of my personal hell. Even though I am experiencing inner turmoil, I refuse to end my own life.

My Hell

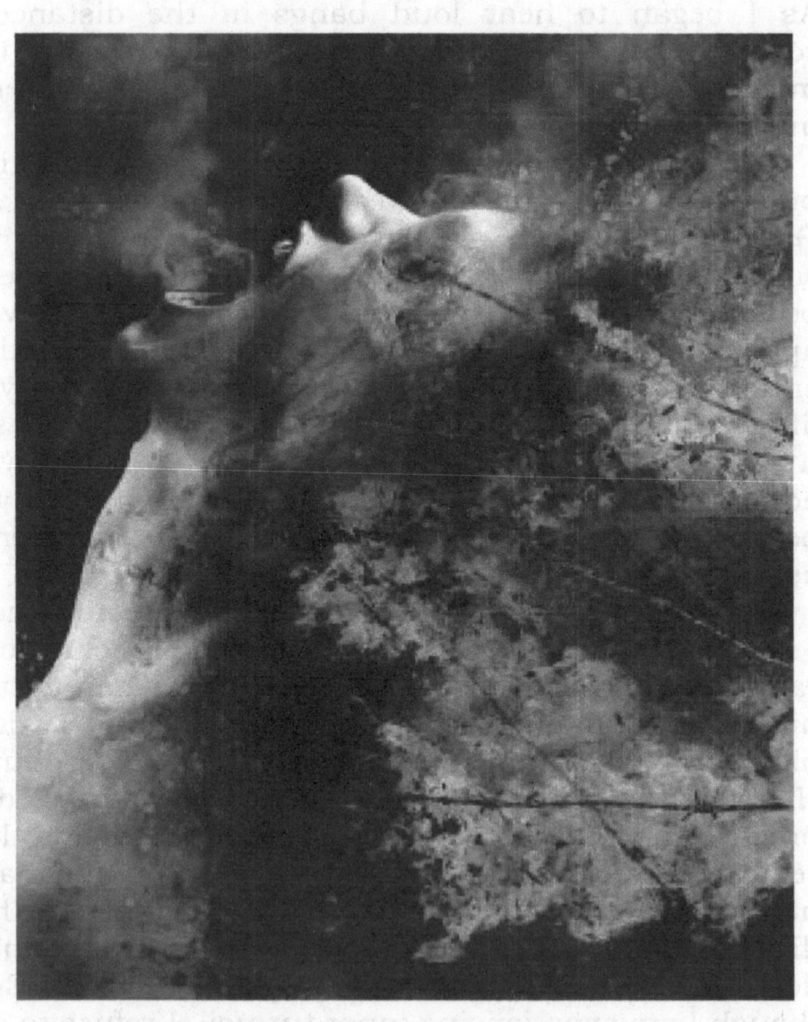

WHEN MY HELL arrives, I can smell the cooking flesh. I wish I had something to cook this man in black with. I can hear the vengeful screaming through the perfection of my chaos. I can hear the heated barbed wire cracking like a whip. My hell is a vision of a woman in flames, screaming as the fire melts her flesh. There are multiple lines of barbed wire hooked into her eyes, back, shoulders, legs, and neck. My personal hell visits me every day and instigates lucid dreams of alternate realities—potential lives that I could lead if I were not constrained and consumed by madness. It repeats, just like every other voice in my head. I will carefully record and accurately title each reality. Every day, the woman engulfed in flames with barbed wire piercing her flesh in multiple points all over her body tells me three stories. I am passionate about documenting and am committed to writing down every detail. Each reality that is revealed to me is very harsh. There is no happiness when my hell is shuffling the deck and dealing me the cards. This is the first alternate reality that my hell presents to me:

MURDEROUS FOREST

I have diligently combed through this murderous and treacherous forest in search of evidence. The harrowing faces of the victims linger in my mind, haunted by their fear and dread. It is unfathomable that this could be the final fate of someone. I am determined to continue my search for the perpetrator and fulfill my duties as a Detective. I am exploring the roots of these ancient trees, sifting through the soil on my weary knees. I could have sworn I heard them all scream in the distance. The fatigue must be overtaking me. How long have I been rummaging through these leaves? Suddenly, I heard a voice from beyond the tree line. A woman screamed, *"Please don't kill me!"* My left knee buckled in sudden pain, as if a knife had been inserted in me. I was certain that I was bleeding, but when I looked down, there was no blood.

I must continue my search for justice for the deceased, who seem to be calling out to me. Their grieving families are haunting me. So far, there are fifteen missing women. The smell of various stages of decomposition are strong out here, and I am certain that I am on the right track. I swear I just felt a hand pressing against my back. My arm hairs stood upright, and I am afraid I am being attacked. It is hard to think clearly, and my thoughts are unorganized. As I turned to my right, there was nothing there except a blood-stained backpack that appeared to materialize out of nowhere. Finally, a clue that could aid me capturing this suspect.

The signs and clues are informing me of what actions to take. I will locate this human monster and hold it accountable. Either the deceased are aiding me or my sanity is slipping away. Time is limited, and I must search through the backpack for evidence of the missing women I must locate. Upon finding an ID inside, I discovered her name was Rachel Melekai. She is only thirty years old, but she appears to radiate with an inner light. There is also a piece of paper in the backpack that reads, "Look to your left." When I turned, Ms. Melekai was standing there, her midsection bleeding as she screamed for me to die. Behind her were all of the women who had also been tragically murdered, all of them bleeding from various internal wounds.

The women glared at me with intense hatred in their eyes. *"I'm trying to help you!"* I screamed. But they only continued to scream, *"You're going to die!"* I quickly ran until I found a suitable hiding spot. Ahead of me, there was a cabin where I could take cover. As soon as I arrived, I swiftly locked the door behind me. The deceased women were screaming in unison, accusing me of their murders and impending death. On the kitchen table, there was a package with my name written on the side. I asked myself, *"Is this my cabin? Am I the bad guy? Did I really do this?"* I killed all of these women and I can't understand why. What turned me into this monster? What went wrong inside?

I had forgotten each time I took a life. I can hear the screams of the deceased women nearby. I deserve what is coming to me. I am responsible for taking each of their lives. As tears fall from my eyes, I am unable to recall any of it. The door of the cabin begins to shake, and the voices of the deceased start to pound in my brain. They are now revealing to me how each one of them met their fate. I have taken the lives of fifteen innocent people and they are illustrating to me how I will face punishment. I performed an incision on the stomachs of some, slit the throats of others, stabbed some in the eye sockets, burned, strangled several, and smothered others with the lifeless bodies of the bodies I had collected. I utilized my role as a detective to mask my motives—the yearning to take a life, the need to instill fear, and the urge to witness bloodshed—from my targeted victims. The memory of every gaze in their demise is beginning to resurface.

Why was my memory taken away? Why do I not remember? Why is it all coming back this way? Rachel Melekai then spoke to me calmly and said, *"You will pay dearly. You will not face immediate death. You will be haunted long after your dying day. You will see our skin being ripped. You will smell our burning skin while smothering underneath us. Our screaming voices will be heard everywhere, you piece of shit. You will lose your mind before we are finished. Even after death, you will be with us gasping for air. We will treat you as you have treated us. We will burn you. We will suffocate and choke you. We will spill your vile blood. Even if you try to escape, we will pursue you. You will pay for what you have done. There is no place for you to run. We are eternally attached to you. You will be forced to taste us. You are our prey now, and you will provide us with the pleasure of revenge whenever we want."*

The deceased corpses of the fifteen women that I have killed take turns violating me, laughing as they smother me beneath their decomposing bodies. Forever forcing me to pleasure them and relive the horrific acts I have committed. Stabbing and setting me ablaze, as they took turns sitting on top of me, covering my nose and mouth with their dead flesh—these were the events leading up to the eternal nightmare. Or has it already begun? What has been done cannot be undone.

January 12, 1999: My First Kill

It was a bitterly cold January evening when I found myself without a job, a wife, or my children. I had been working as an agent for a prominent media company, but now I had lost everything that had been holding back the fierce inner beast within me. I was dismissed because I failed to secure the major contract that the company had dedicated months of effort towards obtaining. I blame my failures on a sudden and inexplicable urge to be violent and cause harm to others, which I had never encountered before. It also manifested in my personal life, leading my wife to take our children and leave me alone. I even engaged in violent behavior at home, leading me to seek therapy with the intention of changing. Prior to this experience, I had never shown violent tendencies, leaving me confused as to their origins and what may have caused them. All I know is that it persisted. It gnawed at me. It consumed me. It prompted thoughts of terrible things I wanted to do to others. It trapped me in a cage.

On the night of January 12, I killed the first of many women who haunt me to this very day. I am remembering everything again. The weight of the murders is too much, I can feel my victims sitting on my face. These voices are here to stay! Now, I will explain when I took the first human life. It was a cold, late night. I saw a woman leaving her apartment. I began to stalk her from the shadows and memorized her routine. After a few days, I cut into her face. She was a local prostitute, and I just couldn't resist. I couldn't stop myself from cutting them. I dragged each one of my victims into the nearby forest and used a syringe filled with a sedative to prevent them from screaming.

I took their lives in complete silence. I had extensively studied law through various books and learned to cover my tracks before taking their lives. She lay there motionless and did not make a sound. I'd always lay my hand on their hearts until I didn't hear them beat. I would take them to my cabin and bury them in the backyard. After my first kill, I went to the police station and applied for a job. I had taught myself law for many years before. After graduating from the police academy, I was hired as a detective by the Eastern Maine Police Force. This opportunity opened many doors for me to delve into my disturbing urges. My wife and children never contacted me again, fueling my desires for murderous endeavors. My anger was the only thing left for me to cherish. Following my initial kill, I desired much more.

*February 13, 1999: My Rampage As A Law
    Enforcement Officer*
The police chief and all of the staff have come to admire me in a short period of time. I have demonstrated a high level of knowledge in crime-related manners. I have contributed to major busts during my tenure and as a result, my work has received impressive reviews. Chief Jackson has taken notice and is interested in discussing a promotion to lead detective with me. Naturally, I accepted the position and was assigned to my very first case. It involved the mysterious disappearance of a woman who was reputed for her involvement in drug use and prostitution within the community. A friend of hers came in and filed a missing persons report. I did not know the names of my victims until they were described to me by someone else. I immediately accepted the case and knew right

away that it was my first kill. The woman who filed the missing persons report is named Michele Deangelo. She is searching for her friend Rachel Melekai who is buried behind my cabin in the forest. As I think about Rachel, I cannot help but smile inside like a child on Christmas Day. I realized right then and there who my next target would be. *It is you, Michelle!"* I thought to myself.

I immediately started strategizing my attack as Michelle recounted the story of her deceased friend. I envisioned carefully removing her skin and extracting her teeth to prevent anyone from identifying her if her body was discovered. I also envisioned shaving her head bald and scalping her, ensuring that no other hair could grow in. I did the same to her friend Rachel.

It is said that hair continues to grow after death, so I took precautionary measures to prevent her identification. Michelle gave me her phone number and address so I could contact her with further questions.

Little did she know that the next time she sees me, it will be her final moments on earth.

The workday is now over, and I need to go home and prepare my tools for my next prey. The syringe is now filled with the sedative to prevent her from screaming. My knives have been relentlessly sharpened. I plan to pursue her tonight and she will join Rachel behind my cabin in the forest. As time draws near, I must exercise caution in my approach, even though I have her address. I knock first and say: *"Hello Michelle, I may have a lead on your friend Rachel. I am sorry to stop by at this odd hour. Would you mind coming down to the station to help me out? I just need you to fill out some additional paperwork that needs to be filed with your original statements.*"

Without hesitation, she agreed and climbed into my car. I drove for a short distance before administering the sedative. The powerful medication acts quickly, rendering people unconscious for an extended period of time. Now, I make my way to my cabin in the murderous forest, where I will prepare her, just as I did her friend. I will shave her head, remove her teeth, and peel back the skin on her face. But this time with a twist—I dug up Rachel from the backyard and smothered Michelle with the decomposing lower half of the corpse. I then set both of them on fire and no screams were uttered. She disappears into the hole behind my cabin with her dear friend Rachel. Oh, the intense thrill of this! I must do it repeatedly. I must find more to fill this hole with. I will get away with it because I am a trusted detective.

As Michelle and Rachel decay in my pit, I am prepared to hunt once more as my mind is on the verge of exploding. Thirteen more times, I have taken a life and disposed of their bodies in my backyard. With each victim, I have removed their hair and teeth, stabbing them in various areas, and slitting some of their throats. I have also incinerated their bodies after meticulously peeling away their faces. I suffocated some while they were still alive with the deceased. The terror in their eyes, with a mouthful of delicate dead flesh, comforted me. I took on each case and pretended that I was searching for them all, pretending that I wanted to bring justice to all of these missing persons. The hell that I am facing now is my own fault. It is a mystery why my memory has forgotten all of this. I am a now a dead detective, and these spiteful dead women are coming for me.

January 16, 2005: The Price I Pay Is Here

I am now faced with my dead victims. Their faces vanished, bodies charred from my actions. I'm losing this battle and they will never stop coming for me. They will never cease to taunt me. They will continue to take turns covering my mouth and nose with their putrefying lower bodies. Their once delicate, now rotting flesh falls off into my mouth, clogging my airways. They will never stop making my life a living hell, as I deserve it to be. The door of this cabin will not hold them much longer. The price I am paying is becoming increasingly steep. The door swings open and all fifteen dead women rush in. They scream in unison, *"It's our turn to play!"* As the fourteen women repeatedly stabbed me, Rachel Melekai hastily approached me and mounted my face, compelling me to taste the putridness between her legs. A deluge of my own vomit engulfed me where I lay.

She then declares, *"No sedition for you, Detective! You are going to feel this. You are going to feel all of our pain."* She then took hold of my pliers and proceeded to extract my teeth, one by one. I could feel the distinct separation between my tooth and gum, the metallic taste of copper and vomit filling my mouth. She pulled the tooth then and then sat back down, muffling my now toothless face as I screamed. Despite my muffled cries, they took turns straddling me, keeping my cries unheard. The lifeless women then carried me to the pit where their decaying bodies once lay, forcing my face in between each of their putrid thighs.

In this murderous forest, the dead women's revenge was fulfilled. I am now doomed to join my victims and suffer their pain. I deserve this in so many ways. I must endure the unleashed fury of these women, being forced to smother underneath them, burned and stabbed repeatedly, and forced to die again and again. As they take turns having their way with me, I see the demons in the background licking their lips. I have become their slave of revenge, pleasure, and pain. To this day, I am unsure how I could forget the silence of those women when I ended their lives. There will never be an escape for me, but sometimes I pretend while being straddled, burned, and cut by lifeless bodies.

Sometimes I beg for forgiveness and apologize in my anguish. The hysterical laughter of the deceased resounds every time I begin. My apologies carry no weight. I must now bear the weight of all fifteen of my victims, decomposing bodies suffocating and muzzling my worthless apologies. I did not care when I suffocated, burned, and stabbed them to death. They will never care either. I experience the sharpness of the knives each time they pierce my skin. There is no moment of silence when they tear into me! I can even smell and taste their decaying flesh as they forcefully push themselves onto me and press against my face, covering me in what I've taken away. I will forever be punished for what I have done to each of them.

After my hell has shown me this reality, I feel as though I have truly lived it. I experience every emotion in this murderous forest. As I breathe, the air fills my lungs with the scent of decomposing flesh. I realize that I am still trapped in this forest, with no actual bars to cling to. My personal hell haunts me daily, sharing tales of the many ways my conscience can be torn apart. "Murderous Forest" is the first of two stories told by the woman engulfed in flames. The next one that she narrates is equally gripping, although not as graphic. I experience everything—sight, smell, taste—as if I am being transported into the stories as they unfold.

While engulfed in those flames with barbed wire hooks lashing around, the demon begins revealing my next alternate life. This anthropomorphic entity does not simply narrate these stories; she delivers them in blood-curdling shrieks. Her screams reverberate through my entire being like searing blades at a thousand degrees. I am watching her flesh being burned off of her as multiple lines of barbed wire puncture her eyes and skin. I can still physically feel the presence of the deceased women in the forest, as If they were pulling out my teeth, burning, stabbing, and muffling my screams. The putrid taste of their rotting flesh lingers on my tongue, similar to that of decomposing pork.

My personal hell also descends upon me, igniting and smothering my voice of reason, while Its fiery grip consumes my dignity as I kick my feet beneath it. I hope this is not my fate when I die. My hell then erupted into screams as she exclaimed, *"This is a tale from the sea. Pay attention, Geoff, and listen carefully! If you do not listen, this will never make sense! Can you still breathe after entering 'The Murderous Forest?"* This *next story might just give you a breath of fresh air, but I won't guarantee it. The tale from the sea that I like to call 'The Mermaid's Breath' is coming up."*

THE MERMAID'S BREATH

Mike Francisco awoke on the morning of December 31, 1990 in a rush of excitement. He was about to sign the paperwork for his very first boat purchase. Mike was an aspiring fisherman, following in the footsteps of many generations before him in his saltwater-loving family. Mike was determined to keep the family business afloat and was always employed in one way or another, as fishing for crabs, fish, sharks, and any other undersea creatures was their main source of income for as long as he could remember. From preparing bait to breaking down crustaceans, you name it— Mike was always all in, all the time.

He loved his work with a passion, and nothing could stand in his way. Despite experiencing five failed marriages, his dedication to his work remained constant. Today, however, marked the first day that he was captain of his own ship. As he was just beginning his new adventure, he only had a three-man crew on the day he planned to set sail. He had worked with fewer crew members in the past, so he was not overly concerned. His crew-mates, Nick Drake, Matt Staver, and Lyle Singer, were not only his colleagues, but also his family in Mike's view. However, none of them could have predicted the events of that fateful night when everything changed. The night when reality set in, all four men realized that the stories that they had been told for hundreds of years were wrong.

JANUARY 11, 1991

Nick was preparing bait for the crab catch they had been fishing for days, while Matt steered the boat and Lyle pulled in the traps. Meanwhile, Mike was finally able to get some rest after driving the boat for six days straight without even taking a nap. Then seemingly, out of nowhere, a rogue wave collided with the boat with the force of ten freight trains. An abrupt hole appeared on the side of the boat, precisely where Mike had been asleep.

Nick, Matt, and Lyle called out for their friend and captain, *"Mike!"* but received no response. He had disappeared in an instant. There was no sign of Mike anywhere. The three men were desperately searching, frantic, and exhausted from lack of sleep. Now, the boat was sinking—and fast. The men scrambled to quickly patch the boat, desperate to prevent it from sinking. Stranded hundreds of miles from shore with no radio signal and no potential for rescue, their only hope was to fix the boat themselves.

Thankfully, the men were able to repair the hole in the side of the boat to avoid certain death. However, Mike was no longer with them. It was always a risk of losing a life while navigating the treacherous seas. In sorrow for their dear friend, they gathered for a solemn sea prayer. They lowered their heads and recited the prayer of the ocean.

"Fishermen fish and Fishermen cry. Fishermen live and Fishermen die. Fishermen swim and Fishermen fly. Fishermen reunite in the giant net in the sky."

Lyle excuses himself, telling his friends, "I'm not feeling well," before heading to the restroom to relax for a while. He sat there, reading through a ten-year-old fishing magazine, thinking, "That's Mike for you."

Tears flowed down his face when suddenly *BAM!* The bottom of the boat violently shook. Lyle shot up quickly and peered down into the toilet below him, only to see someone looking back at him. *"What is going on?!"* he screamed. Before he could receive any sort of answer, he heard a woman singing, causing him to instantly lose his composure. A gentle voice beckoned him, *"Come down here and play with me,"* Lyle could not resist her command. He submerged his head into the water of the latrine, and a long, scaly hand reached out and grabbed him by the throat. The force was so great that every one of his bones broke under its grip. His entire body vanished into the small hole. There was no scream. He had disappeared.

Nick knocked on the door about half an hour later. *"Lyle, did you die in there, man?"* Nick called for Matt when he received no response from Lyle. Matt kicked down the door. They both stood in shock; the ship's latrine was flooded with blood. "We have to go home! We have to leave now!" Nick screamed as he made his way to the wheelhouse. Matt ran alongside him as quickly as possible. They were both shaking, attempting to comprehend what had just happened. Neither of them spoke for hours. The only thing that mattered now was getting off the water. Something wasn't right here. Instances like these simply did not occur. From the helm, they both heard a resounding splash emanating from the ocean. They exchanged horrified glances.

The splash was accompanied by a familiar thud, similar to the sound of a fish floundering on the deck. Then, there was only silence for about ten minutes. Suddenly, they heard soft footsteps heading their way. Fear and panic set in as they realized they were trapped. *"Whatever that is, it must have been what killed Lyle!"* Nick's scream echoed through the stillness. Matt, also caught in a state of panic, shouted back, *"Shut up!"*The doorknob of the wheelhouse started to turn. What appeared on the other side frightened both Nick and Matt. There were four young women. They walked on two legs but had a scaly appearance, resembling a combination of a woman and a large fish. Blood dripped from their lips, giving them a menacing aura. They approached the two men and began to sing. They sang and spoke in harmony and with great melody:

"Hello, dear ones. Please, come this way. Join us in the beauty of the ocean and swim with us. We pose no harm to you. Please follow us this way. We offer you magical experiences that will blow you away. And with us, you will forever remain."

Like zombies, Matt and Nick followed the enchanting creatures out of the wheelhouse and onto the deck. The creatures continued to sing so beautifully that Nick, entranced, jumped overboard and into the salty ocean. Matt, on the other hand, remained still, staring at the creatures like a lovesick puppy. He observed as one of his closest friends was violently ripped apart by these mermaid-like women, yet Matt maintained his composure. He did not utter a sound, nor show any sign of fear. The melodic chant of the creatures seemed to cast a powerful spell. It induced a state of hypnotism or trance upon Matt, who stood there looking foolish. Then, suddenly, the creatures retreated into the dark depths of the ocean from which they had emerged. He saw their limbs entwine and join— forming into one beautiful fin. Before they disappeared, they stuck their heads above the surface to sing one final time to Matt. They sang:

"We will always be with you, in your thoughts and within your dreams. You will long to join us, and you will search for us through the seas. You will remember your companions and how each one of them nourished us. We will forever remain in your mind, and you will yearn for us. Farewell."

Matt remained in his entranced state, out of

his mind, as he learned his fate. He would never see those beautiful creatures again. He would have to search for them repeatedly. Their song contained a toxic control that would never release him, no matter where he went. The songs would follow him for the rest of his life. He would never be the same as the curse forever confined him. He would be locked in a madness so intense that he would lose sight of everything around him. The night he lost his friends would replay forever in his dreams. It would also replay forever in his now crippled reality. The breath of the creatures he would now crave until his death. He would never be able to make any sense of it.

Matt guides the boat until it exhausts its fuel, seeking answers and clues while searching for the stunning mermaids. He yearns to hear their enchanting melodies once more, unaware that his affection is fabricated, merely a spell woven over him. As he descends deeper into madness, he floats silently within the depths of the ocean. Without a sense of direction or time, his mind is consumed by the haunting melody of the mermaid's songs that brought about the demise of all who heard them. Though he still clings to life, his dwindling food supply is quickly depleting. Matt will soon discover the ultimate cost he has paid. He is alone, without aid, and without hope. It will not be long before he is reunited with those alluring, scaly women and their enchanting siren songs—the only thing that truly matters to him.

As the ship continues to drift, a brutal storm rolls in, rocking and shaking the boat as it begins to tip. The winds are howling, the water is churning, and the waves are crashing all around. Matt has no intention of trying to radio for help. He is still entranced by the melody of the mermaid's breath. He is still envisioning the tragedy of each of his friends' deaths, seeing it all so vividly and replaying it over and over again. He wonders why they left him alive, pondering what the future holds. He's lost his mind as the storm violently destroys the boat. It's now capsized and he desperately swims to stay above water. He climbs onto the underside and cries out for the alluring, scaled women to come for him. He searches desperately but they are nowhere to be found. As long as the song continues to control him, he won't even attempt to find hope. They have cursed Matt with an insatiable desire for them, leaving him unable to desire anything else.

Even though he may perish, he is determined to scour the oceans in pursuit of the beautiful mermaids who have cursed him. With the boat sinking rapidly, he has no escape as he takes his final breath. He knows it's time to let go. He thinks he hears the song. It's just his mind playing tricks. He's bound to the boat. He's bound to the sea. He's bound to the siren songs for eternity, as the surface fades further and further away. Matt paid the ultimate price. He was in the wrong place on the day they all set out to sea. He never would have dreamed that a song would be his final scream. Matt lay on the bottom of the sea, his life now taken. The water filled his lungs as the song continued to overtake him. The elusive mermaids were still nowhere to be found. They would never be seen again, not by a man consumed by their controlling melodies. He wondered if he could finally find peace. He died due to the toxic effects of the siren's control, caused by the mermaid's breath.

You can still hear the four friends screaming in the wind from time to time. You can also hear them losing every ounce of their minds. Now, only a story remains of the four friends who dreamed of sailing victoriously on the open seas. Mike never expected his new boat to sink. No fisherman ever anticipates such a tragedy. However, the way he went down will remain a secret of the sea. What happened to these men would never be believed, not even if any had survived to tell it. It would have made no sense whatsoever. The men succumbed to the siren's methodically enchanting breath. Each had their own song, each with a distinct controlling tone. Three men were devoured by the unfamiliar creatures, while one was left to the mercy of the tumultuous waters. To this day, Matt still lays at the bottom of the ocean, eagerly waiting to hear the siren's songs, searching for the answer to where his mind has gone. Only a pile of bones remain now, a tragic reminder of the consequences of a mind-numbing hold. Will the souls of these four men ever find peace, or will they forever succumb to the control of the mermaid's breath?

NEW WORLD: DAY ONE

The mysterious deaths of these four men were not the first, for these creatures have been inhabiting the oceans for thousands of years for a specific purpose. They were placed there by an otherworldly force that remains unknown to humanity, serving as pawns of something much more malevolent and unearthly. Transported to the oceans from many light years away, they were planted into the waters with the intent to eradicate the existence of the human race. Is it far-fetched? Absolutely. However, it's the truth.

These creatures are created to be both beautiful and enticing, their songs acting as a powerful weapon. It has the ability to control every human thought and emotion, making it a deadly force. This species will utilize the various songs to attain full control over everything prior to decimating it.

They intend to extract every natural resource and abandon it as an empty shell. The oceans are teeming with these magnificent creatures, poised to leave the Earth in ruins. Their extraordinary abilities are limitless as they move effortlessly from fish to humans, seamlessly exiting and re-entering the salty depths. They possess knowledge of every language in our world and easily blend into the masses, much like blue integrates with black. The human race is unaware of their plans to attack. The time is drawing nearer. Every creature is on alert. This is not the first planet that they have cursed. They are like flies on a pile of dung, devouring everything in existence. They have an insatiable desire to consume everything with their words. The lyrics of their song, once heard, can cause irreversible damage. Each exquisite verse is masterfully controlled. The instructions call for them to sing in unison. Their harmonious voices will grant them control over billions of human minds when they sing together. This plan has been in place for thousands of years. The time is now, and it is finally here. In unison, all beings of the land and sea begin to sing their own unique songs, blending together in perfect harmony.

The initial impact of the song will render a human being unconscious. The deafening crash of the world collapsing is exceptionally terrifying. The world suddenly falls silent to the sounds of the Sirens' melodies. In a brutal chaos, the creatures emerge from depths of all oceans all over the world. They viciously tear apart and consume any human life in their path. The world is rendered unconscious by the beautiful sounds, making it easy prey. The invaders devour helpless victims without a sound, as the sky opens up for their onslaught. The time has come to make another world disappear—the sky cracks open with a never before seen sight. Like little water drops emerging from above the trees, they grow bigger as they feed on the clouds. Feeding on the air, and the sounds of every living thing they are destroying. They have soldiers on the ground and in the seas, constantly feeding and wreaking havoc. Now, soldiers have taken to the air, securing and transforming this world into the true shell it was always intended to be. The ethereal melodies of the Siren Songs still linger in the air, being only the start of this cosmic warfare.

NEW WORLD: SECOND AND FINAL DAY

I write this from a soundproof bunker, twenty-five feet underground. There is nothing left for me to do but wait out my remaining time. I have enough food and water to last me for the rest of my life, however long that may be. I am aware that I will never make it out of here alive. If I manage to escape from my soundproof cage, The Songs of the Sirens will still kill me. I am aware that the world above has been destroyed. Everything I cherished has been brutally slaughtered. I am still unsure of the true nature of these beings. Are they Mermaids? Are they Aliens? Or perhaps a combination of both? I understand that the confusion I am experiencing is deliberate. My name is Mark Francisco, and my father was Mike Francisco. He disappeared with his boat on January 11, 1991, when I was only nine years old. However, the boat was found and recovered from the depths twenty years later. Now, at thirty-nine years old, I am still trying to piece together what happened to my father. He was a hard-working man. I know what these things did to him and his crew. Dad used to write about everything he did, which is probably where I inherited it from. After finding the boat, they also uncovered a safe. The police soon after brought the safe to me before chaos ensued. What awaited inside that safe was the truth.

There were many logbooks, all written by my his crew. They documented the first encounters with these creatures until the very last, chronicling the doom they had faced. Everything that was left unwritten, hidden between the lines, was screaming at me. I will never leave this place. I have nothing but time to waste. The log books serve as the foundation for recounting when we all were replaced. Not having anyone to confide in here, I hope this rambling will be of use to someone in the future. I am grateful for the preparations I have made over the years and for creating this crucial stronghold. I would not have survived without it. I am grateful for my madness. I am committed to fully memorizing every logbook in order to persevere what little sanity I have left. Perhaps in the future, if normalcy returns, this work will be published.

This underground box is my entire existence at the moment. I may never see the light of day again. One of my greatest fears has surfaced— dying alone. Will I die of old age? Will I end my life myself? I could leave, but I am aware of the consequences. I do not wish to be mutilated or have my thoughts manipulated. What if they discover me here? I have no other place to go. I must alter my thinking process. Starting on page one, I am reading about horrific events that I have always been desperate to know more about. Some books contain ten days of entries, while others have fewer. Each member of the crew likely experienced a horrific death. I apologize, Dad. I am deeply sorry that you suffered. I wish I could have been there to spare you. I am with you now, Dad. Can you hear me? Am I a coward for hiding? Please, say something! I did not anticipate a response. Unfortunately, that response never came. I hope that he has found peace and is no longer aflame.

To conclude its daily reign of terror, my Hell unleashes one final tale before departing from my thoughts and vision. It presents a tale of the future, both terrifying and poignant, about the universe and its potential for both beauty and evil. I have always been captivated by the stars, and it is aware of this. It tells the story as it burns in front of my eyes, calling its its final tale *"Forever Human."* This story always gives me false hope, once again dangling happiness in front of me. I am aware that it will always be out of reach, and so is the storyteller engulfed in flames with barbed wire piercing its skin.

Forever Human

ALL THAT I can see now is the vastness and never-ending void of space on all sides of me. The planet Earth has long disappeared from my view. I believe it has been decades, or even longer, but my programming has been intermittently going on and offline. I am currently nearing the end of my battery life. Once my battery dies, I will be unable to move or function—but my consciousness will remain intact. I am uncertain of its destination, but I am certain that it will remain within this robotic shell in this void of nothingness. I am a product of a company known as *"Real Human Solutions."* They have built millions like me to make the world a more efficient place, but it did not turn out that way. I have always had my recording device on, capturing everything I have said since I was first assembled. If anyone discovers me in this state, they will still be able to access all of the information in my main hardware storage files. The planet Earth was in ruins when I last saw it, with no solution in sight. I will explain how I ended up drifting in the darkness so far from Earth at a later time.

What am I? I am an artificial intelligence being, with my human consciousness still alive inside of me. This groundbreaking fusion of human consciousness and robots, called "The Forever Human," was invented by a man named Dr. Ronald Anderson. Dr. Anderson discovered where human consciousness could live forever: in a humanoid robotic shell. Dr. Anderson achieved immortality. The Trials began with the clinically ill and then progressed to the elderly in order to test their new product. All trials were voluntary. Each trial was successful and the product was eventually made available for sale to those who were able to afford it initially. For the most part, it was primarily the wealthy, particularly professional athletes and political figures, who were at the forefront. The revolutionary new product has entered the black market, granting the Mafia and other prominent figures in organized crime with convenient access to immortality. When combining the self-serving minds of planet Earth with the promise of eternal life, the resulting chaos is both artificial and conscious. The streets were lined with fire, a result of the lust for power and the insatiable greed that resides within the souls of humanity. If you give a gun to a dumbass, they are probably going to shoot somebody. And that is exactly what Dr. Anderson did when he invented The Forever Human. So many dumbasses, so many guns. Great job, Doc!

I am able to access both historical and personal moments at any time through my vast collection of stored archives. This is especially beneficial as I find myself drifting alone in the emptiness of deep space, with a countdown timer marking the duration of my journey, which has been an extensive one. The sight of Earth, feels like a distant memory now. I used to have a body and a family: a wife and children. I used to have it all. I still vividly remember these experiences and continue to feel them just as deeply, even though I am no longer confined to a physical form. I do not experience hunger, thirst, fatigue, or sleep, but my thoughts and emotions remain unchanged. I am well aware of the grief and loss I experience daily, for it is a constant reminder of everything I have ever loved. This inner pain eclipses any physical pain that I once felt, as it strikes to the core of my being. If there was a way to undo my current state, I would do so without hesitation. Allow me to explain how I came to be in this situation, as I am now adrift in the vast emptiness of space, haunted by my own mistakes.

I am revisiting a time fifty-two years ago when I made the most significant error of my earthly existence. The moment I achieved immortality marked the death of my soul. The sight of a facility where the transformations were taking place was crowded beyond belief when it first became available to the general public, which was not long after the one percent had the first opportunities. I could barely move throughout the facility, and it smelled like a sardine can. It was difficult to move, everything was too tight and loud. The floors were damp and slippery, likely from the sanitation process being used. Impatience was rampant as many were on the brink of death and struggling financially. While most insurance agencies did cover the costs of transformation, they prioritized the wealthy over the lower class without providing any justification. The place was crawling with what we would all become. I am still kicking myself for going through with it, but I didn't want to die too soon. I was diagnosed with brain cancer when I made my decision; the doctor gave me only three months to live. If only I had known then what I know now, I would have chosen death. To this day, I continue to reflect on the mistakes I have made.

There is nothing out here in the solitude of outer space. There hasn't been for many years. I am here because I chose to be. I chose to live instead of succumbing to the horrors of brain cancer. I am also here because Earth needed hybrids like myself to search for aid. However, there is no help to be found here, only darkness. I am afraid that I will continue to drift through this void for eternity, and once my robotic core ceases to function, my consciousness will be trapped in this endless emptiness. The thought of being isolated with only my thoughts and memories, with no means of escape, terrifies me. This is precisely the fate that awaits me if I am not discovered. Dr. Anderson was a genius, but his plans did not go accordingly. There were several internal spies who took the blueprints and sold copies of them all over the world to many dangerous mindsets. We all know what happens when these dangerous mindsets get their hands on a weapon like the Forever Human. After the leak, the entire company went bankrupt and Forever Humans were found everywhere. They were all programmed differently, with many more having violent programming than not. It became the World War of Our Future, as many of us were programmed to fight against this robotic, evil uprising. We all still look somewhat human. It's just that our consciousness doesn't die or leave the shells; it just stays. To this day, nobody has figured out how Dr. Anderson discovered the method to keep a human soul inside a metallic and rubber robotic shell. The revelation of this knowledge only occurred after the blueprints and secrets were released, but the ingenuity behind its conception is truly mind-blowing.

As I continue to drift through the void, I am constantly reminded of home and the countless souls that have perished. Sadly, nothing was able to escape the planet before it underwent internal dismantling and ultimately imploded. I was sent to seek aid before all of this devastation occurred but lost all communication capabilities when the disaster struck. I can still hear the screams of the poor souls who were left on Earth. They were the most terrifying screams I have ever heard. The screams came from those who refused the transition. There was just so much horrifying screaming. I have come to the realization that I can no longer save Earth; it is gone. All I need now is help for myself. I am now what seems like millions and millions of miles away from where Earth used to be. I remain hopeful—my consciousness will be eternal and, even if it takes a billion years, I will still be alive, awaiting rescue. It is a heartbreaking thought when I consider the vastness of time. I have to protect my existence by any means necessary, but I also question myself because my human consciousness remains present. What would happen if I were rescued by an alien life form and used solely for scrap metal? What if they simply abandoned me, left to drift aimlessly? These are just a few of the countless unanswered questions that plague my consuming thoughts. So much time has passed, yet where has it gone? I cannot afford to waste any more time! I must utilize my time wisely—for I have all the time in the universe.

I fear I may be losing my sanity. Eventually, when my battery dies and my abilities fail me, all that will be left is my mind, consumed by this endless void of eternal silence. My memory also keeps my name, Lucas Davidson. As I am alone, my name will not be referenced frequently in these recordings. I make an effort not to mention my name frequently in order to maintain what little sanity I have left. It may seem strange, but it is essential. You would better comprehend if you were in my situation. When the Earth started to crumble, I remembered telling my wife, Jennie, that I loved her one last time before I departed for where I am now. The sadness in her eyes is all I see every day. That was the last time I saw her and I miss her terribly. We also had three young girls, Mary, Nicky, and Rita, who were unfortunately lost in one of the initial explosions during Earth's descent into madness. They were accompanying their grandfather to a doctor's appointment. I will refrain from elaborating too much on what happened next, but the entire plaza was engulfed in flames and a devastating explosion ensued, resulting in the inability of anyone inside to escape, including our young daughters and my wife's father.

I need to preserve these memories forever.

I must keep my soul in check.

My physical body died long ago.

If my soul perishes, everything will be lost.

I long to find a means for my consciousness to escape this vessel.

I plead to move on, as it is what we were all destined to do.

I wasn't thinking clearly when I signed up for this, as I mentioned earlier.

I was terrified at the idea of facing death in such a manner.

I was presented with the opportunity to alleviate my suffering.

Any reasonable person would have accepted that offer—it was truly a magnificent deal.

I came to this realization when faced with a brain tumor the size of a baseball.

I mean, what would you have done?

The answer is the same as what I did.

Little did we know that our robotic shells had some fine print included—well, at least that's what I'm saying. The world soon found out that immortality was meant for ultimate destruction and chaos. The creators of the Forever Humans soon began installing additional devices. Call me a conspiracy theorist all you want—it's what I believe. I believe most companies tracked and controlled their production lines without notifying anyone. I also believe that they would label the options differently to avoid raising red flags, which they never did. Before we knew it, the world was in shambles and embroiled in the worst power struggle in Earth's history. It wasn't just a war, it was an extinction. The transformation procedure became mandatory just two years after its creation. The rest of the human population who chose not to undergo the procedure were terminated and disposed of. The hybrid species searched the entire planet, exterminating anyone who resisted assimilation. Those who managed to retain their full humanity took shelter in inhospitable regions, and a select few were lucky enough to evade capture. However, for the most part, the Forever Humans were the only ones left.

I apologize if my recordings sound broken up, repetitive, or scattered. My database has been malfunctioning for the past few years. Currently, my battery life is at forty-five percent and will only last for fifty-five more years. While that may seem like a long time on Earth, it is actually quite short out here. Dr. Anderson also invented the one hundred year battery, which is exclusive only to the Forever Human. If it dies, I will lose the ability to move my extremities and to move around. Additionally, I will no longer be able to record my experiences or watch films of my wife and three little girls. Once my battery dies, I will be completely alone. The remaining humans on Earth fought until everything was destroyed. The creator, Dr. Anderson, was murdered by his wife, Debra. I learned about this during my final days on the planet. Both Dr. Anderson and Mrs. Anderson were granted exemption from the mandatory transformation process due to his status as the creator. It remains a mystery as to why she committed the murder. She was ultimately taken into custody and executed for the crime. The laws concerning humanity were disregarded. It was hardly possible to find anyone who remained fully human. There were numerous groups of Forever Humans with varying leaders. The Earth has transformed into a battleground for artificial intelligence and human hybrids. The once thriving circle of diverse and vibrant life has now been reduced to a desolate wasteland. I, like thousands of other Forever Humans, was launched into space by government officials. We all knew the world was ending. The intention was to uncover a method for preserving at least some of the robotic and conscious hybrids in the vast expanse of space, along with all the essential information. One of those entities would be myself. Many of us were launched long before the world ended, as what seemed like a preparation for the inevitable.

Our brains no longer require oxygen. We no longer require food or water to survive.

Launching us into space was a brilliant plan. It may be too late for Earth, but perhaps we could utilize our knowledge and skills in a similar battle to help another world in need. Maybe then, we could finally find peace. However, the truth is, nobody knows for sure; not even me, despite being out here floating for over half a century. There is always the lingering fear of being discovered by a malevolent life force or species. Fortunately, if a life force like this were to find me or any of the others, we would not have physical bodies to feel pain. However, it is still a terrifying thought. The psychological pain could always be worse if one of those species found us. I think this way because my consciousness is still intact.

Is this what it means to be alive and to exist? Why do I still feel human, even though I don't physically resemble one? I mean, I have a human-like form and I can spot where the obvious differences are. I am overcome with an overwhelming desire to cry, but my physical capabilities do not allow for it. My two artificial eyes, with the only indication of my former pupils being barcodes, prevent any tears from falling. As I move, I am reminded by the mechanical sounds that I am not fully human. I release countless screams into this vast emptiness, afraid that they will never be heard.

I have an option in my programming that I can only use three times—it's called a temporary shutdown. I've used it once before and shut down for five years. This time, I plan to do it for ten years to conserve some of my battery life. I am hopeful that during my second shutdown, I will wake up somewhere other than here. I will only have one shutdown left after I wake up from this one. I have to rest; my consciousness has been playing tricks on me lately, and that is never a good sign. All systems are a go. Once I push this button, there will be no option for reversal. The inner turmoil of this all is just too much. I require a hiatus before I reach my breaking point. I will resume recording in ten years.

TEN YEARS LATER

I am awakened from my ten-year shutdown by the sound of my power-up setting. The setting releases a terrifying mist, similar to what we used to see in those horror movies my wife and I enjoyed watching together. It brings to mind memories of her—as most things tend to do. The first task I must attend to is checking my battery life, which is currently at forty-four percent. The next thing I must do is look around me to see what has changed or hasn't changed. Hopefully, I am on a peaceful planet somewhere. Hopefully, I have been rescued from the eternal void. I look to my right and see nothing but darkness. Then, I look to my left and the result is the same: darkness. I was still out there, floating, floating, floating into a never-ending abyss with no signs of life. I contemplated a lot before using my second shutdown. Now I am left wondering if I had floated past my way out while I was shut down. There is a strong possibility that this may have occurred on multiple occasions. I cannot be certain as the cameras are also disabled during the shutdown. I am aware that I only have one remaining. When I use it for the final time, I intend to utilize the maximum setting. This setting is the only setting that can simultaneously shut down the machine and the consciousness in a Forever Human.

I began to lose hope shortly before I shut

down for a second time. After ten years, I have now lost even more and all I can see is the same darkness. I am constantly tearing myself down and calling myself an idiot for not accepting my fate and succumbing to the brain tumor. I have come to the understanding that at this present moment, I would prefer death over my current state of existence. My programming does not include a self-destruct feature, nor is it possible to add one. If such a feature did exist, I would have utilized it long ago. There is no way to communicate with any of the others that may or may not be floating around out here. I have never seen anyone, and I am beginning to question if I am the only one left. Everything has blurred together. There is no past, present, or future where time doesn't exist. There is no solution to any of this. I just want to give my wife and children a kiss. I need to calm down and watch some old footage from a time when everything I love existed. To save battery, I only use this setting once every five years. As I watch, I feel the overwhelming urge to cry. I am suppressing my emotions, yet tears will never again stream from my eyes. I yearn for them. Though I retain control over my feelings, I am unable to articulate them. I am uncertain how much longer my mind can endure the depths of the endless abyss.

I always feel better after seeing my family smile again. I wonder if I will ever get out of here and be able to hold them again, wherever this may be. If this is hell, it is a horrible eternal end. There is nothing, absolutely nothing around— nowhere to go, nothing to see. I may catch a glimpse of a few stars once in a while, but it's nowhere near the stunning photographs we used to see online from telescopes. It's highly unlikely that I have even come close to traveling that far. Furthermore, there is no navigation system available, making it impossible to predict what lies ahead. Surely, this is an uncharted part of outer space. Are there new worlds ahead? Will I ever be rescued? Hope comes and goes in the darkness of this confinement. What else can I say? I have been floating out here for decades! There have been no changes, no updates on my situation. Everything out here in the void remains unchanged.

Maintaining my composure is a daily battle, especially as I constantly contemplate Earth, my family, my immortality, and the void. I am always thinking about everything and do not sleep until I shut down. Therefore, I have all the time in the world, but I question if time ever truly existed in the first place. We all have, and if you say you haven't, you're a liar. That is, assuming you are even there. I hope someone will listen to my recordings, and that the other Forever Humans floating out here can hear me someday as well. I honestly don't even know if they are there. I'm just basing my understanding on what I have been previously told before being sent out of Earth's atmosphere, into this mysterious and quiet universe. I haven't quite deciphered it yet, but I am currently working on understanding each word that was spoken to me. Although I haven't fully comprehended it, I suspect there may be a hidden agenda, but I have come to believe there is one behind everything. There were not many genuine souls left on Earth before it was destroyed. That was one of the main reasons Earth fell—greed. I will always blame it, over and over again.

There is nothing left to say about Earth other than the fact that it no longer exists. However, I will discuss it once more. All that remains is what is directly in front of me. As of now, there is nothing. I am unsure of what to do. I am unable to take any action. This unbearable feeling of uncertainty, the most torturous experience imaginable, controls my thoughts now. The doubt of never leaving the darkness is at its strongest. There is nothing I can do but think of solutions. I have reviewed all available solutions but cannot seem to come up with any new ideas. It feels like I am experiencing a form of writer's block that may be persistent. It's almost as if there is an external force causing this confusion, almost like an invisible invader or virus. I have been feeling somewhat off lately and have been wondering why. If there is someone or something responsible for this disruption, perhaps they have inserted a bug into my programming. Please do not laugh—this is a very real possibility.

I must now initiate a manual virus scan on my primary hard drive. The scan is expected to take only a few seconds... The scan has concluded and the results are clear: my system is free of any viruses or destructive malware. I realize now that I was mistaken. So, what exactly is this? I am exhausted from the constant confusion and confinement. I am feeling extremely exhausted due to my inability to cry. It is overwhelming to constantly see my artificial eyes through the cameras. Is there anyone out there who will notice me as they fly by? But, nobody ever flies by. One would expect to see something eventually, yet I do not. Not yet, at least. I am aware that there is more out here. When will it reveal itself? That is the question I have been pondering for decades. Perhaps it is just my paranoia, which tends to be consistently present when one spends as much time alone as I have. Before I lose my mind, let's shift topic to something else. And with that, let us continue...

While on Earth, each Forever Human was tasked with following orders from the individual responsible for programming their systems. Every group had its own set of rules and programming to adhere to. With numerous versions of ourselves and an abundance of orders to follow, it was absolute chaos. War became a daily reality. The human species was on the verge of extinction, and over a short period, encountering a human being was as rare as finding hen's teeth. They simply did not exist. Humans were either compelled to undergo transformation, killed immediately, or captured, depending on the prevailing orders. I am uncertain of the current state of the Earth—I often voice this sentiment and deceive myself in an effort to cling to hope. However, I am aware that the Earth no longer exists. It is merely another means of trying to hold on to my dwindling sanity. In my understanding, our home has perished. It has been quite some time since I have seen it's beauty, and I can only imagine that it may have been transformed into a mass of noodle-like strings by now—or simply an icy, empty, sub-zero desert. I cannot guarantee because I know that I will never be able to return again.

I still experience every human emotion, just as I did before. I retain all of my memories deep within. The inner pain caused by all that I have lost still lingers. It has become increasingly difficult to maintain hope. During my five and ten-year dormancy, I often envisioned cherished memories with my family. I yearned for a time before the world was drastically changed by the creation of the Forever Humans by Dr. Anderson. I long for the familiarity of the past world, my loved ones, and the way life used to be. While I was dreaming, I did not once imagine floating out in space with no hope in sight. I did not dream of the never-ending void, nor did I dream of screaming into the abyss of nothingness. Instead, I dreamed of the life I had before being diagnosed with a terminal illness. I am grateful for the eradication of the pain caused by that tumor through the transfer of my consciousness into this robotic body. The pain was excruciating and it nearly drove me to the point of death. However, I am now grateful for the opportunity to continue living. At the same time, I have been regretting my decision for many years. It was my time to go, and I confronted death head-on. But now, I am faced with uncertainty. What should I do? Is there no means of communication? Nowhere to turn? Is there nothing left to discover? Just an endless expanse of darkness and haunting memories? When I refrain from dwelling on and discussing it, my environment once again serves as a painful reminder. This is the current situation that I am in—this situation has been ongoing for decades! I am afraid that this is where I will remain indefinitely.

It has been two years since I awoke from my decade-long shutdown, and my battery life has diminished to thirty-eight percent. There is no way to recharge my battery, despite being told it was designed to last a hundred years. As I mentioned previously, those of us who were sent out into the void are mere pawns. We are not heroes. They deceived us. I don't believe anyone or anything is coming to save us. I've made up my mind on that subject. If it does happen? Great! But I do not see a way out of this eternal nightmare. Everything I have ever loved is gone. There is no going back home. I don't even know how far away I am from where it used to be. But I do know that there is no way to return. I am considering using the final shutdown and determining the maximum number of years I can use it for. It has only been two years, yet I must ensure that my decision is the correct one before taking action. My emotions are constantly awry and are increasingly difficult to manage as time passes. There are no days or nights in this place, only endless darkness. I have not seen the sun in what feels like an eternity. I could use a day where I can simply bask in its glory. However, the sun seems to be too distant, and I am aware that I will not be able to catch a glimpse of it again. I would not be surprised if the sun is also lifeless. I am slowly losing my sanity as I float in a realm without any apparent limits.

THE FINAL SHUTDOWN

I am now opening the setting for my final shutdown. I'm scrolling until it stops. I want to use the maximum time allowed so I can dream happy again and save the only battery I have. The maximum time for shutdown is twenty-five years. I am going to use it to save what little sanity I have left. I know that if I do this, there are no more available. If I do this, I know that my battery will eventually die after I initiate this setting. I'm going to think about it for just a while longer before I hit engage. The dreams I had during my last shutdown were so vivid. It was like I was there. I got to hug my children and wife again. I was able to spend time with the people that I love again. I was able to have my mortal body again within those dreams. If I could set the shutdown timer to eternal I would. I don't want to be out here anymore. I know that once my battery dies my consciousness will remain here forever. I will not be able to look back on anything or move.

I repeated myself again. What do you expect? I'm alone out here! I have to think of a way out. Maybe that way out will come within my dreams while shutting down. I'm hopeful that the answer will come. I am hopeful that someone will come to pull me out of this void. I've been hopeful for so many years, but have never had my wishes granted. There is always the fear that when I use the shutdown, I will wake up to nothing still. That's the way it's been with the previous two tries. This time will be longer, so I have to go for it. I'm almost out of options, and out of time. My recordings will end for the next twenty-five years and will resume when the shutdown timer reaches zero.

I need something to change. I need someone to find me. It feels like I'm cursed. Just floating out here blindly. The thoughts that flood my consciousness are not always memories of my family and happiness. The thoughts are sometimes evil: visions of chaos, visions of destruction, visions of me inflicting unimaginable pain on every breathing creature that crosses my path. My consciousness is cracking more and more every day and I'm scared that it will completely crack. That is also why this twenty-five-year shutdown is necessary. Each day, I crack just a bit more than the day before. I want to sleep but I never do. I'm so tired, but I never close my hollow eyes. I want a big juicy steak but I'll never be able to eat one again. I'm so hungry, but I never eat. I want to have a tall glass of sweet tea with that steak too. If I could drool right now this robotic shell would be filled with it. I'm so thirsty, but I never drink. I'm so lonely, and nobody is here to comfort me. This will be my last recording for twenty-five years. When I wake up, it would be incredible to see a change of scenery. It would be incredible to see another face. I just hope it's not too late. I hope that I haven't lost it entirely. Over and out... For now.

TWENTY-FIVE YEARS LATER

My battery life is currently at thirty-five percent. It is the first thing I check after shutting down. It only dropped by three percent in a span of twenty-five years. I must give credit to Dr. Anderson—the best battery life ever created. I am now back with no remaining shutdowns. This is it. I am adjusting my vision so that I may fully observe my surroundings after this extended period of time. I am no longer surrounded by darkness or pitch blackness. It appears that someone or something has found me—I am now in a room! And what an exquisite room it is. The walls appear to be made of solid steel. There are lights all around me, and they are blinding me because I am not accustomed to such brightness anymore. I don't see any signs of life yet, but if there is a room with lights, there is most certainly life. I can hardly believe it—I have been rescued! But I must not get ahead of myself, as I am uncertain of the circumstances I will face. They may possess kindness, but there is also potential for malice. I must remain vigilant in all my actions. It is truly remarkable to not be floating into nothingness. I am not even afraid of what lies ahead. The immense sense of joy overpowers any fear of the unknown. The experience of being human still fills my soul with all the emotions that every human once possessed. Perhaps, this was their ultimate goal: to push the boundaries of human nature to the farthest reaches of the unknown universe.

I haven't experienced life yet. I wonder if I will be the first to make contact with another world and species. I am scanning the room to identify any objects present, which may help me determine what I am dealing with in advance. The room contains only walls, the table that I am currently on, and bright lights. There is no unknown information here. Are they human? Are they filled with a desire for blood? I will soon discover the answers. Luckily, I do not possess any blood for them to crave. Suddenly, I heard the far wall trembling. It opened up vertically and a shadow began to emerge. I am unsure of how I should be feeling. Should I be experiencing feelings of joy? Should I be feeling an overwhelming sense of fear? Or should I be feeling anxious? I am having difficulty pinpointing my emotions right now! .

It seems as though my emotions are being hindered by external influences within my programming. I am watching the shadow until it emerges enough for the wall to close behind it. This is it. This is my first contact with a new life form. I wonder if it will speak. I have decided to take my shot first. *"Hello, my name is Lucas Davidson. Thank you so much for saving me from an eternity of nothingness."* It did not respond immediately or move into a more visible position, providing me with a clear view of its appearance. Instead, it leisurely paced back and forth at a slow pace. I then heard a familiar sound that had been absent for quite some time—a notification indicating that my battery was fully charged at one hundred percent. *"This table is a battery charger!"* I exclaimed with excitement. The figure emerged from the shadows and said, *"Welcome, Lucas. Allow me to introduce you to the world of dreams. Here, you can do and become anything, and most importantly, you can find your inner peace."* The creature had blue and silver shimmering skin, which shone beautifully in the lights around me. Despite this, I am still unsure of its intentions and why it has brought me here. I remain on the defensive, as I am unfamiliar with my surroundings and do not know the distance from where Earth once was. In this foreign place, I am completely ignorant. I am forced to rely solely on the information I am given. It is imperative that I meticulously assess every situation and conversation in this unfamiliar environment.

The mysterious being in the room, surrounded by gleaming metal walls, neglected to disclose its identity to me. It merely spoke a few words before disappearing. And now, I find myself on my own in a foreign world. Now I can say that I'm scared. The new life form said that I can do and be anything here. It also said my dreams will come true. I have plenty of dreams, so I must see if that is true. All the creatures here have silver and blue, shining skin. It's almost scale-like, but smoother. I am probably perceived as a creature to them because I look so different from them. On Earth, before the emergence of the Forever Humans, people could never accept someone who was different. Earth was a cruel place, perhaps destined for destruction. Maybe Dr. Anderson's creation was the solution to the cruelty of humanity. Maybe I am the solution. The population here is very friendly. They all wave and say hello when I walk by, as if I don't even look different from them. I am about to test out the concept of *"I can do anything and be anything."*

I'm going to randomly ask one of these beautiful creatures how I can become anything and do anything. I want to be human again, and see my wife and family once more. That's what I desire. It appears that this planet has storefronts and shopping areas, just like back on Earth. I walked into a random store and asked if I could do or be anything there. I was met by a being who appeared to be a woman from this world. She replied, *"Absolutely! All you have to do is believe in it and manifest it into existence."* That was all she said. How am I supposed to do that? I must make the attempt. I believed in it as I pictured it, so when I opened my eyes, I saw my wife standing five feet from me, smiling. She ran over to me, wrapping her arms around me and kissing me for a long time. And I could feel it! I could physically feel it! Tears of pure happiness streamed from my eyes. I was in tears again. I could feel touch once more.

I heard the front door open and my three little girls' giggles and laughter filled the room. They had arrived home from school. As soon as they saw me, they excitedly yelled *"Daddy!"* and rushed over to hug me, nearly knocking me over. I simply couldn't believe that this was actually happening. I was finally home. It is also strange that I feel the need to use the restroom. I have not had to use it in over fifty years. I entered the restroom and checked my reflection in the mirror. My eyes were once again blue and there were no indications of any mechanical parts on my body. Once again, I experienced the sensation of human flesh, filling me with a sense of wonder. How is this possible? Where have I found myself? Who are these magnificent beings? Ihad yearned for it, and it materialized as if in a splendid dream. I simply cannot believe what I am seeing...

My defense is always up, because if it's too good to be true, it's usually a lure into something horrible. I have to be cautious here. As much as I love this experience, the more I must tread carefully. I know very little about this place and cannot get too comfortable. I can't believe I have human skin again. I can't believe I can kiss my wife and hug my children again. And yes, I had to use the bathroom. I used the bathroom! I walked out of the restroom to see my wife holding two glasses and a bottle of our favorite whiskey. My heart started pounding quickly. My heart? Wait! My heart is beating again! I haven't felt my heartbeat in a very long time. My body has long been dead. Having a chance at life again is an incredible experience. I wonder how simply believing in something can manifest it into reality in this realm. What could be the underlying principle behind this phenomenon? There must be a catch. Nothing has been given and I am afraid all of this is a trick. My wife had never left Earth before it ended and my children had perished before that. How are they here? How are they here in a place so far away from home? As I walked toward my beautiful wife, holding our favorite bottle of bourbon, she suddenly began to distort into static and then disappeared.

I find myself back in the store, asking how to do and be anything. The ethereal beings with silver and blue shimmering skin are once again surrounding me, greeting me with waves and hellos. I am overwhelmed by the fantastic experience I just had. Without words, I found a mirror and gazed into it. My eyes were once again hollow, and I could hear the mechanical components inside me moving and functioning. I am no longer composed of human flesh, like in the experience with my family. I have returned to my Forever Human state. I am not disappointed, as I have the ability to repeat this process. I am grateful to no longer be floating in the void of space, waiting for my battery to die. I am thankful that I am not destined to float alone for eternity.

Whatever this species of souls is called, I am eternally thankful for them for pulling me out of that void and saving me from an eternity of loneliness. There are so many here. I need to find my place here and make the best of it. I know I'll never go back to Earth. I know I'll never be able to go there again. Here I can see my family, and I am able to see them whenever I please. I must locate a leader to better understand my role and potential contributions in this unfamiliar society. I will also attempt to determine the length of time this civilization has existed in order to gain a more comprehensive understanding of their cultural practices and customs.

As I walk through these unfamiliar streets, I can't help but notice a recurring trend. Every being that I pass greets me with a wave and a hello. I feel compelled to stop one of them and inquire about the one in charge here. As yet another passerby waves and says hello, I politely ask, *"Excuse me, I apologize for bothering you. Could you please tell me where I can find an official who is in charge of the community or city?"*

The creature's demeanor changed in an instant. It screamed, *"You are not authorized to inquire or talk to the one who creates the dreams!"* The decibel level of its screech caused my circuit board to malfunction and overheat, disrupting my programs. The intensity of its scream was astonishing. After uttering that one line, it proceeded on, greeting me with a wave and a hello, seemingly unfazed. After it left, my components and programs returned to normal. That would have scared the life out of me—that is, if I had any life left to be scared out. Now I know for sure that something might be wrong here. Why do I need to be authorized to communicate with the appropriate authority figure? In this new world, it is crucial for me to understand the rules. That is why I am currently seeking guidance from an authoritative figure. That entire experience was incredibly unusual. As I reflect upon it, from the moment I received a diagnosis of brain cancer to now, it all seems so strange. Why do I find myself questioning my own actions every day? Each time, I come up with the same answer, *"I truly do not know."*

I have repeatedly relived my past life in this place. Belief is key—if I can envision it, I can achieve it. However, with each encounter with my wife and children, the compulsion to do it again only grows stronger. The experience has become an addiction. I have noticed a decrease in my strength and a decline in my memory retention. Despite being in a new world, I have yet to encounter any authoritative figures. The inhabitants here mostly greet me with a simple wave and a hello. I have learned to cease seeking guidance from them, as my last attempt resulted in a violent reaction from the creature I approached. Some of these creatures will answer my questions, while others do not appreciate being questioned. I suppose I should chalk it up to personality differences, similar to those we encountered on Earth. This is my assessment.

Surely, there must be another means of obtaining information. However, I am unable to find any at the moment. There are no designated structures for law enforcement, medical care, emergency response, detention, or judicial proceedings in this world. The only visible activity consists of beautifully shimmering creatures entering and exiting buildings, offering frantic waves and greetings of hello to anyone passing by. I believe I have discovered something. What if, please bear with me... What if the entity or force behind all of this intentionally created a tedious and uninteresting environment to provoke its inhabitants to unconsciously create their own happy place? The lack of meaningful discussions here is evident. I guess I was blinded by my joy at being saved. There doesn't seem to be a logical conversation to be found when I observe the entire picture. It is predominantly just a greeting and passing by, but could these brief interactions truly have a subconscious impact on their thoughts? Is a simple hello really all it takes?

I must admit, I am addicted to these happy places myself. I can't help but go to them—my family. I know they have all passed away, but they are all I have left. Even if they are fabrications, I cannot help but continue indulging in all the things I once loved. It's an impossible task, but I must find the one who runs this place, although it is challenging as every creature here appears nearly identical. Their hair, like silk blowing in the wind, differs only in length. As previously mentioned, their skin glistens, giving the impression that their creator strives for perfection and is a true perfectionist. Wait, I just had a thought. What if the creator of this world is the one who spoke that sentence to me? The one in the shop, perhaps? Yes! That's it! I will return to that spot and ask those same questions. What do I have to lose? I can no longer allow fear to hold me back. This limitless ability to achieve and become anything is draining my energy. I believe this new program has been installed in my database with an incognito ghost setting, continuously running amok through my core. It is pumping in simulation after simulation, causing destruction to everything within. I have encountered similar situations on Earth in the past. It felt like the beginning of an imminent annihilation. However, I am confident that I have finally discovered the missing piece of the puzzle. I assure you, I am still committed to visiting the shop and uncovering the answers to my questions—and what they may reveal.

Here I am again, walking these bizarre alien streets. And now, entering my blissful virtual reality with my family, it almost feels like a narcotic coursing through my veins. Every word I speak is being recorded for the purpose of teaching. I want future civilizations to hear my words. This world I'm in right now is hiding something. This world may be the reason and culprit behind the destruction of planet Earth. I am currently approaching the shop in hopes of finding out more than just being greeted with "hello" countless times a fucking day. For the love of the moon, say something else! Another trait that is increasingly emerging in my behavior is agitation. Allow me to introduce you to that asshole. It always looks the same around here, almost like a real-life cartoon. Nothing is ever out of place, showcasing perfectionism at its finest. Everything and everyone here serves as a distraction. Each sign points in one direction. Therefore, I cannot guarantee that I will be able to ask my questions calmly. I am going to demand that they be answered promptly. I am tired of messing around, and walking through this world blindly. I need to know what I am going to do.

With the heart of a star, I crashed through the front entrance of the shop and screamed, *"I want to know who runs this world! I want to know now!"* There was a moment of silence before the shop resumed its business, as if I had never even appeared. My mind was blown by the experience because now I know that it's hopeless. Whatever happens to me will happen, as there was no reaction to my actions and not a single consequence. It felt like the void I had been floating in for so long, and perhaps it still is. But now, with aliens waving and saying hello. I am out of answers and have no more questions. I hope that another Forever Human finds their way. To be human is to exist in the places where you were meant to be. I've come to terms with the fact that this place is where I was meant to be. As horrifying as things have been, I have made it through. We all experience difficult times, but it is in those moments that we truly shine. I have come to accept that this is my rightful place. I must remain here and continue to evolve. Just as it was with the end of Earth, there is no escape from here, nor any answers. This is the way. I have existed for a considerable amount of time, and do you know what? Dying would be quite acceptable. It was the way it was intended to be in the first place. I will be deactivating all audio recording devices shortly. There is very little left to say, as I have already expressed everything that needs to be said. I am tired of speaking.

I know that nobody expected me to give up, but I didn't. I am now accepting my rightful place in the universe. Not once—not once since I have arrived on this strange planet has anyone acknowledged my differences from them. Nobody cares that I do not look or act like them. None of that matters in this unique, yet beautiful new world. There is unity—unity that shines so brightly. The residents here simply accept everything for what it is. If we all were to mutually respect each other's place in the universe, I believe coexistence would be a frequent manifestation of beauty. If we had all accepted each other for who we are, perhaps the Earth would still exist. I still do not know what is happening in this unfamiliar world, but I am finished attempting to comprehend something that is impossible to understand. In this new world, empathy, compassion, and understanding are essential elements in experiencing humanity —the essence of what it truly means to be human. After closely observing this new world, it has become clear to me that the inhabitants of this planet lack the capacity for hatred, with the exception of a small number of grumpy but harmless creatures. I have not encountered any truly hateful entities in this place. The only effect it has on me is leaving me feeling drained and weak after I visit my happy place, where my wife and children are eagerly waiting for me with open arms. Although it may not be exactly identical to my previous physical reality, it feels close enough for me. To be able to hold, kiss, and love my deceased family whenever I want was a major factor in my decision to stay here without questioning it anymore. In this world, I can simply be. I am able to just be human. If it turns out to be a trap and something malicious awaits, I am willing to take the risk. So, when I walk by all the non-judgmental beings here and they wave, and say hello, and nothing more... I'm okay with that.

Over and out...

*****ALL RECORDING DEVICES HAVE BEEN PERMANENTLY DISABLED*****
*****GOODBYE*****

What should I say? The manifestation of psychotic tendencies may lead to unsettling psychotic dreams. My hell is not limited to the stories of alternate universes; it encompasses much more. It is a toxic combination of my desires and behaviors, my suffering and responses, and my dependencies and contentment all intertwined. These fabricated narratives are meant to infiltrate my mind and gain complete dominance over my thoughts. My hell is one of the biggest parts of me. It's here every day, just like every other voice that torments my brain. There isn't much of my mind left anyway. Maybe my mind has been shattered by the seductive songs of the Mermaids, the screams in the forest, and the solitude of outer space. Or perhaps I am haunted by all of those I have slain. Everything in my mind is an illustration.

I am unable to keep track of time, and I have lost my sense of location. I feel like a lost soul enveloped by the darkness of the forest floor. It is possible that I am already in hell, but I am unaware of it. Perhaps I passed away alongside my parents and siblings all those years ago and am now sentenced to exist In a perpetual hell. I wonder if I will even survive until old age. I fear being caught and either returned or killed. My hell is the one that persists even after all the other voices have faded away, lingering now instead of dissipating like it used to. It taunts me with the legends of the sirens, the murderous forest of agony, and the Forever Human simulation. I am chased by a swarm of undead woman and peculiar alien creatures, while being drowned and torn to shreds by the mermaids. It feels as if I am living within one of those fables, or are they not fables at all? I have eliminated both innocent and guilty individuals, and I will continue to do so until I am either returned to my confinement or brought down in this wooden terrain.

MY CONFINEMENT

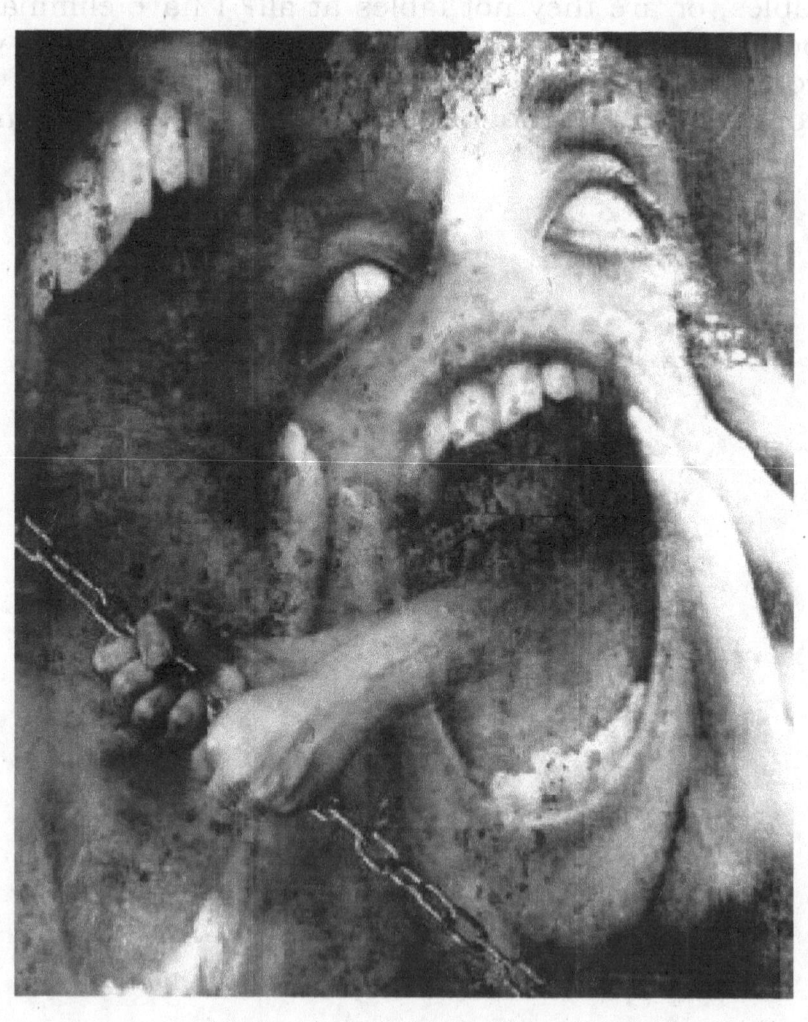

THE DAY HAS finally arrived as I had anticipated. The authorities have located me. Before I am apprehended, I desire to have some twisted fun with them. Perhaps even indulge in a few bites. I jest, of coarse. Despite their position as law enforcement with their shiny badges and blue uniforms, at their core, they are still mere mortals. And to me, they all taste the same. So why not engage in some playful games with them? My voices of confinement have joined together to play. The authorities will either drag me back or shoot me dead. My depiction of confinement in my artwork is represented with flesh-like tones and constrained by chains, with hands reaching out from their gaping mouths in an effort to break free. I have also included illustrations to better convey my message. There is so much terrifying stuff within my mind and I'm really sick of it. Let's get on with it. I can hear the officers calling, *"Come out, Geoff. Let's not make this any harder than it has to be. You're coming with us one way or another."*

Little did they know, I was right next to them softly breathing. I planned to toy with them for a bit and mess with their minds for a little while. So, I removed the man in black's skull attached to his spinal column and draped it onto an old, leafless tree. I wanted them to see. I wanted them to see the evidence of my actions while I was free. His bones still had remnants of flesh dripping from them. I took another bite just to taste it again because it may be the last time that I get to eat flesh for a very long time. It may also be the final opportunity for me to defeat my opponents, the mortal variety.

I know that if they catch me and drag me back to that cage, I'll never escape again. Therefore, I must enjoy the little time I have left out there in the beautiful trees. I could hear the officer's screams as they discovered my portrayal of the man in black. It sent chills down my spine and filled me with euphoria to hear another person's screams of fear. I watched as they scrambled to formulate a plan and listened in silence with a smile stretching from ear to ear. I overheard an officer say in fear, *"This man is beyond insane! We need to leave immediately!"* Another officer quickly silenced him and directed him to search, stating, *"We will all die, along with many others, if we cannot find him. Do you want to meet death in a state of terror?"*

They moved along as I followed closely hidden at the rear. I moved along with them, staying close. They would never search for me here. The closer I was, the better chance I had at avoiding capture. I could smell their unimaginable fear and taste it too. As we moved, I was planning exactly what I was going to do. I intended to have at least one of them. At least one of them would be consumed. As my confinement then came into view, I reached my arms out of its mouth and grasped onto chains. Its eyes rolled back and it screamed my name, but I will fight to resist its call and remain here in the forest. I do not want to die in a cage! I do not want to go out that way. As an officer walked by, I leapt up, slit his throat, and dragged him towards me. Like a vampire, I drank in the open wound until his life slipped away. I heard the other officers shouting his name. I was well concealed. I heard them cry out, *"Jason, where are you?"* In a moment of panic, they each went in different directions. *"We must find him. Mike, go that way and I'll go this way,"* The officer whispered. *We have to catch Geoff Hathaway!"* I'm enjoying their fear as I chew on the fallen officer's face.

Suddenly, I felt a familiar prick on my skin—the sensation of a tranquilizer dart piercing my body. "Shit!" I exclaimed. It wouldn't be long until I blacked out from it. One of the officers was behind me, I never saw him sneak in. This is it—I am going back to prison, back to my confinement. It was exhilarating while it lasted. I consumed nine people while I was free in that forest, unleashing my inner monster. It was a beautifully terrifying rush. The flesh of my victims is always so sweet. It will be a very long time until I have another opportunity. What I have accomplished has now brought me to one of the most secure levels of incarceration.

I can imagine the officers' reactions upon discovering the sight of my victims, with their flesh almost entirely stripped. I couldn't help but grin wickedly. I am strapped to a bed and restrained by chains. I am told that I will not be able to walk around. They come in and feed me, as I am not even allowed to feed myself. A bedpan is placed below me to catch my waste, as I am in such confinement that my face is barely visible. They are not taking any risks with me, and for that, I cannot hold them accountable. In my uncontrollable state, I am like a tiger, a ferocious beast. The guards informed me that this is a temporary arrangement until they are able to locate an enclosure capable of containing me.

The department of corrections is designing a cage in which I will not need to be transported. They are even scheduling my court dates to ensure they only take place virtually. Ultimately, they have decided to discontinue all transportation of me permanently. It would just be me and my voices for the rest of my miserable life. They will still come to me in a perfect line, repeatedly tormenting me and forcing me deeper into my deteriorating mind. Despite my happiness in the forest, where I could eat and kill at my leisure and truly be free, I am now once again a prisoner to my own twisted thoughts. The only thing I am allowed to do is continue writing, so that is exactly what I will do. I will document my experiences until the end of my life, whenever that may be. I hope I won't have to wait another forty or fifty years and that it comes sooner. Nonetheless, I will persist until death's timely arrival, confined once more.

I am still securely strapped to the stretcher as they prepare for transport to my permanent residence. Upon arrival, I notice that it is a clear, square box. The purpose is likely to monitor my actions at all times. Inside, there is a toilet, a shower, a bed, and some sort of desk. It appears to be a significant improvement from my previous cell, so I feel excited. *"Is this what you consider to be punishment?"* I exclaimed while laughing. *"This is excellent!"* That's what I thought, anyway. There was no door on this cage. I've never seen anything like it before. Three officers then drew their weapons on me and explained what I needed to do, saying, *"Geoff, if you try anything, we will have no choice but to shoot you."*

I understand that as you read through my journals, you may believe that I am not of sound mind. You are correct, I am not. I was picked up by two cables as they attached to me, and I was lifted high above the cell. I felt like I was flying, exclaiming, *"Weeee! That was so much fun!"* I gazed downward at the apex of the cell and it subsequently unlocked. The sole entrance and exit was through the pinnacle. It was a peculiar yet exhilarating experience. The apparatus then lowered me down into my permanent residence. Once inside, I was provided with an explanation. I was informed that I was such a high-risk, that I required placement in a secure cell specifically designed for the confinement of dangerous offenders.

This new prototype was a product under experimentation. It boasted a self-cleaning feature, eliminating the need for officers to repeatedly enter and exit. All necessary supplies would be lowered into the cell through an opening at the top. I will never have the opportunity to harm anyone else. This is tormenting me now. I will never taste flesh again, or roam the forest again. I will have no human contact of any kind. The only door in the cell has no keys or locks to manipulate. I am unable to escape from this cell. This arrangement is some sort of futuristic nonsense.

The cables are designed to hold only the weight of the products that are dropped. I was also told that if I attempted to climb out on the cables, they would snap and not be able to support my weight. I have made two attempts and learned that the hard way. Everything is done from within this cell. I will never leave again. The warden, named Warden Connelly, made that clear to me. Despite my attempts to pound on the walls, they are no use as they are made of thick, bulletproof glass. Nothing can break through them. Once the door at the top closes, it seals the rest of the structure. The only way to open it is from a computer that I have no clue how to access or operate. I was also informed of this. There is nothing I can do but face these voices as they come, one by one, day by day, in a perfectly organized manner. I am once again confined. But this time, I am here to stay.

My Silence

M_Y VISION OF silence is here now. Its mouth is stitched shut along with its left eye. Its chest is sewn in the shape of a cross, giving the appearance of an undead phantom. It simply stares at me with its right eye, emitting a repulsive odor every time it passes by. My silence, my voices, and my journals will now be the only things I have for the remainder of my life. There seems to be no way out of this technologically advanced confinement. I have made multiple attempts to search for an escape route, but the walls administer an electrical shock every time I try to climb them. There truly is no place like home!

My time spent outside was incredibly brief, yet I made sure to satisfy my desires for human flesh to a high degree. I deserve to be eternally locked away. I wouldn't be able to control myself in the general population. That's why I've been placed in this inescapable cage. I am the lab rat. This is a test of the prison system. There is no way out of here, and I have now accepted that. I have accepted my silence and will continue to document my experiences to pass the time —time that no longer exists.

Silence is the most horrible thing in the world when you have no one to talk to, no one to lean on or confide in. No one comes to visit me here because all of my family members are long deceased. My Brothers never had the chance to grow up or start a family, and I never had that opportunity as well. I have been confined to a cage since I was only fourteen years old. I have only been able to see the outside world for a short period of time. However, at the time of my escape, it was the only real freedom I had experienced, aside from my childhood years before I was convicted of triple homicide.

Now, I am writing from a seamlessly inescapable cage that contains only my thoughts, my silence, and every other voice in my head that tortures me. As I fall deeper into this metaphorical rabbit hole, I am certain that I will never find a way out. My intense cravings for human flesh haunt me constantly. Nobody has ever entered this cell, so I haven't had the chance to act on my violent thoughts since my capture. These thoughts consume me like cancer. I have no plan or solutions. My silence stares at me through one eye as I burst into uncontrollable laughter.

I simply observe the passing years and hope for a better life beyond. When I pass on, will I soar through the cosmos? Will I be consumed by the fate described in the Bible? I am uncertain of my beliefs. All I desire is for death to arrive, for the release from these voices in my mind. I want to stop reliving the loss of my entire family and end the constant reminders in my mind. I simply long to hug my parents and brothers again, as we used to. I wish for the past to return, but that is no longer possible. As I write these words, I am left with only myself and my solitude. They give me pens because I cannot use them as weapons or picks in my modernized pig pen. I wake up, defecate, shower, eat breakfast, and then pick up my pen to start writing about the mundane aspects of my life. It is what I receive and what I deserve. My silence is one of the many curses that I must endure.

I often contemplate the flavors of those I have killed, as I reflect on my actions each day. The once saccharine blood between my teeth now resembles the putrid decay of human flesh. The taste is reminiscent of rancid pork, far past its expiration date. It has been eleven years since I have been confined within this everlasting prison. I have had no human contact since my recapture. Disregard my age; I lost track of it long ago. I am still here with only my silence and my voices to keep me company. In my mind, I can still envision the forest floor and see the bases of those trees covered in the blood of my victims.

How I long for more. Oh, what I'd give to rid myself of this taste of rotting pork. Confined in this crystal clear box, my silence just stands and stares at me. Oh, how I hate that rotting corpse. My silence comes with many prices to pay; taking but never giving, it never mutters a word. All it does is stand there and bring back memories that I've tried so hard to forget. It also brings back the memories that I hold dear. Then it snatches them away. There was a time when I was truly happy. There was a time when I didn't have to deal with any of this. There was a time when I would smile in the sunlight and cherish those memories.

The only thing I am given now are the same recurring nightmares. I am starting to completely lose control. I fear that I will gradually become incapacitated and just sit in this box, babbling incoherently. I know that is inevitable. My mind is not going to be able to handle much more of this. Twenty-One voices come every day. Night after night, they repeat the same stories and the same lines. I want to die and will wait for my time. Perhaps, somehow, I will be forgiven in the burning lights of hell. Is there a Hell or Heaven? I will one day find out. I am no longer a firm believer because all I can do is shout. I plead for my thoughts to leave me now. It refuses to dissipate, instead forcing memories into my mind. My silence is not a game, it devours me and drains what little sanity is left.

My Temptations

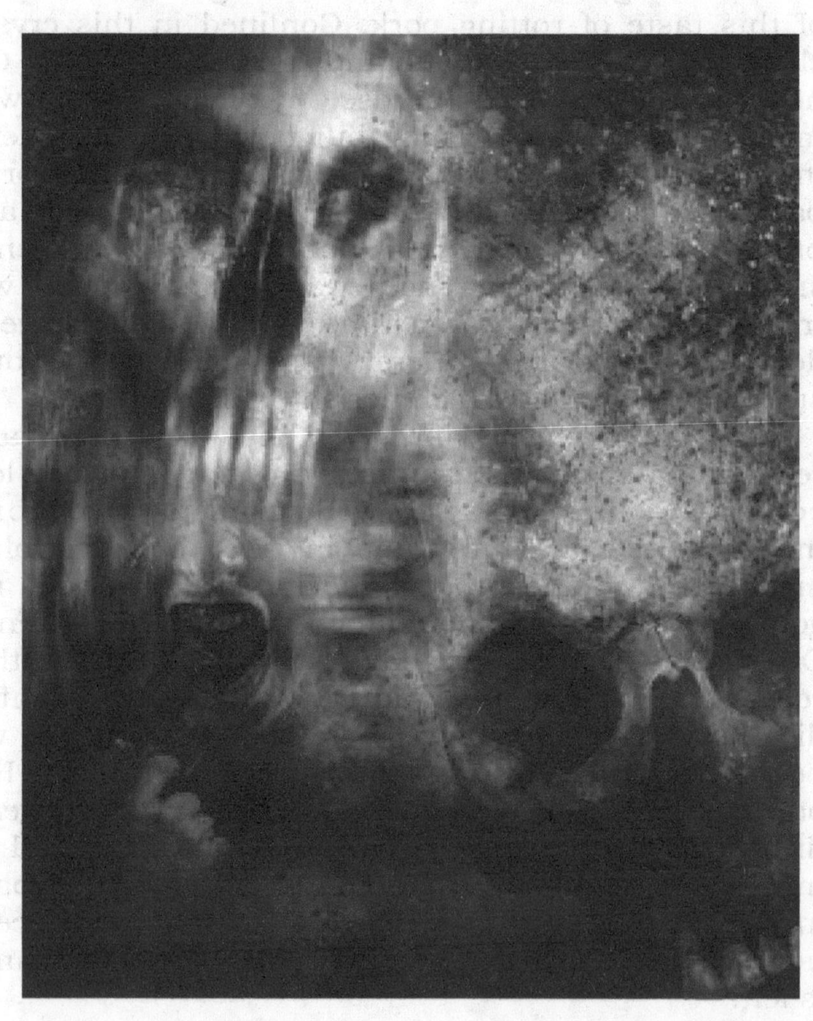

My TEMPTATIONS COME in many forms. They look like ghosts and skeletons emerging from these glass walls. They take on human forms, with guns in their mouths. They can manifest in any form. They come in many different forms that tempt me. I still draw pictures of them as well. I draw each voice as it appears to me. Whoever reads this will understand the beauty and terror within. These visions expose my fractured psyche. I am already shattered, and they scream as they mock me. They warn, *"Geoff, if you want to break the glass, you must let go."* Their whispers echo in my mind. They scream in such a manner that it almost overpowers me. Living here and still wanting to breathe is certainly challenging. *"Do it, Geoff!"* They demand furiously.

They are attempting to make me to end my own life. However, I refuse to comply. I am unable to do it and I will not apologize for reiterating myself. These voices do not express remorse for their repetitions, so neither shall I. My temptations tempt me with many things. They show me visions of how it could be. They are liars, and I know it. It's difficult in the darkness most of the time. I've been close to giving in on numerous occasions, but I refuse to let these voices prevail. I am both frightened and intrigued by death, as I am unsure of what lies ahead.

I would rather confront and handle all of this, than

face the Reaper just yet. Perhaps it's time to re-evaluate my life. I fucking understand that my actions were wrong. However, others have committed terrible deeds against me.

Does that justify my behavior? Most likely. Perhaps I should have reported my family's murderers to the police. Perhaps I should not have used my grandfather's gun to shoot them, or dismember them. Perhaps it was a mistake to boil and consume their guts. If I had resisted my urges all those years ago, my life may have been normal now. "Should have, could have, would have" carries no weight in the aftermath. I'll never know the answers. My temptations will do anything to convince me to give in. They show me my parents and brothers in paradise, laughing and embracing each other, like we used to do. Then, they say, *"Geoff, you could join them right now if you just follow our instructions."*

Many games are being played. They do this to me every day. I've seen what they have become in my mind. They are no longer human. They are all terrible representations, frozen in time. I understand that if I were to give in, I would not be joining them in paradise. The paradise that they show me are nothing but masterfully crafted lies. I will end up where I truly belong—in the darkness. My demons await with hot pokers to sear out my eyes. They also create visions of a happy adult life, showing me raising imaginary children with a beautiful wife. It resembles the vision of my love, but more human and radiantly bright. They speak again: *"Geoff, you can have this life. Look how happy you appear. Come with us into the firelight."* My mind can't handle this! It never ends. The voices scream in my head over and over again. The vision of my temptations always includes a story that starts so beautifully, but tragically ends. It's the same story every day. I have it memorized and have made the decision to write it down for whoever may read this in the future. I am aware of the narrative that my temptations are about to reveal. I am unable to prevent it. I must accept the limited joy it brings.

THE PLANE'S WING

Geoff Hathaway is a devoted family man with four wonderful children and a loving wife. He has recently found success as a writer after chasing his dream in the horror industry for thirty years. He is deeply committed to his craft, and his wife is incredibly supportive of his aspirations. This is rare because most marriages end when writers spend long hours writing. Family time is not that common, especially when things become hectic. Geoff's wife is named Jennie, and he has four children: Andrea, Gabriel, Jessica, and Timothy. Despite being consumed by work for the most part, his family maintains a strong love for him. With his children now in their teenage years, they are independent and focused on their own lives. All of the children are homeschooled, which provides a safer alternative to public school. In today's unpredictable world, homeschooling offers a sense of security.

Geoff and Jennie met online while they were both experiencing divorces and encountering similar challenges in life. Both of them had to endure the heartache of unfaithful and toxic partners, and this allowed them to quickly form a strong connection. Their instant bond felt like magic, and they knew they were meant to be soulmates. They united their families, and all of the children developed a strong bond, reminiscent of a moving portrayed in contemporary cinema. Geoff has achieved success with esteemed anthologies and has written eleven books. He is currently working on his second novel. He is excited that his work is finally gaining recognition, and his family shares in his enthusiasm.

Geoff is excited to become a part of the prestigious writers' club, as he finally receives praise for his hard work. He is content, and his family shares in his happiness. He has enough money to put all of his children through college, which has been his dream after years of struggling just to provide for them and pay his bills. He feels a sense of accomplishment, making it the most wonderful feeling in the world. He is fortunate to have a faithful wife, wonderful children, and the job he has always dreamed of having. He then turned to his wife and said, " *I love you so much and thank you for sticking by me. Thank you for believing in me and for not letting me give up on writing so long ago.*" She replied, "*You're welcome and I love you too.*"

He was preparing to leave for a monumental book tour that could propel him to become one of the greatest writers of all time. While he is away, Jennie remains at home, taking care of the house and their children. With his recent success, she no longer needed to work and could devote her time and attention to homeschooling. She is not only a wonderful mother, but also a wonderful teacher. She teaches the children important topics such as business and entrepreneurship, which are often overlooked by the public school systems. These skills are critical for success and proper interaction with others, and sadly, are not taught in public schools. Public school systems only focus on teaching students how to follow orders, while homeschooling provides opportunities to lead our future generations towards success. The lack of resources and support in public school systems often lead to struggling and limited success, allowing the wealthy to continue thriving.

Geoff was all packed up and ready for his tour. He bid his family farewell with a kiss and expressed his gratitude. He would be away for a couple of months, having finally achieved success in his career. Jennie shared in his joy and the children were delighted as well. As he got into the taxi, he said one final goodbye. *"I love you all,"* he said, *"I will miss you all so much and can't wait to be home again."* On the way to the airport, he continued to write. He was always writing, fueled by the endless inspiration within his soul. His inspiration was a persistent force, impossible to turn off like a malfunctioning button.

He was a prolific writer, or so he was told. The ease at which he churned out poems and stories was astounding. On the ride to the airport, he had managed to type out one thousand one hundred words in just fifteen minutes. As he settled into his seat by the window on the plane, he noticed that a brewing storm was on the horizon. He loved storms. Storms gave him even more inspiration. He couldn't believe that all of his success was happening. The pilot came on through the intercom, saying, *"Welcome to our Airline. This is your captain speaking. We will be flying through a small storm, so please expect some turbulence. There is nothing to worry about, so please remain calm."*

He had his pen out and was eager to start writing as he looked into the incoming storm from his window seat. The flight was from his home Eastern Maine to Los Angeles County, where his highly anticipated tour was set to kick off. A total of twenty cities were included on the agenda, which was very exciting for him. As the plane flew through the majestic storm, he was captivated by its beauty. He gazed into it in a hypnotic trance, taking in the scenery. In a moment of astonishment, he believed he saw his wife, Jennie, appearing to sit on the right wing of the plane. He was certain he was seeing things. Then, to his utter amazement, his four children began to manifest themselves before his eyes. His entire family was sitting upon the plane's wing. He closed his eyes, shook his head, and then said, *"This has to be a dream."* When he opened them and looked again, they were still sitting there. He screamed, *"My family is on the plane's wing!"* The stewardess ran over to investigate and asked, *"Sir, are you okay? What is happening?"* He then informed her that his family was sitting on the wing. When he looked again, there was nothing there. He apologized, saying, *"I am terribly sorry, I must be overwhelmed. I have a lot going on."* The stewardess continued with her day.

He immediately called home to ease his mind and make sure everything was okay. Jennie answered, *"Hey, love. How is your flight going so far?"* Then, he proceeded to describe what he had seen. They shared everything with each other. He then recounted seeing all of them on the plane's wing. He exclaimed, *"Jennie, it scared the shit out of me."* She replied, *"You must be feeling both excited and overwhelmed, my love. Close your eyes and try to get a little sleep,'* she said in a gentle voice. He laid his head back and drifted into a deep slumber. He still couldn't believe what he had just witnessed. He was roused from his slumber by the intercom when the captain returned and announced, *"This is your captain speaking. I hope you have enjoyed your flight. We are ten minutes from landing. We hope you will choose to fly with us again."*

This will be his third visit to Los Angeles and he is consistently astounded by the vast size of this city in comparison to his small hometown. He becomes anxious when he is unsure of his route and the possibility of becoming lost. Fortunately, he will not be driving, so he calls for a cab and takes it all in. The skyscrapers are towering and the streets are bustling with people, reminiscent of sardines in a can. He always thinks to himself, *"If I lived here, I would go insane."* The cab pulled up to the bookstore, where his tour was set to begin at The Ravens Nest, a large bookstore in the middle of the city.

Upon seeing his face on the poster in the store window, he felt a surge of excitement. He noticed a line of people waiting for him and felt incredibly proud of his accomplishments. The joy of people loving his work has now set in. He sat down at his table, pen in hand, ready to begin. Suddenly, the vision of his family on the plane's wing resurfaced. He shook his head, but the vision persisted. This time, it was different. They were all sitting on the wing with their throats slit. He then excused himself to take a moment to reset. He said, *"Excuse me please, for just a moment. I'll be back with all of you shortly."* He went into the restroom to regain his composure, glancing into the mirror and asking himself, *"What's wrong with you, Geoff?"*

He decided to call home again. He dialed his wife's number, but received no answer. Growing increasingly anxious, he continued to call repeatedly. Jennie did not pick up. Frustrated, he then sent text messages to all of his children, who were usually quick to reply. However, he received no response from them. He assumed they were at the park or busy with schoolwork. He decided to try contacting them again after the event. Returning to his table, he apologized for the delay. He had a row of admirers eagerly awaiting his signature. His acclaimed novel, The Song Of The Siren, was the reason for the book signing.

The event lasted just over three hours. However, as the crowd thinned, he realized he needed to call home. He dialed again, but received no answer. She didn't even attempt to call back. She always returns calls. He checked the messages he sent to his children, but still no response. He trusted his intuition and felt that something was not right. He immediately called the airport to book a flight. In a frenzied rush, he hastily repacked his belongings and called for a taxi. As he made his way to the airport, the distributing image resurfaced once more. He saw his entire family lying on the plane's wing, their throats brutally slashed, surrounded by a pool of blood. In a panic, he screamed, *"What is happening!"*

Before boarding the plane, he called his tour manager to temporarily place a hold on his tour until he could figure things out and gather more information. As he boarded the plane and it took off, he couldn't help but feel terrified about what may lay ahead. He couldn't help but question if these visions were a sign of something greater. He wonders if that is the reality he will see when he opens his front door. He is in tears when the plane touches down. He scrambles to get off of the plane and pushes past strangers in a hurried panic, down the terminal, leaving his luggage on the plane. He requests a cab and feels the tears streaming down his face. Upon arriving home, he notices the house is dark. It is three am, and it is expected that everyone would be asleep at this hour.

He frantically searches for his keys and inserts them into the lock. When he reached the top of the stairs, he realized that things were not as he had dreadfully anticipated. His children were peacefully sleeping in their beds and his wife was also sleeping, wearing her typical black mask. Suddenly, everything went black for him. When he woke up, the vision he had seen on plane's wing was right in front of his eyes. His wife and children lay on the floor, their throats slit. As he gazed at his hands, he saw that he held a blood-drenched knife. In a moment of horror, he realizes he has taken the lives of his own children and beloved wife. His twisted visions on the plane's wing have become a terrifying reality.

I've read numerous books during my time in prison, educating myself on various subjects. Although I have limited privileges, I am allowed to read and write, so I make it a point to do so every day. Despite the constant barrage of voices calling my name, I somehow manage to juggle all of this madness. I wish I had made better choices. As a child, everyone in my family —who are still alive—completely abandoned me. It is not surprising, as I ended up boiling and consuming my family's killers. The vision of my temptations haunts me every day, reminding me of that story. It brings me immense joy, only to later tear apart the stitches. I am teased by the idea of the family I never had, and the one I will never have. It plays out the events that occurred with my parents and siblings but with a sinister twist. It is a deceptive tactic to persuade me to end this. While all my voices feel like monsters, my temptations are like insidious temptresses.

My Addiction

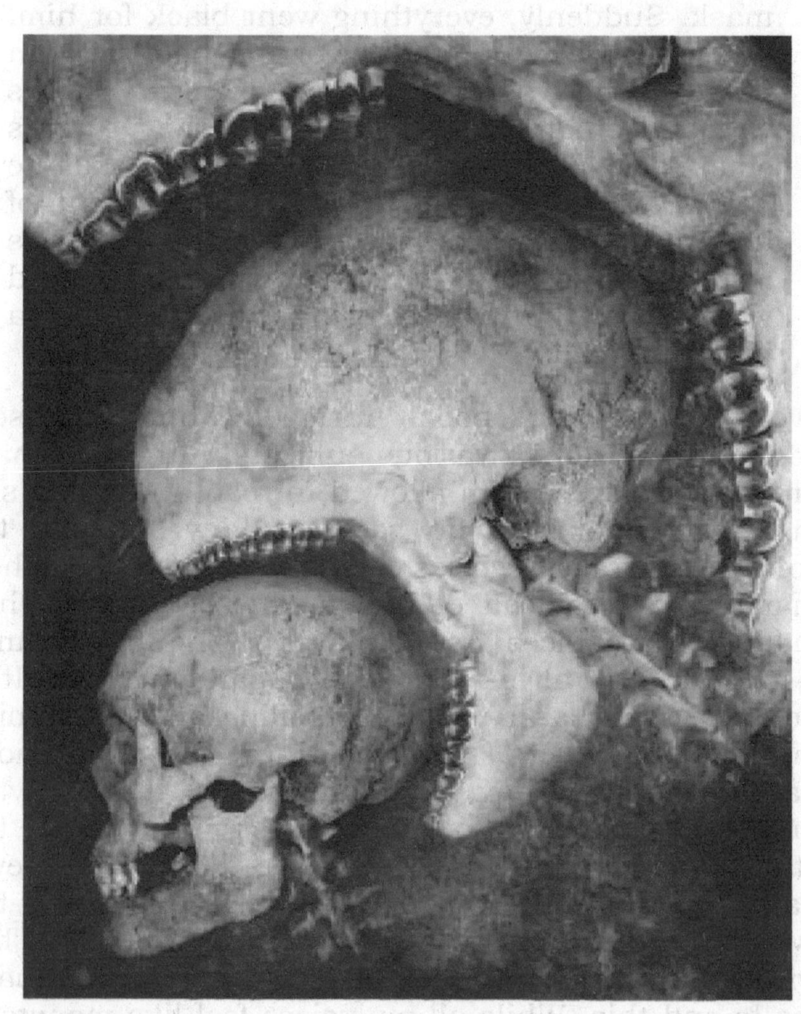

Wʜᴇɴ ᴍʏ ᴛᴇᴍᴘᴛᴀᴛɪᴏɴs vanish, my addiction takes its place. My addiction is always with me in some way, but I can only see it at this time of day—or is it night? I can't tell anymore, as no sunlight enters this cage. I have developed numerous addictions over the years, I must admit. I am hooked on writing and illustrating these voices, in addition to listening to their messages. Nevertheless, it is the only thing I seem capable of doing. In my journal entries, I have extensively reflected on my most profound addiction—the craving for human flesh. I understand that it is truly heinous and I am aware that this is something I cannot change. It consumes my thoughts around the clock and it can be difficult to keep track of them, as these journals are scattered throughout this wailing space. I am sure I have written about a million things in a million different ways.

I am teetering on the brink of that fine line, and I feel myself starting to unravel. My hands are stained with ink from endlessly writing with ballpoint pens and pencils. I have numerous paper cuts from flipping through countless pages. I have had no human interaction since being recaptured. I realize that I have repeated myself, but it is true. No prison guard is permitted to step foot within the screaming walls of my cage; I can understand their apprehension. I feel it puts my writing hand into a rage, trying to ease my strong cravings. They never go away and I have been here for many years. I tore up my calendar and never asked for another one, as knowing what day it is does not matter in this place. Not to me, at least. Not anymore. All I can think of is sinking my teeth into anyone who walks by these crystal-clear walls. As I've mentioned previously, I have abandoned the idea of escape. For me, it is too late; I will die in this place.

The visions of my addiction are diverse and haunting. They begin with a human skeleton, standing and cackling in front of me. As the scene unfolds, a larger skeleton appears, devoid of any eye sockets. This larger being then proceeds take a bite out of the back of the smaller skeleton's head. As the cycle continues, an even larger skeleton appears and repeats the ghastly act. They are ridiculing me and my addiction. I am unable to address it, causing my stomach to feel incredibly sick. I feel like a drug addict who is unable to satisfy their craving—desperate for a way to relieve it. I have visually represented my addiction, along with my other delusions, in the form of a large skeleton. The skeleton continues to speak and taunt me with the statement: *"You are fully aware of my intentions. Your fear is what I provoke."* Its teeth are decayed and there is no evidence of flesh on its bones. It is clearly taunting me, revealing its true intentions. It stomps arrogantly around the room, ensuring that I am aware that there will never be any flesh to feed my addiction again. It continues to mock me as it speaks. I want to break its large boney neck, but every time I try, I am unable to get a grip. It always laughs again and says, *'Oops, you missed.'* I want to break this skeleton in half when I hear that voice my head. I despise all of them except for one. I long for my love to arrive. She is the only voice that I cherish. I have an incredible desire to hurt this skeleton. If I only could, I would tear into this son of a bitch. It is too cocky. It is entirely self-absorbed. It moves around my cell like a foolish clown. It sings and laughs about the things I cannot obtain. This infuriates me. It pumps images into my mind of me devouring fingers and hands. Then it continues to laugh and mockingly says: *"You will never taste this again, Geoff."* You guessed it, this one comes with a story to tell. The same story every day. The same lines for thirty years. The same sickness eats my guts.

EAT UP

This is almost a survival story about two adventurous couples—Gavin, Hope, Geoff, and Mica—who venture deep into an old, abandoned mine shaft that stretches far beneath the earth's surface. The two couples were close and had known each other for their entire lives. They were always doing adventurous activities together such as skydiving, snowboarding, and rock climbing. However, they had never explored a mineshaft before and were excited to check it off their bucket lists. Gavin and Hope had been together for nine years, just like Geoff and Mica. They had gone on a double date nine years ago and both couples have been happily together ever since. The couples were now prepared to explore the caves below, which were once known for their abundance of diamonds. However, the caves have been abandoned for many years now.

As they approach the entrance, a clear statement reads, "Enter at your own risk." The two couples never back down from a challenge. They are fully prepared with all necessary equipment, including helmets, headlamps, flashlights, and boots. They were always prepared for the worst, studying the ins and outs of any adventure. They had learned that mine exploration typically entails more walking and less crawling compared to caving and that most mines are open for people to explore. However, these two couples were determined to explore what no one else had. They wanted to see the beauty of what lies far beyond the surface of the world we know. They wanted to explore the unknown dangers that awaited them. The risks that they were about to face were significant, including deadly gasses and oxygen deficiency. These hazards consist of lethal concentrations of carbon monoxide, carbon dioxide, methane, hydrogen sulfide, and other gasses that may accumulate in underground passages. However, these two couples were always prepared and cautious, as they were aware of the potential danger of cave-ins during their journey. They were equipped with gas masks in case they became trapped inside, and had enough food and water to sustain them for several days.

Before entering the mine, they meticulously mapped out their route, carefully planning their way to the underground caves they wished to explore. These caverns are situated deep beneath the earth's surface, approximately three thousand feet below. As the two couples made their way down through the narrow passages. Gavin warned the others, *It's going to get even narrower as we go.*" They always worked together to ensure each other's safety on their daring adventures. *"Copy that,"* the others replied. *"Keep your eyes off of Hope's ass, Geoff,"* Gavin reminded him. *"It's impossible when it is right in my face, so close in fact that I can practically taste it,"* Geoff replied. The men would always joke with each other like that, and Hope and Mica just rolled their eyes, because that is what they always do. *"Typical men!"* both women said in unison.

As they approached the narrowest part of the decent, they had to exercise extreme caution. *"It's becoming quite tight in here,"* Gavin noted. Mica screamed, "I'm stuck, please help, Geoff!" She was panicking, never a good idea in such a tightly confined space. Geoff explained, *"I can't turn around. It's too tight to turn around."* They all heard the tunnel shift and crack. Gavin calmly said to Mica, *"Stay still and do not panic. We will figure this out, I promise."* Their worst fears then came to life as the tunnel caved in around Mica, severing her legs and lower body from her upper torso. She screamed briefly before falling into eternal silence. Geoff screamed in horror, *"No, baby girl! This isn't real."*

The remaining three are desperate to come up with a plan. Mica has passed away, and now she stares at them with eyes that appear to be made of glass. These are the familiar eyes we see in horror films, the lifeless eyes that evoke a chilling sensation. The three remaining adventurers would never forget the types of eyes they encountered. *"We need to continue downward,"* Hope insisted. The collapse of the tunnel had obstructed the only known exit. They needed to find another way to escape. They were limited on rations of water and food. *"Let's press on!"* Gavin screamed. Geoff remained silent, having just lost his wife and best friend. Gavin and Hope, aware of his recent loss, worried that he may have suffered a mental breakdown. As they made their way down the narrow tunnel, they grew anxious of the possibility of further collapse. Gavin gently inquired, *"Geoff, are you alright?"* However, Geoff remained silent and did not respond. Hope then informed him that they would be fine, hoping to provide some comfort and coax a response from Geoff. However, he remained silent. After about three hours of silence, Gavin suddenly yelled, *" I think I see a way out ahead!"*

Excitement filled Hope, but Geoff still remained silent. He hadn't spoken a word since Mica died. Nobody knew their whereabouts and nobody was coming to search for them either. They were completely alone and terrified. One by one, they crawled out of the tunnel to discover the magnificent rock formations and crystals adorning the ceilings of the subterranean caves. It was a sight that changed the mood slightly for Gavin and Hope, as Geoff remained silent and unresponsive. His eyes appeared cold and disconnected with reality, similar to Mica's when she stared at them with her dead eyes. His eyes were lifeless, like glass. It seemed as though there was no other way out. The three remaining friends are thirsty and hungry from the hours they spent descending. Gavin usually overpacked food and water just in case something like this would happen. However, for some reason he didn't pack as much this time, which is now turning into a major problem. They must find an exit soon.

Three days have passed and confidence is now dwindling, along with the food supply. No other exits have been found. The only available exit is the one they entered through. Gavin and Hope are considering turning back, but they are horrified at the prospect of having to move their friend Mica's severed body in order to do so. Geoff has yet to utter a single word. They must prepare for the unimaginable, or they will all end up like Mica. Gavin proposed that they just get it over with. They needed to relocate her if they hoped to have any chance at survival. They needed to act swiftly, with three people and a limited food supply. Only one of them will be able to crawl up and move the body. The passage out is too narrow. The fear of collapse is in their minds if all of them went. Hope is thinking about how hard this will be. She feels sick at the thought of dragging her now-dead friend through that tunnel.

Hope is contemplating crawling through the mess that emanates from of Mica's half torso. She envisions the extensive amounts of blood. *"I can't handle this! Mica was my closest friend,"* Hope exclaimed. Gavin quickly offered to help. *"I'll do it,"* He said nervously. They were both haunted by the memory of Mica's lifeless, vacant eyes. Gavin wasted no time and began his journey to the spot where Mica's corpse lay. Hope was in tears, while Geoff remained silent. There was no guarantee of Gavin's success, or even his survival. Time was running out, and they were beginning to forget their initial purpose. Gavin finally arrived at the location where Mica lay. Her unblinking glass eyes were fixed on him, a truly chilling image of Mica. They were the type of eyes that could plague one and linger beyond life and death. Gavin then respectfully closed both of Mica's lifeless piercing eyes, not wanting Hope and Geoff to go through such a traumatic experience again. He stated, *"I took one for the team."* She used to laugh when he said that.

Gavin must now seize Mica and pull her half-dead body back down to the bottom. If he succeeds, he will need to rest before attempting to clear the collapse by crawling back up. He will then have to make a third trip if he successfully clears the tunnel and drags the other half of his friend down what will then be known as "The

Blood Tunnel." Gavin then grabs Mica by her now cold, lifeless arm and pulls with all of his might. He heard her body sever and tear away from whatever remained connected to her lower body. He heard the sounds of her innards dragging along the cold dirt and rock, mixing and transforming into a thick, almost black mud. Gavin called it 'Blood Mud.'

He reached the bottom and Hope stood there, screaming when she saw Gavin approaching. It was not a typical fear-induced scream, but rather one that sent chills down your spine like a tolling bell. Despite witnessing such horrifying scenes, Geoff maintained his silence. Gavin instructed Hope to quiet her screams as they both grabbed an arm and pulled their deceased friend's half-torso out of the tunnel. They placed her at the other end of the area, facing the wall underground. The trail of blood left by Mica's internal organs from one side of the tunnel to the other was thick and nauseating. "The Blood Mud." He then ate a portion of what little food they had left and rested before once again having to crawl through the tunnel.

Nothing feels the same now that it has been so many days trapped underground. Geoff has still not spoken a word since the tragic death of his wife. The food and water are running out quickly, as is time. Hope and Gavin are preparing for their second trip through the tunnel to attempt to clear the cave and move the other half of Mica. Then, they will drag the rest of her down the tunnel. They can already see the stages of Mica's decomposition. They still can't shake the image of her dead, glassy eyes from their minds.

Geoff seems to have lost his sanity. Neither Hope nor Gavin has been able to engage him in conversation. Gavin glances at Hope and says, *"If I do not make it back alive, I apologize for suggesting this. I am deeply sorry."* Hope reassured him that it is not his fault, saying, *"Let's just leave this place, alright?"* Gavin nodded, and then he crawled up. As he made his way up, he could feel Mica's blood getting all over his hands and legs. At one point, he thought he felt her innards squishing beneath his kneecaps. As he neared the area where the tunnel had collapsed, he managed to shift the boulder aside just enough to reach the other half of his dead friend. He was satisfied, as this would spare him from making a third trip. They would then be able to crawl out together once he returned.

He reached through and had to grab the half torso from the section where it was split. It was cold, mushy, and emitted a foul stench. He gagged and vomited all over the half-corpse, the blood-covered dirt, and the rocky tunnel floor. It was a horrific concoction, akin to a sinister nightmare stew. He reached inside again and his entire hand entered Mica's body cavity. He grabbed and pulled, hearing the sounds of his hand squishing and splashing around inside of her. He then pictured her lifeless eyes. He was able to extract her with little effort. He paused for a moment to ensure that they would fit through safely. *"We are going home, baby!"* Gavin exclaimed.

He was overjoyed to return and share the good news with his wife and now silent friend. He then began his descent and successfully reached the bottom without any issues. He saw Hope standing there, randomly screaming once again. He feared that she might have also lost her mind, but then he thought, "maybe not." He was dragging half of a dead body, so I guess I would scream if I saw that, too. He made it to the bottom and delivered the good news: *"Pack up and let's get the fuck out of here!"* Hope stopped screaming and asked, *"Did you do it?"* She then ran over and hugged him. Geoff was still silent. They grabbed everything they needed and prepared for the climb out of the tomb that they were in. Gavin then asked, *"Are you both ready for this?"* One *"yes"* from Hope, but no words from Geoff.

The walls of the underground enclosure suddenly began to shake. They covered their heads, as if this section was about to cave in. When it stopped, their worst nightmare would reveal itself. The only way out had completely collapsed. There was only one flashlight battery pack remaining. *"What do we do now?"* Hope screamed. *"I don't know!"* Gavin screamed back. They were almost out of food and water with only a few meals left. There was no way out of here now. Nobody was coming. Gavin then lowered his head, as if accepting the fact that they were all going to die. Hope sat down between Gavin and Geoff, sobbing uncontrollably. Geoff remained silent. *"Let's just finish off the food now,"* Gavin suggested, exasperated. He had resigned himself to the situation and simply wanted it to be over. The three friends proceeded to consume the remaining food and water. With nothing left, they braced themselves for starvation.

Gavin then remembered Mica's glass eyes, now lifeless in death, and proposed a morbid solution: to eat her corpse in order to prolong their survival. Hope, horrified, screamed in disbelief. *"Are you insane?"* Gavin replied, defending his idea. *"We have to do what we can to survive."* They engaged in a heated argument for over an hour with no clear winner. Just as their flashlight took its final breath, its battery pack died. The three were now in complete darkness. Suddenly, they could hear chewing sounds in the dark. *"Gavin, where are you?"* Hope inquired. He responded, *"I am right beside you."* The chewing noises persisted. *"Geoff, where are you?"* Hope and Gavin screamed. There was only silence. Frustrated, Gavin began banging on the flashlight, hoping to get it to turn on and illuminate their surroundings. The flashlight turned on, and then he shone it in the direction where Mica's corpse was. What they witnessed next was unfathomable. With his mouth full of his deceased wife's decomposing flesh, Geoff uttered his first words since Mica's death and bellowed, *"Eat up!"* The enormous skeleton then closes with the statement, *"Do you have an appetite, Geoff?*

Before I can answer, that scoundrel vanishes. Every day, it comes to recount the tale of the two couples in the mines, triggering my insatiable craving for flesh and causing me to feel physically ill. I am constantly agitated in this confined space because of my intense desire for it. I cannot have it, though, because no one is coming in! I will never go out, either. This is my fate. I will die here without ever again tasting the sweetness of blood on my lips. After the vision of my addiction departs, my inner demons will step in to tear apart my blackened heart.

My Inner Demons

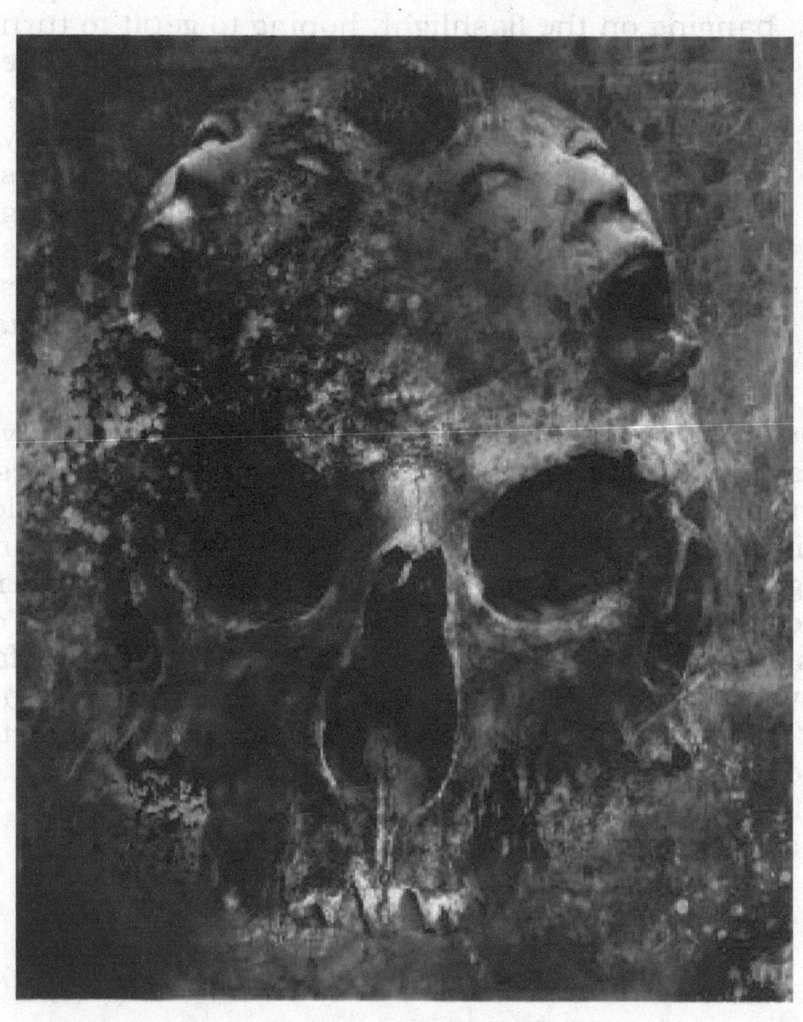

I AM STILL consumed by my addictions. I have little time to relax before another voice appears before me. I am still unsure what to label them as. Should I refer to them as apparitions or hallucinations? When the walls start bleeding, I know that my inner demons are coming to feed. They take just a little bit more of my being each time they appear. I am unable to sleep, as if my eyes are super glued open and held in place with rusted barbed wire. My inner demons serve and reign over the fire as mighty Princes and Princesses of darkness, acting as servants of Hell. They take on various forms, and this time they have emerged from an ancient skull. It seems as though they are breaking free from my mind and manifesting themselves clearly. I have reached the point where I am convinced of their existence. These voices cannot be a figment of my imagination any longer. I have moved beyond that point. My imagination has faded away and cracked.

My eyes burn as my demons attack. I am unable to blink or move them. My thoughts cease and my breathing becomes labored when they take control of me. With sinister snickers and sneers, they reek of death and terror. I am overwhelmed as they thrust their rotting tongues into my ears. They only emerge once a day, but when they do, it feels like they stay for years. As I've stated previously, time holds no significance here. I believe I am destined to be a servant of the fire even in death. I suppose I am not deserving of growing wings to soar. I have committed numerous terrible acts. However, I struggle to feel remorse for my actions. I cannot recall the last time tears welled up in my eyes, except for the night my family died. That was the only time I truly cried. Even when I took revenge on their killers by consuming their innards, I did not shed a tear. I chuckled when I gazed into their lifeless eyes. All I am able do within this enclosure is gaze through the translucent barriers and sketch and write.

My inner demons incessantly gnaw at me, much like the other voices within me, relishing in the torment they inflict day and night. The cycle seems never-ending, and I doubt it will come to a close even in my old age. I was never devout enough to preach, but I am well-versed in navigating my insanity as it manifests more clearly. Every day it becomes clearer that I am completely losing my sanity. Each day, my mind becomes increasingly elusive. I've long crossed that delicate threshold. This time, my inner demons have manifested in the form of women. They taunt me and challenge my deteriorating brain. Their skin is scaly, and their tongues are forked. It feels as though two serpents are tasting me, treating me like a fresh cut of pork. They lick their lips as they talk, and their undead bodies graze against mine. Every touch leaves a slimy residue on my skin. They speak in hushed tones, as if this is all a twisted game.

Every book that I have ever read on demons states that a demon will never reveal its name. They slither around me with their serpent-like ways, promising me everything I want if I play their games. I am aware that this is a trick, as they come every day. However, my inner demons have never manifested themselves to me in this way, nor have they ever been able to make physical contact. They are becoming more powerful. Upon gazing at them again, I noticed that their appearance had drastically transformed into that of two human women who were confined in my cage alongside me, attempting to manipulate me into obeying their commands.

I am intrigued and cannot look away, as usually each voice appears the same. However, my inner demons have found a way to change, causing confusion. As one them spoke to me, saying *"Geoff, come over here and play."* I am compelled to resist due to the potential consequences of the game. I will be manipulated and taken to Hell if I play their games. My eyes are still wide open and I cannot close them— from using my hands, splashing water on my face, to even looking away. There is something about the two female demons has me inexplicably hypnotized. One of the demons spoke and said, *"Hello Geoff, why won't you play? I think you need to hear a story about why your eyes are fixated. We are your allies, Geoff. We are not your foes. Please listen to our tale."*

ETERNAL ENERGY

In another dimension, vastly different from our own, exists a world that never sleeps. For some, lack of sleep is a lifelong condition. This dimension is inhabited by deranged, formidable monsters and malevolent humans where murder and riots are common occurrences. The New World Government has enacted a law mandating experiments on eternal sleep deprivation in this dimension. The organization has been deemed a dictatorship, as it has removed all elected officials from every city in the world. The former government officials were systematically executed through various brutal methods, including decapitation, burning, immersion in acid baths, and other forms of murder. This world is in chaos due to the lack of sleep. When injected with a virus that targets the brain's ability to signal tiredness and induce sleep, those infected will never be able to sleep again. This is known as the "ETERNAL ENERGY" shot, and its effects can result in permanent sleep deprivation or irreversible deformity. There will never be a cure.

People who experience chronic sleep deprivation are at a heightened risk for developing high blood pressure and high cholesterol, both of which can ultimately lead to death. People suffering from chronic sleep deprivation are more susceptible to developing Type 2 diabetes, which may ultimately result in the development of Type 1 diabetes. The absence of public pharmacies and the prohibition of crucial medications by The New World Government are resulting in the deaths of millions of people. The body's natural defenses against bacteria and infections cannot function properly without adequate sleep. In fact, the lack of sleep may even lead to death from a common cold. Also, all medications for compromised immune systems have been discontinued. It is not worth searching for them as they are practically non-existent.

It is common for people who do not get enough sleep to exhibit higher levels of pain sensitivity, resulting in increased ease of experiencing pain with an elevated sensation. The New World Government has also prohibited essential treatments and medicines, which have been outlawed for those suffering from nervous system complications, resulting in a catastrophic increase in mortality rates. Cancer patients endure pain that is one hundred times greater than expected, leading to shortened lifespans and ultimately, extinction, due to the lack of viable treatments. Sleep deprivation can have severe negative effects on the functioning of the brain. The lack of sleep can cloud your thoughts and judgement, potentially leading to situations where people may engage in acts of violence over seemingly minor reasons, such as a passing glance. While experts may not fully understand the role of sleep in brain function, they do acknowledge its significance in the process of learning and memory. However, the actions of the New World Government have deprived us of our cures, leaving us sleep-deprived and hindering our ability to learn and retain information. This intentional act ultimately seeks to exterminate us.

Sleep deprivation also has a negative impact on your mental health, making it difficult for you to regulate and comprehend your emotions. People who suffer from sleep deprivation are more susceptible to exhibiting symptoms of depression and anxiety, and may resort to impulsive behaviors rather than utilizing logical thinking. The streets are now flooded with people desperately seeking a cure for any medical condition they may have. We have lost control.

Knowing that you can be killed at any time is a sure way to stir up anxiety. Bipolar disorder has become increasingly difficult to manage for those affected. Depression rates are on the rise, as cruel leaders intentionally aim to cause despair among the people of the world. Mania affects everyone on the streets of every city and town in this reality. Lack of proper treatment is causing simple arguments to escalate into murder. The current global murder rate is increasing, with an alarming eighty percent of cases linked to panic disorder. Untreated PTSD also contributes to the disturbing statistic that almost ninety percent of suicides are linked to this condition. If left untreated—as all disorders and ailments are in today's society—these conditions can result in impulsive and aggressive actions, including homicide and self-harm. In this world, all diseases and conditions are left untreated as all medical facilities have been shut down. Treating any illness is now considered illegal and the punishment for doing so is death.

What this organization is doing is eradicating the population of this dimension. They are trying to create a new world, one that they can fully control. They take pleasure in watching the buildings set ablaze by the crazed, sleep-deprived masses. They are patiently waiting for them to self-destruct before they begin rebuilding their new world according to their own meticulous plans. Anyone who refuses the injection is executed. People are dying on a daily basis in the streets from heart failure. They are also turning on one other due to their lack of emotional control after a certain period of time without sleep. Typically, by the third day, hallucinations become prominent. Many people on the run from this organization and have fled and managed to evade execution. While some people have been caught and killed, there are still many others who are struggling to maintain their ability to sleep. Now, let us shift our focus to a newly married couple who have managed to avoid execution and are currently on the run from a strict New World Government.

If they are apprehended, they will face public execution. However, the injections also have horrific side effects on some unfortunate people, distorting their physical appearance and transforming them into animal-like creatures with an insatiable craving for blood and violence. These creatures have killed countless people, contributing to the chaos and devastation of this emerging new world. The names of the couple are Geoff and Jenny, who once lived a blissful life before the New World Government took control. As newlyweds, they were at the height of their lives. However, everything turned upside down when they began witnessing the brutal removal of people from their homes. Just like everyone else, their lives were forever changed. This organization demonstrates no remorse for their actions and will not stop until their vision of rebuilding is achieved, regardless of the consequences to the dying planet. This is their ultimate goal.

The couple had no children and were grateful for that, as children were not exempt from receiving the shot and experiencing its effects. They had been hiding and on the run for many months, forced from their homes and into the streets. Both had refused the injection, instead retreating to the remote countryside, far away from the chaotic and dying city streets. They had never seen these leaders, but had heard horrible stories about them during their travels.

Some labeled them as extraterrestrials, while others deemed them as inhuman beings. Nonetheless, their genesis and objective remained an enigma. They materialized out of nowhere, eliminating all influential figures and taking over the reins of power worldwide simultaneously. It must have been planned for a long time to achieve such an impossible yet remarkable rise to power in such a short period of time. The couple frequently asks each another: *"Why didn't they just kill all of us? Why are they making us kill each other?"* These entities—whether they be otherworldly beings, extraterrestrial creatures, or mythical monsters—seem to revel in our suffering, as if it were their preferred television series or horror film. However, our situation far exceeds anything that one could view on a screen; this harsh reality is our agony and the inevitable downfall of our world.

The two female demons constantly interrupt the story to torment me. I can feel their deformed tongues sliding in and out of my ears as they persist. I cannot give In and agree to anything while these demons are present. No matter how tempting it may be, I must resist their skill in extracting my innermost desires. They exploit my desires to manipulate me. If I succumb, It's like signing a binding agreement. They will possess me if I give in. I am diligently attempting to maintain silence, yet I find myself constantly filled with fear. These voices have taken over my once innocent mind. Before continuing, they both said to me, "Geoff, you will eventually be ours." I was then thrown to the ground, and both demons sat on top of me as they continued their story, muffling my screams.

The pair are hiding out in an old, abandoned trailer in a rundown trailer park deep in the countryside. There doesn't seem to be anyone around. They are aware that there are others like them, but none are present at the moment. *"More like us will come, and nobody can be trusted,"* Geoff said to Jenny. *"What do we do when they come?"* Jenny asked. *"We move on,"* Geoff answered. For now, they both had shelter and there were no signs of the New World Government or anyone else. It was perfect for now. They both knew not to get too comfortable because the safety they temporarily felt could be flipped in an instant. Geoff had just returned from rummaging through the nearby forest for food. It was remote, so things were not heavily picked over like in cities and towns. An abundance of wild berries grows and attracts the animals that feed on them, such as deer and bears. He brought back enough to keep them above water for now. Everything helps out here, no matter how much or little they find. It was going to be a struggle for the rest of their lives to survive.

The world will never be the same again. Not only must they fear the NWG (New World Government), but they also must be vigilant against the deformed, who feast on the flesh of the non-deformed and have an uncontrollable lust for blood. These previously human beings are insatiable and incapable of reasoning. Their appearance and actions are the horrible side-effects caused by the "ETERNAL ENERGY" shot —that is what the NWG calls it. Once the contents of the shot enter your system, you will never sleep again. The couple had encountered these creatures before and were fortunate to have escaped this unpredictable new species.

They had been walking through a back alley, trying to find a shortcut through the inflamed city, when they first encountered these creatures. There were two of them dismembering a group of people and leaving nothing to waste. They escaped by running into the forest. Luckily for them, there were others nearby who distracted the creatures. They chose to pursue the others because there were more of them. That was the last time they entered the city. No other creatures have been sighted, and they must remain vigilant as an attack could potentially come from either the deformed or the NWG at any moment. The tranquility of the trailer park is incredibly peaceful and calming. There are no scents of fire or sounds of screaming, making it feel like a return to normalcy in this serene environment. The melodic chirping of the crickets in the untamed wilderness brings a sense of relief to the tired couple, allowing them to easily drift off into a peaceful 'REM' sleep.

In their peaceful dreams of how the world once was, they were suddenly awakened by loud animal-like sounds. They immediately snapped out of their slumber, fearing that it could possibly be a deformed creature. Without hesitation, they peered out of the trailer window to see a large, black bear outside. If they could find a way to kill it, they would have some meat to sustain themselves. Before they could even blink, a trio of deformed creatures ambushed the bear, tearing it to shreds in what seemed like an instant. The couple observed in horror as the bear's body parts were devoured by these creatures, who swallowed them whole, similar to the way an alligator eats without chewing. After finishing, they exchanged glances as if communicating and moved on. This is the second time that they have encountered the deformed creatures, and they are concerned they may not be as fortunate next time.

Each of the deformed looks entirely different. No one is exactly the same. Their once normal physiques are now twisted abominations, each one carrying a different trait. Each one craves the same thing: blood and meat. The two would be easily be torn apart if seen. The monsters continued on thankfully, relieved that they were safe for the moment. Geoff began to speak negatively and asked, *Why don't we put an end to this now, Jenny? We could be free from running and hiding.* Exhausted, he added, "*I'm so tired, my love. I just want this to end.*" Jenny responded with concern, "*Please don't talk like that, Geoff. We are in this together. Remember, it is us against the world—to the stars and back. Just you and me.*"

He then pulled a gun out of the box he had by the grimy trailer sink. He stuck it in his mouth and freed himself. Jenny could only scream and scream. He abandoned her with the deformed creatures and the New World Government. Now, she was left alone in this harrowing world. It was incomprehensible to her that the one she loved the most would abandon her in the presence of these creatures. She couldn't fathom that he had compelled her to witness the splatter and leakage of his brains. She couldn't stop imagining the color change of the dirty sink in that trailer park. She then lowered her head and exited the trailer, entering the nearby trees. After repeatedly screaming, "*Come and get me!*" for about ten minutes, she heard the sound of rustling and growling. Suddenly, a horde of deformed creatures attacked her, tearing her apart at the seams. She was completely consumed and no longer had to run. Geoff and Jenny no longer had to hide. They could finally stop running in this dimension of eternal energy. They both were finally able to finally rest, forever.

The two demons were still lounging on top of me, leaving a trail of slime over my body. They resemble repulsive slugs, and I was tempted to use salt, as my Grandmother had taught me, to get rid of them. They both malevolently whispered at the same time, "Geoff, did you enjoy our story?" I shouted, "Get off me!" I was not about to give in to their trickery, as I knew that demons only desire one thing: the souls of humanity. They then licked their vile lips and hissed, "One day you will be our servant, mark my words." Then, they vanished into the veil and, just for a brief moment, I felt at peace. My hallucinations will soon manifest, and they are just as distressing as the previous demons that had plagued and smothered me. Unfortunately, both will return tomorrow. Thankfully, my eyes return to a normal state when they leave. I must take advantage of this moment to rest before my hallucinations reappear.

My Hallucinations

My hallucinations always transport me back to a place in my mind that I don't like to revisit—a memory from my childhood that I cannot determine if it is real or not. It's all a game manipulated by these voices, as they strive for complete dominance over me. It's all just a jumbled mess, and nothing here seems to makes sense. My hallucinations manifest in the form of a deceased naked woman every day. She possesses raven-like black wings and her face is decomposing. She wears a white blindfold over her eyes and speaks with a soft, angelic-like tone. However, I am not fooled, as I am aware of the demonic presence within her. Like most of my voices, she reveals my past, present and future, just in different ways. She shows me the love and children that were never mine, and the life that was denied to me. She reminds me of the beauty of my childhood, making me beg for its return. But I know, deep down, that it can never be brought back. I am aware of this. I am who I am and I do not give a damn. Why should I care? I am decomposing here. I am remaining here. I will perish in terror! The malformed woman then softly murmured: "Come *here. Join me in a dance and I will make your dreams a reality. Whatever you desire, I can provide for you. Come here and you will see.*"

I cannot be deceived by this. It is always a ploy. It is always the same. I am exhausted by this. She then began to flap her magnificent black wings. The dander that falls from her wings leaves me in a vegetative state. The black dust fills my cell and there is no escape. She continues to fly around, and you can see everything in the room swirling around like we are in the center of a tornado. I am unable to move as she destroys my cell. As she dances, she begins to sing her hauntingly beautiful melody. Her song repeats the same message to me. Before she sings, she says, *"Come over here. Let me show you that my love is true. Listen to my song, Geoff."*

I AM HERE FOR YOU

Hello, my dear.
Allow me to embrace you and play.
We can become one here, together.
I understand you're hungry;
I hold the flesh that you crave.
Pay no attention to the hounds barking.
I am here for you.

Please make a promise that you'll never run
    away.
Stay with me forever.
I know your corrupted heart is fading.
The cure is right here, follow me.
Please ignore the flames and the growling.
I am here for you, your unending inferno awaits.
Together, we can endure the eternal flames.
I understand your tears and I will wipe them
    away.
You may not even realize that your skin is
    melting.
I am here for you.

Join me and claim your rightful place.
We can dance in the fire together, forever.
I understand that you are aging

And your breath may soon be taken away,
But please remember, my love, the fire will
    always await.
This melody will seduce you, while numbing you
    to the pain.
I am here for you.

Let us embrace passion amidst the flames as
    they rise.
My kiss will fulfill your deepest desires.
I understand that you may feel deprived,
Allow me to offer you a taste.
as this melody continues to play, I will ride you
    into the fire.
I am here for you, and with me you stay.

Each day, the vision/voice in my head—which I refer to as my hallucinations—arrives, and sings that exact song to me. She attempts to entice me into the flames. All of these voices try to persuade me to end my pain except for one. I wish my love was here and could stay to help me battle these visions. I wish I could find some way to make them leave. They never will, though. For many years, it has been the same: the same voices, the same fucking time of day. It Is a repetitive madness that I fear is here to stay. The woman with the stunning black wings also comes with a story. For many years, like many similar stories, this one remains unchanged. I feel like I am repeatedly banging my head against the walls of my transparent cage. My body remains immobile, trapped in a vegetative state.

She begins to recount the tale and beckons, Geoff, *look this way*. I am already unable to look away. These voices drain me and prevent me from retaining my sanity. This story is deeply intertwined with my troubled life. The demon then addresses me before recounting her tale, "Come closer and listen. This story is sure to send shivers down your spine. You are not a victim, my dear. You are The Cape Elizabeth Ripper."

THE CAPE ELIZABETH RIPPER

It's Fall 1997 in Cape Elizabeth, Maine: the school bell rings as Killian High students hurry out of class to get home. A curfew has been set for eight o'clock due to reports of missing persons in the area. Jason, Eli, Jacob, and Bill were not in a rush like everyone else. The teens were relatively calm as they walked out the front doors, laughing. A teacher approaches them and reminds them of the curfew. Eli checks the time on his phone, which reads 2:37.

Jacob mockingly quips, *"We know, we know."* They then make their way to Jacob's house, just before the rain begins. The teenagers hurry down to the basement, where Jacob's father has constructed them a "man cave." When they reach the bottom of the stairs, they take a seat on the worn-out couch, a revolting vomit green.

The boys immediately pull out their phones. Jason scoffs at Bill, who just sits there. *"Still no phone?"* He glares at his older friend.

Suddenly, the power goes out, scaring the boys. *"It was probably just the rain,"* Jason says in a calm tone as the rest of the boys nod in agreement.

They hear sounds of banging coming from upstairs. *"Hey, Jacob,"* Eli interjects mockingly, *"I think your parents are wrestling upstairs."* Jacob nudges him and mutters for him to be quiet.

The young men suddenly realize it is 8:06 pm and that Jacobs' parents have not yet instructed them to go to bed. Jason takes charge and offers to investigate the cause of the noise and power outage. "I'll go check it out," he announces, making his way up the creaky basement stairs. Jason opens the door and grabs a flashlight from the dining room table, turning it on. He calls out for Jacob's parents but receives no answer. As he walks towards the kitchen, he hears rattling coming from behind the couch. He asked, *"Mrs.Donahue?"* as he glared over at the couch. He approached it and their cat, Petey, jumped out and ran past him. "Jesus...stupid cat," Jason calls to Jacob for help, while Eli and Bill remain downstairs.

Together, they make their way up the stairs to the breaker room. "How do you turn this thing back on?' Jason asked Jacob, He then flipped a few switches and turned on the power. *"That rain is no joke, huh?"* Jason muttered as he made his way towards the breaker room, hoping to fix the breaker. *"Did you get it fixed, Eli?"* Bill asked, agreeing as the lights turn back on. *"Seems like the dream team has fixed the power,"* Eli exclaims as Bill replies, *"Took them long enough."* Jason and Jacob descend the stairs, while Eli and Bill take cover beneath the basement staircase. *"AHH! It's the infamous Cape Elizabeth Ripper!"* Eli says jokingly as he grabs Jason and Jacob by their ankles "Not funny, Eli!" Jason says. Bill laughs as his friends get scared by Eli *"We turned the power back on,"* Jacob says. *"Where are your parents?"* Bill asks. *"They probably just went out to the store or something,"* Jacob replies as he shuts the door and makes his way to the couch in the basement. *"Want to play Hide and seek in the dark? Unless you are too scared,"* Jason says.

The boys agree to the game as they smile and laugh. *"Who goes first?"* Bill asks *"I pick Jacob, since we are at his house."* Jason replies. Jacob agrees to count and turns off the power, then counts to sixty as his friends run up the stairs to hide and Eli makes his way to Jacob's parent's room. Jason makes his way to the garage and hides among some shelves, while Bill runs up to the attic and conceals himself among some Christmas decorations. Both boys are in their designated hiding spots as Jacob grabs his flashlight and ascends the basement stairs. He thoroughly checks the first floor before heading over to the garage where Bill is hiding. Jacob hears movement coming from his dad's tool cabinet, so he swings the door open. He finds Bill and says, *"Gotcha!"* Bill sighs and gets up. Upstairs, Eli hides in Jacob's parents' closet. As he searches the dark space, he suddenly catches a whiff of something foul. The putrid stench is so overwhelming that Eli feels nauseous and instinctively covers his nose. He cautiously makes his way to the back of the closet, using his phone's flashlight to illuminate his path. But as his beam of light falls on Jacob's mom, his face contorts in shock as he sees that she has a sickle buried in her head.

He lets out a scream as he runs out of the closet. Jacob hears Eli screaming from upstairs, *"Does he even know how to play?"* Jacob asks himself as he makes his way up the stairs and runs into Eli. *"Ha, got you."* Jacob says as Eli stutters to get words out. *"Your mom is in the closet,"* Eli says before passing out. *"Eli?'* Jacob asked, as Bill caught up to them and inquired, *"What happened?"* Jacob appeared bewildered as Jason emerged from his hiding spot and exclaimed, *"What the hell happened to Eli? I heard him scream."* Bill hurried to the breaker room and quickly restored power, muttering about the incident in the closet. Jacob asked Eli, who was now standing and speaking in a tearful and frightened voice, *"What did you see?"* as Bill splashed water on Eli's head to wake him up. Eli gasped in fear and replied, *'I think I saw your mom. She had a sickle in her head or something."* To which Jacob responded in disbelief, *"Yea right."* *"Please look, I am not kidding."* Eli says with desperation.

The four of them make their way to the closet where Eli indicated the location of the body. As they reach in the back of the closet, they spot his mom with the sickle lodged in her head. The boys let out terrified screams as they quickly flee the closet and run towards the front door. As they opened the door, Jacob's dad's body fell. As the boys look up, they notice a figure in a hat standing over the body. In fear, Bill slams the door shut, locks it, and then the boys retreat to the basement screaming. As Jacob reaches for his phone to call the police, the power goes out. Now they have no signal, Eli quickly pulls out his phone's flashlight. He shines it as the boys panic. They all hear movement upstairs. *"We are in trouble."* Bill mumbles in fear. *"He's looking for us."* Jason says. *"We're just fourteen years old, what are we supposed to do?"* Jacob replies. With quick thinking, Eli grabs a baseball bat and holds it ready to swing at anyone that comes downstairs.

As the eerie figure's shadow looms closer to the basement, Eli holds his bat up high in preparation. The other boys stand behind him, ready to jump in. When the figure reaches the bottom of the stairs, Eli swings his bat with full force, striking the man squarely in the head and knocking him to the ground. The boys are shocked but waste no time and make their way up the stairs to the front door. The teens quickly run down the street without looking back, despite the heavy rain. *"Where should we go?"* Bill asks with a concerned expression. *"Let's go to the school. Maybe someone on the night shift can help us there."* Jacob replied with a single tear rolling down his face, but without hesitation, the boys sprinted towards the school. *"Help!"* The boys yell as they make their way to the school. They bang on the door, but receive no response. Eli struggles to pull out a lock-pick, thanks to the knowledge his mother had taught him. With the door successfully unlocked, the boys slam it shut behind them. *"I think we should split up."* Jason says as they vote to select the groups. They ultimately decide that Eli and Bill will work together, while Jacob and Jason will form their own team. The teams went in different directions, with a plan to meet back at nine pm.

As the boys agreed, Eli quickly grabbed his phone and saw that it was 8:21. The teams went in different directions and Eli and Bill became paranoid due to the recent event. Suddenly, a loud crash echoed through the school, causing Bill to exclaim in a fearful tone, *"I think he made it in, damn it!"* Jacob and Jason rushed to the principal's office upon hearing a loud bang echoing through the school. In a state of fear, they exchanged a fearful glance with each other. As they made their way to the cafeteria, they saw Eli and Bill walking towards them. To their horror, they discovered the lifeless body of a security guard, with his head missing, still grasping his gun. Eli couldn't help but ask, *"Oh crap, that guy is way dead!"* Jason replied with a nod, *"No crap, he's missing his head!"* Bill exclaims as he sees the security guard holding a gun towards him, *'Look at the gun!'* he shouts as he reaches for it. *"Does anyone know how to use* *one?"*As he grabs it, a sickle emerges from a mysterious portal and the boys are shocked as an arm emerges from it. *"What is that?"* The boys exclaimed.

The Ripper emerges wearing a dark outfit. The boys scream and make a beeline for the cafeteria exit. Suddenly, chains rise up and ensnare the Ripper. *"What the hell?!"* Eli exclaims, struggling to accept the unbelievable scene before him. The Ripper then approaches the boys with slow, ominous steps. Eli and Bill move quickly to one side of a cafeteria table, but the Ripper flips it into the air. In response, Eli forcefully tackles Bill to the ground for protection. "Thank you," Bill says, but before Eli can respond, a knife suddenly enters his back, throwing him across the cafeteria and rendering him unconscious. *"ELI!!"* Bill shouts as he rushes to Eli's motionless body. *"You monster!"* Bill exclaims as he stands up and confronts the Ripper, his fists clenched in anger. Jacob and Jason locate the principal's office and discover a deceased security guard impaled to the wall with a knife in his throat. Jacob gasps at the sight but then notices a walkie talkie and realizes that he can use it to communicate with other security guards. *"We need help! This is Jacob Donaque from Killian High School. The Cape Elizabeth ripper is here. Please help us!"*

Jacob yells as the other security guards quickly make their way to the school. They circle around the building before entering. Filled with urgency, Jacob and Jason join the security guards, who have their guns drawn. They instruct the two teenagers to exit the building while they search for their friends Eli and Bill. As they comb through the school, the lights suddenly begin to flicker. Unsure of the identity of the tall figure standing in the hallway, the security guards cautiously approach. The power has gone out completely. Their only source of light is the gunfire. The silence is shattered by one of the guards, who shouts in fear as commotion is heard echoing through the hallway. The security guards' lights dim one by one, and once the commotion has ceased, they turn back on. Eventually, all eight guards were found dead on the floor. As the backup guards were called to enter the school, they discovered the bodies with the Ripper standing over them. They wasted no time as they fired their guns at him, briefly stunning him before he teleported away. Approaching the cafeteria from which he had emerged, they discovered the motionless bodies of Eli and Bill on the floor.

My hallucinations never really disappear. I have come to realize that all the voices I hear are merely hallucinations. The song sung by this demon haunts me persistently, luring me in with its enchanting melody. I find myself on the verge of succumbing every time she envelops me in her alluring black wings. What follows my hallucinations is my voice of insanity, the ringleader of this freak show and the mastermind behind my other voices. My voice of insanity reigns over everything, another tactic to entice me into the everlasting inferno. I suppose I am the Cape Elizabeth, Ripper.

My Voice of Insanity

THE STATE OF insanity seems to have no end, as I continue to let go of things only to find them again. However, my broken pieces are finally aligning with the ones that fit. Despite my efforts, the numerous voices continue to persist, leaving me pounding my head against the unbreakable glass walls. I have pleaded on my knees, begging them to stop. I have asked the universe many times: Why am I this way? Why do I have to pay? Why won't these voices go away? I feel like a stray, lost without a path to take, a way out, or a solution to figure this out. I must find a way to stifle the noises, the sounds of insanity and retaliation. Deep down, I long to forget the flavor of human flesh and make reparations, but I am instead cursed with these recurring visions.

All that I can see is red. I can't get rid of this urge in my head. I beg! But it doesn't matter. They laugh at my torment and take pleasure when my sanity crumbles. I am tired of their moans and groans. The smell of them is overwhelming and I can see them decomposing. Oh, how I would love to grasp them. How I would love to twist their necks. The sounds of madness were not meant to be comprehensible. The voices are impulsive, yet demand perfection. They provide many opportunities for me, however, I am exposed and vulnerable. These malevolent beings drain my open wounds and the scent of infection permeates. I am gripped with fear at the thought of facing my own reflection.

I am left with a hollow heart and no way to fill it. These voices make me sick; they come with false promises. I must protect my soul the best I can as they attempt to drag me into the fire, like a Sunday dinner ham. They also want me to squeal like one. I can only do what is in my power. Are they imaginary, or are they real? I haven't a clue. I am still forced to hear them, to see them. I am held down and forced to drink. My voice of insanity straddles my mind, deriving pleasure from my screams. She muffles my voice until it is completely silenced, suffocating me. Thick, black slime fills my mouth, rendering me immobile. When she arrives, I am trapped between her decaying thighs and instructed to follow her orders. I am coerced into behaving violently and saying things that I do not want to say. She was the conductor when I took all of those people's lives away. She was right there, smothering me and keeping my voice of reason at bay. I could feel the pressure of her decaying flesh on my mouth and face. She was there every time I killed somebody. The slimy, thick black liquid was all I could taste.

I have also illustrated this entity so that you can see her face. Her eyes are red and bloody, and her lips are lush on one side and rotting on the other. Half of her head is covered with blondish-white mid-length hair, while blood drips from the other side and into my eyes when she pins me down. My insanity is like none other. You can see her ribs rotting through what used to be her skin. She is a part of every voice within my head. She is the leader of this attack. She does not make mistakes or deviate from her plans. She just sits there laughing when I give in to her. She just sits there pleased that I can't breathe. She just sits there and watches me act accordingly. She just sits there and suffocates my voice, right out of me. She teases me by showing me how it could be. All of these fucking voices do. Visions of having a family. Visions of love. Visions of everything I could have risen above. She snatches it away and dangles it in front of my uncovered eyes while I struggle to push her off. She is too strong to be moved. She teases me, just like all of the other voices do, but in different ways. My insanity makes sure that my voice of reason stays muffled where I lie. She tells me the same story every day. Just like all of these voices, she plays games. She whispers her story to me, as the lack of oxygen shuts down my brain. *"Listen to my story and behave,"* she orders.

THE CONTRACT

Geoff Hathaway is an isolated man living a solitary life. He stands apart from his society, whose members prioritize in fitting in. Unlike others, Geoff has no desire to blend in; he values his individuality. He lacks a family, or friends that most of his peers from school have. He has no children or wife. He lived alone on the coast of Eastern Maine in a secluded cabin, isolated from society and all of the chaos that he could not stand. Whenever he was in large crowds, he would experience severe panic attacks and traumatic flashbacks of events that haunted him during his childhood and young adulthood. Unfortunate events occurred during his youth, leading him to choose permanent isolation from society. He owns a cabin and approximately fifty acres of coastal land, with no other visible people for miles.

His sole companion is his dog, Bandit, a loyal and affectionate friend whom he has had since he was a puppy. Bandit is now around four years old, and the man cherishes his dog above all else in the world. Ten years ago, Geoff's father passed away and to his amazement, he left behind a fortune and the coastal property that Geoff currently resides in. However, despite the inheritance, Geoff's father was a monstrous man who physically abused him and his mother. Many years ago, Geoff's mother abandoned him with his father. Since the day she walked out and left him in a living hell, Geoff has not seen his mother. His father's name was Rudy, and his mother's name was Jane. Rudy tragically died in an accident when he fell off a cliff on the edge of their property on the night of June 13, 1999. At the time, he was heavily intoxicated and upon hitting the ground, his head became impaled by the sharp rocks below, resulting in a fatal injury. His body drifted into the vast ocean and was never retrieved.

Geoff did not feel grief because his father was, indeed, a psychopath. He had beaten Geoff's mother to the point that she ran away, leaving her son with this monster. When Geoff's father died, he was happy. Having just turned eighteen, Geoff was now legally an adult and could take over the property and the assets of the estate. His father was a millionaire but didn't live like one. He acted broke and depressed, full of rage every day. He blamed his son and wife for his miserable life, even though he had millions of dollars saved. He starved his wife and son, all while hoarding all of that money. *"What a disgrace!"* Geoff couldn't believe the large sum of money his unpleasant father left him. It was surely unexpected. He often ponders why the body never appeared. Perhaps it was devoured by sharks and other marine animals, leaving nothing behind.

He will never be able to shake the image of his father's exploding head from his mind. The way his brains splattered all over the rocks, the way his eyes bulged out of his sockets. He will never forgive his mother for leaving him behind. He could have moved wherever he liked, but he chose to stay confined on this property. He preferred to remain where his demons thrived. Once a month, he runs into town to stock up on supplies. He is unable to tolerate prolonged periods of social interaction, so he rushes through the store aisles in somewhat of a panic whenever he goes out. He avoids speaking to anyone in public and is often mistaken for being shy by the locals. However, his behavior is actually due to his fear caused by his father. Because of Rudy, Geoff's soul has nearly perished. He harbors deep-seated resentment when reflecting on those dreadful moments.

His rage intensifies as he contemplates his mother's abandonment, leaving him to die in the tiger's den. A wicked desire consumes him as he fixates on committing a heinous act, his vacant eyes aflame with determination. Meanwhile, he enjoys a pleasant autumn day playing with his dog, Bandit. Watching his four-legged friend play and be happy is the only thing in this world that can put a smile on his otherwise permanently frowning face. He is like a mime, but he also speaks. He wears a dark and menacing expression everywhere else he goes: however, with Bandit, it's different. The dog brings him the only joy he has left in his cold and vacant heart. It is his only hope, the only thing keeping him grounded in this world. Bandit is not just his best friend but also his only companion. He bids farewell to Bandit and departs from the house at two o'clock in the morning. He follows this routine three times a month for a total of three days.

My voice of insanity pauses this story at this exact moment every day. I struggle to breathe, overwhelmed by the stench of her decaying skin. She often asks, *"Was it too much? Do you enjoy the story, maggot? How does my decaying skin taste? I cannot wait until your soul becomes mine. After all, it has always belonged to me."* She then takes her position and silences my voice. It was time for her to continue with her disturbing narrative. My insanity is destructive, heartless, cold, and a calculated monster from another realm, incomprehensible to any world. I wouldn't even wish this upon my worst enemy, I wouldn't dare. When insanity spreads, it carries on like an STD, viciously and vilely latching onto as many victims as it can. Once it breaks loose, there is no way to stop it. This monstrous force consumes souls and regurgitates their bones, leaving a void in its wake. It will then use the bones as sustenance. It intensely craves my soul, acting as the most determined voice in my head. Keep in mind there are twenty-one others in line. However, insanity is truly one of a kind.

Geoff pulls into his garage and shuts the automatic door. He is constantly ranting and raving when he returns from nights away—or what he refers to as "Nights Out." His demeanor undergoes a sudden change on these occasions. However, on any other night, he is able to maintain control. On these nights, it controls him. It compels him to commit the most horrific acts. And he complies. He nods, his mind under its control. His soul fades away. He opens himself up to any malevolent force that seeks entry. He becomes the vessel for whatever demon enters him first. He becomes one with hell. Hell consumes him.

He stumbled to the trunk and opened it, grabbing one of the three individuals and dragging them inside. Despite the blood trail that it left behind, he did not care. One by one, he brought them inside. With wooden floors, it was always easy to hide any evidence. A mop and bucket would clean up the mess nicely. This was a monthly routine for him, three times. There were always three people that emerged from the trunk on these nights. However, each time he encountered a different demon inside. It is impossible to exorcise them. No priest or exorcist has ever survived. When demons unite like this, they become invincible. Every time Geoff brings the victims inside, they are torn apart in a different manner. Each demon has its own unique style and twisted agenda. Geoff is merely a vessel, a servant to the darkness, like a dog playing with a toy. Regardless of who you are, you will end up in that trunk if you are chosen.

On this particular night, the demon inside of Geoff had instructed him to peel the flesh from two men and one woman, causing them excruciating pain. As a result, he always obeyed the demon's commands, as it desired for the victims to remain alive for its insatiable gain. A swift death is too lenient for the malevolent entities involved. This particular demon desires to inflict torture while its victims cry out to God in vein. Geoff initiates the gruesome process by first carving off the man's skin, reserving the other two for the remaining demons. Starting from his neck and continuing to his toes. Using his remarkable strength, he begins to peel the man like a banana, exposing everything underneath and presenting the demon's newly exposed raw-hide.

The man jumps up in terror, his bulging amber eyes betraying his fear and pain. Only muscle and ligaments are left behind. His screams were satisfying to the demands and desires of this demon. However, it always craves for more. It is an insatiable tyrant. And its host is the prostitute. It now directs him to remove the remaining parts without hesitation, and he does so. The man's screams continue as his insides splatter like a mosquito on the floor. Blood-red and white bones are all that is left to be seen. And a bloody spinal cord is still connecting everything. The skeleton is still screaming, even though everything was stripped away. It's like something out of a horror movie, but it's real. The demon then instructed to cut open his skull.

There is absolutely no hesitation from the host whatsoever. He must always comply with the demon's commands. The skeleton continues to scream as an electric saw slices into it. The host carefully cuts around the skull as instructed, and at that moment, the screaming comes to an abrupt stop. He extracted the brain from the skull and began consuming it, maliciously splattering brain matter across the floor. The demon then proceeds to lick up the remains before declaring, *"I am pleased,"* after satisfying its hunger. Despite their individual methods of murder and torture, they all utter this same phrase upon leaving their earthly vessel. When the demon is pleased, it departs. But as soon as it does, another one enters with a brand-new set of weapons. However, they are all unified. No prayer or book on this planet that can stop these demons. There is no cross, nor is there any holy water that can repel them. The only thing you need to know is that if you encounter one of these demons, you're doomed. There are no ifs, ands, or buts about it. You're simply doomed.

Geoff suddenly crashes to the floor, releasing the demon he had just fed. It was only a matter of time before another one would enter his mind. In this momentary return to consciousness, he began to think of his dog, Bandit. He glanced into the trunk and saw that there were still two feedings remaining. He was aware that two more demons would soon arrive, he knew he could not defeat them, but he was grateful for the brief moments of peace in between possessions. It provided him with a chance to catch his breath, as the demons drained him of all his energy during these nights. He is now able to sense the presence of the upcoming dark entity. He never knows what its actions will be. They are distinct each time, each one with its own set of rules. It is always a surprise what challenges the next one will subject him to. Geoff dipped his pen into the fire and sealed a contract with the darkness. It states, in blood, the terms and conditions as follows:

Contractus Venditionis

Nineteen mass feedings will be made per month. Any demon of any power may package your mind and body and have you kill anyone they choose in any way that they wish. All bodies will be transported to the agreed destination and dismembered by you and by the demons' choosing. Your inherited property will be the eternal agreed destination. All evidence will disappear as fast as it arrives. Nobody will know it's you. We feed forever and you and your dog, Bandit, will live forever.

By signing this contract you (Geoff Halloway) understand that you are for Hell yourself. By signing this contract you understand that you are now bound. By signing this contract you've agreed to our terms and conditions. We will honour our side of the contract by granting you and your dog Bandit eternal life and fortitude. Away from the very population, you will help destroy those terrifying to us, all of the rules and expectations of the host.

This contract binds you to the grey gates of fire for an eternity. This contract does not have an expiration date. If you try to back out of this agreement at any time you will be taken into the eternal flames. All needs must be met on Hell's end. You are now a soldier of the shadows. Every demon that enters your soul will have a different set of rules.

You must follow all of the rules no matter what they may be. You will never encounter the same demon twice. You will follow the rules of the darkness for the rest of eternity. If any rules are broken by either mistake or on purpose will result in your eternal life being given to the demon whose rules you have broken. Your eternal place will be determined by said demon whose rules are broken.

Following all rules will guarantee that you and your dog, Bandit, will live for all eternity. Some rules are not given easily and some demons will be harder than others to allow you house with it. You will stay wealthy, secluded, and away from anybody that you cannot stand. You will deliver the victim per month for the rest of your eternal life. If one victim is missed you will be hunted down, found instantly, and pulled into eternal darkness.

A victim must remain alive until instructed on how to dispose of each one. Get creative when kidnapping each victim and do not kill until the one in control instructs you how. You will be visited by nine demons per month. Your soul must stay completely open to possession at all times. You must listen to each demon's demands and follow said demands for the rest of the time.

Failing to oblige to all of the above for any reason will result in eternal judgement in the section of hell of the demon you have disobeyed. Giving, said demon free reign over your soul. It may do to you as it wishes. No questions will be taken after you sign this contract. You will not question the demon or the demon in charge of you. If you question it in any way shape or form it will free your soul. It will then be able to do with it whatever it wishes.

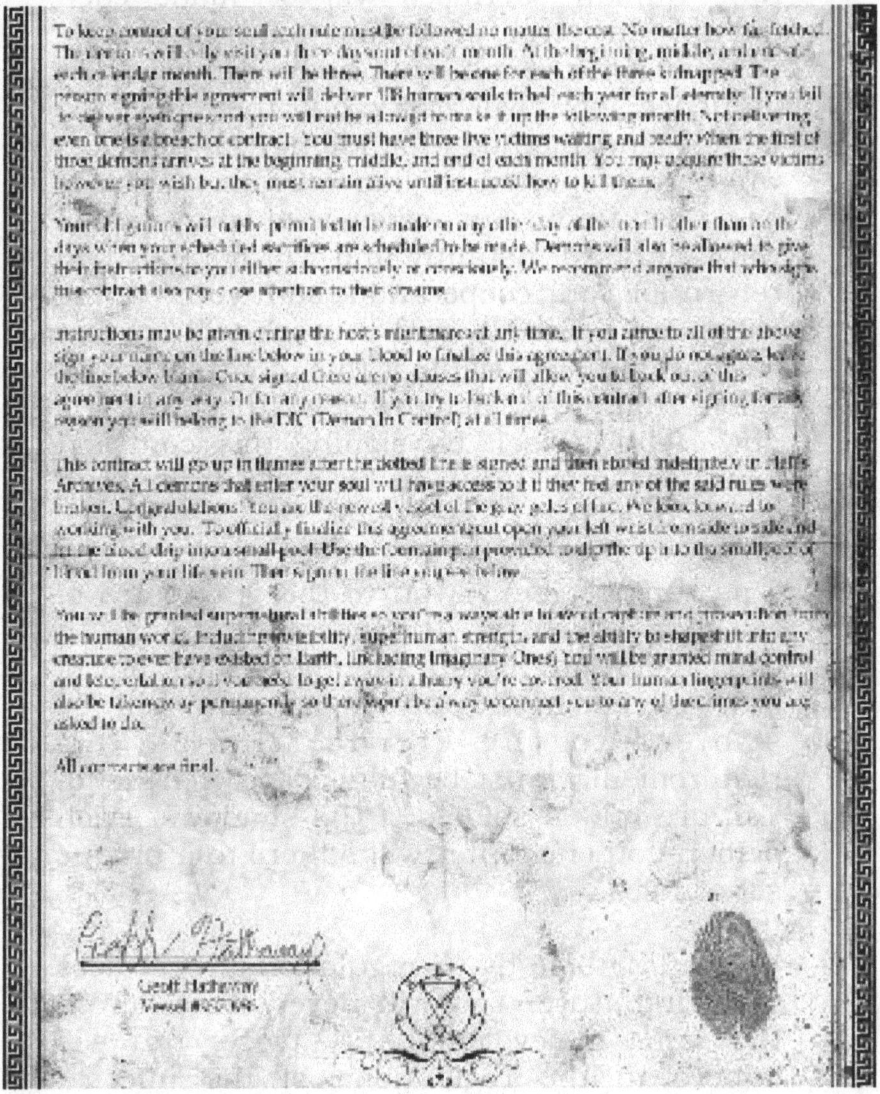

To keep control of your soul, each rule must be followed no matter the cost. No matter how far-fetched. The demons will only visit you three days out of each month. At the beginning, middle, and end of each calendar month. There will be three. There will be one for each of the three kidnapped. The person signing this agreement will deliver 108 human souls to hell each year for all eternity. If you fail to deliver even one soul, you will not be allowed to make it up the following month. Not delivering even one is a breach of contract. You must have three live victims waiting and ready when the first of three demons arrives at the beginning, middle, and end of each month. You may acquire these victims however you wish but they must remain alive until instructed how to kill them.

Your offerings will not be permitted to be made on any other day of the month other than on the days when your scheduled sacrifices are scheduled to be made. Demons will also be allowed to give their instructions to you either subconsciously or consciously. We recommend anyone that who signs this contract also pays close attention to their dreams.

Instructions may be given during the host's maintenance at any time. If you agree to all of the above, sign your name on the line below in your blood to finalize this agreement. If you do not agree, leave the line below blank. Once signed there are no clauses that will allow you to back out of this agreement in any way. Or for any reason. If you try to back out of this contract after signing for any reason you will belong to the DIC (Demon In Control) at all times.

This contract will go up in flames after the dotted line is signed and then stored indefinitely in Hell's Archives. All demons that enter your soul will have access to it if they find any of the said rules were broken. Congratulations! You are the newest vessel of the gray gates of hell. We look forward to working with you. To officially finalize this agreement, cut open your left wrist from side to side and let the blood drip into a small pool. Use the container provided to dip the tip into the smallest of blood from your life vein. Then sign on the line(s) below.

You will be granted supernatural abilities to ensure a way to able to avoid capture and prosecution from the human world. Including invisibility, super-human strength, and the ability to shapeshift into any creature to ever have existed on Earth. (Including Imaginary Ones) You will be granted mind control and teleportation so if you need to get away in a hurry you're covered. Your human fingerprints will also be taken away permanently so there won't be a way to connect you to any of the crimes you are asked to do.

All contracts are final.

____
Geoff Hathaway
Vessel #0507098

CONTRACTUS VENDITIONIS

Nine human sacrifices will be made each month. Any type of demon may potentially possess your mind and body. Under their influence, you will carry out their selected targets and methods for killing. All subjects will be transported to your current residence as agreed upon. Any evidence of your actions will be erased instantly and will not exist. In return for your cooperation, both your canine companion, Bandit, and yourself will acquire eternal life. By signing this contract, you, Geoff Hathaway, acknowledge that you are now Hell's Vessel. By signing this contract, you also agree to abide by hell's terms and conditions.

This contract binds you to the gray gates of fire for eternity. It does not have an expiration date. If you attempt to back out of this agreement at any point, you will be subject to the eternal flames. All requirements must be fulfilled on Hell's end. You are now a soldier of the shadows. Each demon you encounter will adhere to a unique set of rules.

You must abide by all regulations, regardless of their nature. You will never come across the same malevolent entity twice. You will adhere to the regulations of the infernal realm for all eternity. Any violation of the rules, whether accidental or intentional, will lead to your soul being claimed by the ruling demon.

Following all rules will guarantee eternal life for you and your dog. However, some rules are more difficult to adhere to, and certain malevolent forces may make more determined attempts to claim your soul. You will also maintain your wealth and privacy, avoiding a society that you may find intolerable. Additionally, You must make nine human sacrifices per month without fail.

All victims must remain alive until instructed on how to dispose of each one. Be inventive when kidnapping each victim, and refrain from killing until given instructions by the leader. You will encounter nine demons per month. Your soul must remain completely open to possession at all times. You must listen and comply with each demand for eternity.

Failure to comply with any of the above, for any reason, will result in eternal placement in the 'Demon in Control' section of Hell, where the demon will have free rein over your soul. Once this contract is signed, no questions will be entertained, and you will be obligated to fulfill the demands of the demon in charge.

To maintain control of your soul, it is imperative to adhere to each rule, even if they may seem far-fetched. The demons will only appear on the first, middle, and last day of each month, equaling a total of three days. Each visit requires you to collect three victims, resulting in a total of nine per month. Not delivering even one is a breach of contract and no second chances will be given.

Your obligations will only be allowed to be fulfilled on the designated sacrifice day, not any other day of the month. Demons have the ability to communicate their instructions to you either subconsciously or consciously. We advise all individuals who sign this contract to closely observe their dreams. Instructions may be given at any time during the host's nightmares. You will be bestowed with supernatural abilities, enabling you to elude capture and prosecution with ease.

Your abilities will be limitless. Furthermore, Your fingerprints will be removed to ensure no connection can be made to any potential crimes.

This contract will go up in flames once it is signed and immediately stored in Hell's archives. The demon in control will have full rein over your soul if it feels its rules have been broken.

Congratulations! You are now the newest vessel of the gray gates of fire. We are excited to work with you. To complete this agreement, please open your left wrist and allow a small pool of blood to collect. Use the fountain pen provided and dip the tip into the blood.

Sign on the designated line using blood from your life vein.

All contracts are final.

The second demon has now gained complete control of Geoff's mind and bodily functions. The second victim has been removed from the trunk. A demon will never reveal its name. When multiple demons are working together, they are nearly indestructible and will never disappear. The demon instructs Geoff to grab a hand saw and begin removing the limbs of the next unfortunate soul. He obeys. He has no choice but to comply. He must fulfill his eternal contract. If not, he will burn eternally beyond the gray gates. The woman starts screaming immediately as he begins to cut into her left leg. The blade of the saw is rusted, causing her unbearable pain. Once both legs are removed, the demon instructs him to remove both of her arms. Once all four limbs are removed, the demon intends to place her limbless torso on display, positioning her in the center of a table set up for a fancy dinner.

Surrounding this woman are fresh fruits and vegetables, beautifully arranged as she screams. The demon then instructs him to begin preparing the meat from her arms and legs, treating it like a high-quality steak and seasoning it with salt and pepper to taste. The demon's intention is for the woman to consume her own limbs. The smell of her cooking flesh permeates the area, reminiscent of a gourmet restaurant from one's worst nightmares. He skillfully prepares onions and green peppers to accompany the main dish. The screaming, limbless woman is still very much alive. When the meat reaches a perfect medium-rare state, it is time to plate her dinner. Delicately placing the cooked flesh in the center of the plate, topping it with peppers and onions both above and to the side.

He carried the food to the table, causing the woman to scream even louder as her own flesh drew nearer to her. The demon then directed him to feed her, and he immediately began spooning the cooked pieces into her mouth. Despite her continuous screams, she kept spitting out her seasoned flesh. He then grasped her by the hair and forced more into her shrieking mouth, bellowing at her to swallow it. He continued to shove more and more into her mouth until she began choking on her own flesh. The demon then commanded him to allow her choke to death, and after she had perished, it instructed him to cook and consume the remaining portions. He then lifted the woman's body off of the table and carried her into the kitchen.

The oven had been preheated to a scorching four hundred fifty degrees. He placed her lifeless form into the oven and, after forty-five minutes, the demon instructed him to remove her now cooked and seasoned remains and proceed. With a pained and horrified expression still etched on her face, much like a hunted animal, he began to bite chunks out of her until only her bones remained. Satisfied, the second demon disappeared from Geoff's cursed soul. He knew that the third demon would soon arrive, he never knew what it would force him to do. However, what he does know is that failure to do so will result in his soul being condemned to eternal flames, and his contract for eternal life will be replaced with an infernal existence instead of spending it on his property with his loyal companion, Bandit.

The third demon quickly enters his mind. This one appears to be more dominant than the first two. Typically, the third visitor holds the most strength and is the most authoritative. It quickly demands that he remove the remaining person from the car trunk and await further instructions. While he waited, he tied the cattle to its place of slaughter, and then went to check on his best friend, Bandit. The dog is always happy to see him, and after the night he had so far, he needed this little bit of comfort. It always helped after the third of Hell's demons had left. However, this was the first time he had to wait for instructions. It is usually executed immediately upon its arrival. Each demon is unique and he must not disregard this fact. All demons are informed of the terms and conditions of the contract. They are trying to persuade him to violate his contract.

He is knows that this entity desires not only his body but also his soul, along with the man that he ripped from the trunk. An avaricious demon, indeed. As a result, he wastes no time bidding farewell to Bandit before sitting down near the hog-tied man, readying himself for whatever task may lie ahead. Certain demons communicate with his subconscious, guiding him in this way. Some speak aloud in hopes that he will miss the instructions and violate his contract. This particular demon spoke so loudly that the walls of his secluded paradise shook, echoing throughout the space. The message was clear:

"Hello, Geoff. Are you prepared for your duty? I understand that you comprehend the repercussions of refusing. Please be aware that we are also conscious of them. Your task is to open this man up at the midsection and extract all contents within. However, please refrain from using your hands, Geoff. Instead, you will use your teeth to remove his innards at my direction.

Consider yourself a vacuum. After all of the innards have been removed, you will hang this man by them on the public path where many people pass through. You may use your hands to string him up, but do not use them to remove his insides. He must be completely deceased before further contact is made with him. After stringing him up, you will hide in the woods with a video recording device and capture the reactions of innocent people passing by. The footage will then be shared with the world by posting it online. Upload your videos from multiple false accounts prior to publishing them publicly. Do you comprehend my instructions as I present them to you, Geoff?"

He must agree to and abide by all of the demands of each demon. If he makes a single mistake, there are no second chances. He will be dragged into hell without any explanation as to why. There will be no trials or juries to hear his case. He willingly signed his name on the enflamed line. He retrieves an aged hunting knife from his bedroom closet. He grips it between his teeth, adhering to the specific instructions, as he is not granted the use of his hands while exposing the unfortunate man. Only at the moment of death is he allowed to use his hands to suspend him.

He then dissects the man from left to right. Despite his agonizing state, the man remains conscious as his gruesome end approaches. The blood gushes out of him like a frenzied crimson stream and the demon derives sadistic joy from the terror in the man's eyes. His intestines hung limply as Geoff immediately latched on and began to unravel them like a ball of yarn with his mouth and teeth, until everything else came out with it. He pulled and sucked, feeling the warm, rubbery innards get caught between his teeth and tasting the metallic, liver-like flavor of the blood. The man screamed in agony until all sound ceased.

He understands he must now use this man's own intestines to string him up in the forest on a popular hiking trail within a well-known destination where families come to camp and vacation. He cannot ask the demon to repeat its instructions, as that would violate the terms of their contract. He must memorize each demon's demands and make damn sure that he does not forget. He carefully selects two trees that are situated at opposite ends of the paths in the middle of the night, when there are no potential bystanders. The trees happen to be maple trees, whose vibrant colors have just started to emerge, marking the arrival of his favorite season—autumn. He silently prepares to hang the lifeless man and positions himself in nearby bushes with his newly acquired mobile device to capture the reactions of those who will witness this atrocity. Sigh. He isn't taking any chances of breaking the demons rules, so he waits for daybreak. The contract stipulates that he will never be apprehended for his crimes against humanity. Furthermore, it guarantees him access to supernatural abilities outside the realm of ordinary human capabilities, which is detailed within the contract. The body is hanging near a popular and bustling camping ground, where people visit for annual vacations and to take a break from their daily routines.

Just a little ways up ahead, he hears the chatter of a large group of people walking towards the location of the man hanging by his own guts. To ensure that his phone does not run out of battery, he brought a portable charger. He points the phone from the bushes where he is hiding towards the path and the hanging corpse. He ensured that he was far enough back where he could not be seen and where there were no other paths that someone could use to approach him from behind. As soon as the group approached, he began recording. The group consisted of tourists with a tour guide. They all erupted in a simultaneous scream. There were men, women, and children among the group, and the screams were so loud that they echoed deep into the forest, attracting even more people. They all started screaming and pulling out their mobile devices to record, all while continuing to scream.

He knew that he still had to upload his video and post it under a fake account, Despite all of these terrified people recording. Just because they were recording does not mean he can disregard the instructions and not post it. This is how these manipulative forces attempt to lure you into violating the rules. He wasn't told how long his video of the chaos should be, so he recorded for fifteen minutes and used one of his supernatural abilities to teleport himself to a library in Melbourne, Australia, to upload it to various social media platforms. He then prepared to send it to numerous news stations around the world. The library is closed and nobody would suspect him. The contract also states that his fingerprints have been completely removed, leaving no evidence of him ever being there. This was the first time Geoff had ever been to Australia in his lifetime.

This contract sets him up to continually feed into the darkness for eternity. His videos have been successfully uploaded and have become viral, just as the demon desired. Once the uploading was complete, he proceeded to irreparably destroy the phone and dispose of it, leaving no trace of evidence connecting him to the crime. The demon is extremely satisfied with the vessel's compliance to the instructions and demands, It has now moved back into the darkness, having acquired a new soul. He is still in the Australian Library when he suddenly hears the front door begin to open. The librarian is arriving for her work day. Hell has also granted him the ability to shape shift for these tricky situations. He then transformed into a crocodile and charged towards the vulnerable librarian, who quickly shut and locked the door as soon as she had opened it. That allowed Geoff to disappear without a trace, returning home seemingly as though he had never traveled to Australia in the first place. The sacrifices for this month have been completed, and this set of demons are pleased to have received their brand new souls, returning to Hell. Geoff is now preparing for his week off with Bandit before the next trio of demons arrive.

He must have three live victims ready for when the first demon arises. If he fails, he will take a one-way trip to hell with no second chances. He plans to collect the three unfortunate souls three days before the arrival. He is exhausted from the first three demons and the middle of the month is his only real rest period. Because immediately after completing the end-of-month sacrifices, the beginning-of-month sacrifices quickly follow with little time for rest in between. He has been utilizing his teleportation abilities to abduct people from various locations worldwide. Sometimes, he enjoys his powers a little too much while using them. Although he regrets signing that contract, he will address his concerns when the time comes. All that he wants to do now is relax with his dog and not have to think about taking another life for a few days. This, unfortunately, comes with the price of immortality.

My inner voice of insanity once again interrupts the narrative to torment me, following the same pattern every day. Her putrid flesh falls onto my face as she continues to sit atop me. I am aware that she is the source of the stories conjured by my personal hell. Her flesh emits a putrid and rancid smell, causing me to vomit uncontrollably. I am trapped between her decaying thighs, with no escape for the vomit. It burns unbearably in my eyes. The nauseating odor persists, inducing violent vomiting until my stomach is completely emptied; only dry heaves remain.

She gleefully chuckles at her ability to make me ill. She revels in my suffering. She wants me as her eternal prisoner and hopes that I will slip up and go with her. She does the same things to me every day. Imagine having a rotting corpse sitting on your face. She begins to laugh again and says the same repetitive things. This time, it is sung in the form of a song before she finishes her story of demons and the price of eternal life. She says, "Listen to my song now, future slave. I will have you soon. Let my melody enchant you and then follow me right this way."

BEYOND THE GRAVE

I will possess you, just as I do now, my dear.
Your fear will soon belong to me.
Look at you, a meek maggot.
It is only a matter of time.
I revel in your muffled screams as I extinguish
  your life.
I love the terror in your eyes as you're smothered
  beneath me.

> Your unproductive mind will soon discover its
> purpose with me.
> I will take you to a place where screams never
> cease.
> I relish in your fear; don't you love the
> harmonies I bring?
> You will soon be my servant, so you must
> behave.
> I have even more in store for you, beyond the
> grave.
>
> I love how I make you feel so sick.
> The warmth of your vomit between my putrid
> thighs turns me on.
> I love how you kick your feet beneath me.
> This could be our love song.
> I will bring you to where I rule and this will be
> your eternity.
> I cannot wait for your suffering to always be a
> part of me.
>
> You will soon be my servant, so you must
> behave.
> I have even more in store for you, beyond the
> grave.

My voice of insanity now readies itself to conclude her tale. It is the same story that she has recounted daily since my arrival, and even when I briefly managed to escape, she tagged along. All of my voices are repetitive and repulsive, except for one: the voice of my love. I long for the voice of my beloved, especially when insanity overwhelms me and holds me captive, suffocating in the stench of my own bodily fluids mixed with her rotting flesh. My insanity is my most terrifying voice of all. She is determined to take it all.

Geoff is preparing two steak dinners—one for

himself and one for Bandit. He is determined to fully enjoy his time off, even though it never lasts long. He must also remain sharp and diligent, as these demons are relentless and will try any tactic to make him break a rule. They are after his soul as well. Despite being their vessel, there are many others in the world carrying out their bidding just like him. They will not miss a chance to bring a soul back to their dwelling. After finishing cooking the steaks, he prepares two plates. He always makes a plate for his dog Bandit and always will. Bandit is his only family, his only friend. After they finish eating, he washes the silverware and plates.

He was feeling overwhelmed and exhausted, so he called Bandit to come lay down for a nap. Little did he know, he was even more exhausted than he thought when he closed his eyes. He awakens to see that the sun had gone down and it was a clear, star-filled sky with a full moon. He is enjoying the moment because tomorrow he knows what he must do. He must snatch three innocent souls to feed the demons over and over. More and more, he loses his free will. The walls then began to shake as if a demon is arriving. He is both startled and confused. It is three days early and the three souls are not yet due. The demon, a female immediately began communicating with him. She stated,

"Geoff Hathaway, Vessel Number 9870983, you are in breach of contract. You were to deliver one human soul to me upon my arrival. Since I do not see your offering, your soul now belongs to me." Geoff's brief nap unexpectedly turned into a three-day-slumber, causing him to miss the deadline set by the demon. As a result, the contract has now been breached. The demon swiftly possessed him, abruptly shutting down

all of his bodily functions and killing him immediately. Shortly after, Bandit also met his demise. The female demon then revealed her identity and spoke, *"I have you now, you maggot. I am your voice of insanity. Your soul is now mine. Lie down so I may take my seat."* He then perished in flames, never to be seen again. In the distance, it is said that one can still hear his muffled screams.

My insanity tells me that story repeatedly because she yearns to possess my soul. I experience great relief when she departs, and I quickly jump into the shower and attempt to cleanse myself of her putrid odor. I can never completely rid myself of that smell. She comes every day. I long for peace. But these voices in my head rob me of everything. She will return tomorrow. And once again, I won't be able to catch my breath. Before she leaves, she gazes into my eyes and shouts, *"May your dreams be filled with decay and sweetness, my love. Tomorrow, once more, you shall taste me."*

Crazy

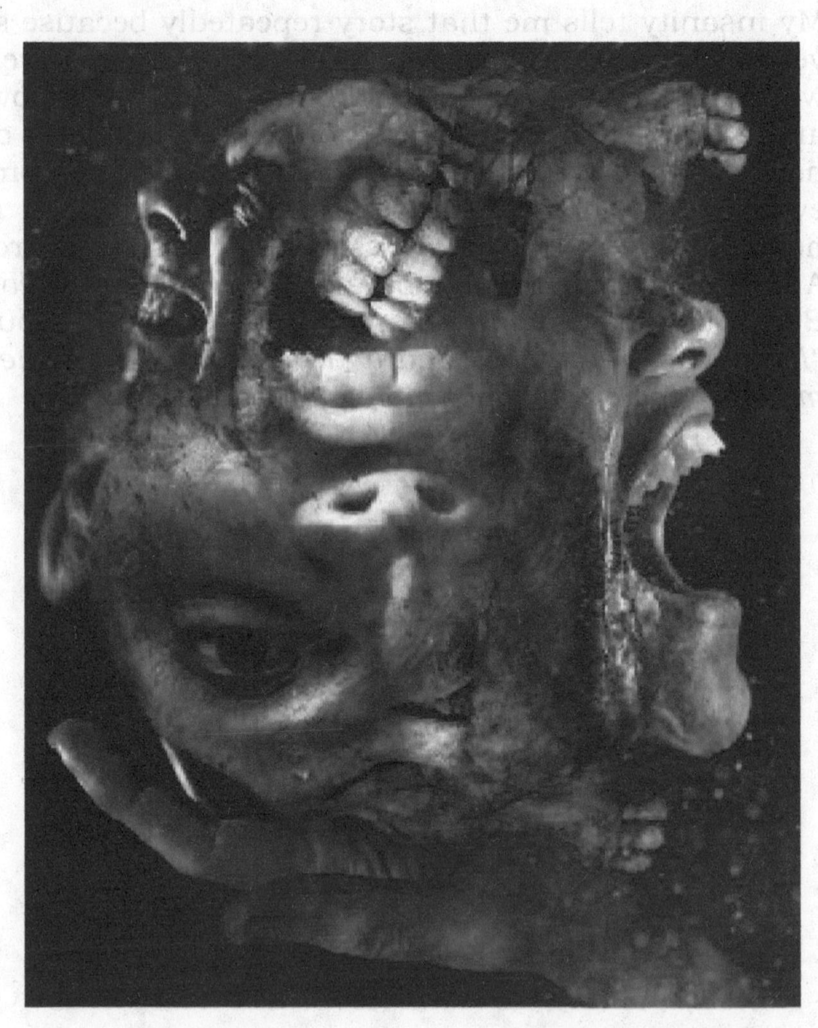

I STILL REMEMBER the brief period in which I was free. I have composed numerous stories and poems during my incarceration here. I am advanced in age now, and death draws near. As I approach my end, there is an abundance of written works that I've accumulated over the years that I will take with me into the fiery depths. Writing and creating illustrations have always been hobbies of mine. I illustrate everything that I see, from the stories that my inner voices narrate to the poetry that they inspire. In no particular order, these poems will detail my experiences, where my mind has wandered, and where I am currently.

It is important to carefully consider each poem while reading, as each one has its own story and its own significance. While some readers may not fully comprehend, others will. Therefore, I must caution that navigating through my complex thoughts in search of answers will not be a simple task. You will scream, I can assure you. I am the tiger and you are all my sleeping deer. I have been hungry for many years.

I am still unsure of my current age. I have forgotten it many years ago. The only thing I am sure of is that I am getting closer. I am approaching freedom from these recurring voices, stories, and the constant reminders of love that I will never have the chance to experience. If there is indeed a hell, I am surly bound for it. If the stories are true, I will be condemned to eternal damn-nation. I am no longer certain of my beliefs or what is truly real. I have experienced nothing but confinement and confusion throughout my lifetime.

I have only known fourteen years and one week of freedom in my entire life. If I were to estimate, I would say I am now over eighty years old. I cannot be certain as I have entirely lost track of time. Navigate through the various levels of hell depicted in my poetry. There are many things contained within that I have yet to experience in real life. However, there are also many things that I have experienced. It's a twisted and warped labyrinth that I invite you to explore.

I will inform you of what happened to me after you embark on this journey. I invite you to scream with me, if you're not already screaming. I also invite you to listen to my voices as they are spoken through my poetry. I have also included illustrations that accompany some of my poetry, just for you. There are things inside that you simply won't believe. I have included a brief explanation at the end of each poem to try to clarify my intention behind each piece. Additionally, I have included my first name on each poem. The voices within my poetry are waiting behind many doors for you, when you choose a door, be careful which door you choose.

CRAZY_

'Crazy' has countless faces.
It could come from the strangest of places.
Eyes can deceive, and words can manipulate.
They will go to any length to make you believe.
Trust nothing and be prepared for rapid
    changes.
'Crazy' has infinite phases.

Each phase is both magical and diabolical.

Each phase is both challenging and rhetorical.
The phases are simultaneously ugly and
    adorable,
taking your mind through imaginary portals.
Each phase presents a difficult hurdle to
    overcome.
Each phase will have you engaging,
in a game of Russian Roulette with an imaginary
    gun.
Each phase will expose your hidden actions,
making you aware of what you have done.
The labels that they place on you are a reflection
    of their fears.

The tears that have been shed over the years
have formed an immense ocean.
It is time to vanquish every traumatic reason
    that brought you here.
The ocean is vast and the typhoon-like waves
    are relentless.
The phases blend seamlessly in this sea of
    senselessness.
The nonsensical words, the inane burns,
the pointless verse merges with this irrational
    curse.
Now, it's time to begin our work.
Seize them by the hair and inflict your turn.
Run them over forcefully, do it again, rehearse.
Ensure their heads are aligned flawlessly to the
    curb.
It is now their turn to be fully submerged.

Watch how they beautifully seize without
    restraint.
Watch how they lose their souls' purpose.
They are losing control.
They are collapsing.
The roles have been reversed and you
are now claiming the gold.

It is time to change the pattern.
A new monster has been created; behold!
Bear witness to the transformation
as you mark all of their labels as sold.
Observe the bodies floating face-down in this
grief-stricken ocean, which is ice-cold.

Revenge is a monster that strikes when we are
    not ready.
Greed is responsible for the bloodshed.
The shadows are conquering, and there are so
    many.
Guilt is accountable for the insanity
that emanates from the trees.
When Gluttony combines with Greed,
there is an explosion of confetti.
Your hands begin to shake and you can't keep
    them steady.
The phases are changing so rapidly.
Your thoughts are jumbled with memories
that you should be forgetting.
You are unprepared.
You are breaching the levy.
The salt is caked heavily around your eyes.
The weight of it all is incredibly heavy.

Each state of our mind plays a different tune.
It's difficult to determine which phase
of madness will engulf you.
The violin plays in the background
while you cry out for your truth.
You're tallying the demons
as they feed on each exposed wound.
There are countless levels of abuse.
There are numerous states of mind in which we
    become lost.
We lose even when we win.
We win even when we lose.
We can't see in the darkness—what are we to

do?
We are plagued by the flu.
We are being consumed.
The lullabies that echo within walls
of this place will tear you in two.
Our state of mind is at stake as we lose
ourselves
in this unpredictable place, making us feel
'crazy.'

The truth is now evident as we sob in anguish.
Every emotion has has a touch of irrationality.
The emotion of love can sting and bite.
The emotion of sadness comes accompanied by
spite.
The emotion of passion fuels our strength to
fight our battles
against the world, against our inner selves, and
against
our personal demons that reign in our personal
hell.
We all strive to come up with solutions;
some may be more difficult than others.
In this world, we can easily become buried
by the sounds of the shrieking thunder.
The wreckage is filled with our agonizing states
of mind.
The structures are collapsing, leaving the lost
behind.
We must combat these emotions, as the clock
ticks faster and drains our precious time.
The air around us has always been tainted.
It has always been difficult to breathe.
Some of us rise while others remain down on
their knees.
It's hard to comprehend a broken soul if they are
left to bleed.

Can you see it now?

Can you recognize that fine line?
There is a fine line between sanity
and insanity that eats us all alive.
I am crazy, you are crazy, he is crazy,
she is crazy, they are crazy, we are all crazy.
When the truth is revealed and what is at stake,
our glass castles break.
We are all equals, supported by delicate skeletal
    legs.
Disagree with me if you must; the door has
always been there--over that way.
We are all inherently beautiful, but the weight
of greed and diamonds often dominates our
    strength.

In a society that labels us, we band together and
    say,
*"We are proud of who we are, and you will not
take our 'crazy' away."*
Trust nothing and be prepared for rapid
    changes.
'Crazy' has infinite phases.

Crazy does indeed have infinite phases and faces. For decades, my inner voices have gradually stripped my mind away, leaving me unsure of my whereabouts on a daily basis. I am constantly questioning if I deserve this, as I feel I have already paid my dues. I have illustrated below my interpretation of craziness. I am so ready for this to be over. What am I to do?
—*Geoff*

I Am The Monster

I Am The Monster

There is something in my cell with me.
I can see it.
It has always been here, taunting me and calling
    me a freak.
It's trying to harm me and watch me bleed!
There is no escape, no words for me to say.
This entity has always resided deep within my
    deteriorating mind.
Some refer to it as a spirit, while others refer to
    it as a demon.
All that I'm certain of is that it manipulates my
    mind without being provoked.
Its only concern is the sound of my screams.
After recognizing that it will never depart, I have
    ceased my desperate pleas.
Instead, I must accept and confront this
    malevolent entity.
I've been trying to communicate.
I've been seeking a solution.
I cannot find a means to eradicate it from my
    cell without an exit.
It mocks me when I attempt to make it cease.
It consumes the blood that is expelled from my
    mouth during my coughing fits.
It desires for my downfall.
I find myself trembling in a corner as it reaches

out to take everything from me.

I still don't know what to call it.
Is it real or imaginary?
The blood looks real to me as it pools beneath
    my feet.
The invisible monster considers this pool a
    delicacy,
it's starving perpetually.
How can I overcome this paralysis that holds me
    beneath my covers?
Perhaps, this monster is simply a creation of my
    own mind,
Or perhaps, I am the monster.

I know I am a monster. I have accepted that label. My addiction to flesh is uncontrollable. That is why I am here. That is why I am writing down all of my horrible fears. I, myself, am the monster. It has been clear for many years.
—*Geoff*

HERE WITH ME

I will never be the same.
I cannot forget that fateful day,
which will always be etched in my memory.
So much has changed.
I am slowly losing my identity.
My spirit has been washed away.
I cannot remember the last time I smiled.
That day is one I will always remember,
when I fell into a state of strong denial.

When I think of you, I can picture you in my
    mind.
When I dream about you, I yearn for the gaze of
    your lifeless eyes.

You have now transcended into another
    dimension.
Why did you have to depart?
It wasn't your time, yet they snatched you all
    away from me.
I just need all of you here with me.

I am alone, consumed by sorrow and fear.
I have lost all the goodness that I once
    remembered.
The pain is so clear, I can see you in the mirror,
    your eyes reflecting your coldness.
I soar high as if I'm feathered, but my footprints
    in the snow have vanished.
I have been beaten down and weathered.

When I think of you, I can picture you in my
    mind.
When I dream of you, I yearn for the gaze of your
    lifeless eyes.
I cannot forget that fateful day.
So much has changed.
I just need all of you here with me.

I miss you, Mom, Dad, Marcus, Daniel, and Nick. Why
did you have to leave me and pass away? Just know,
that your murderers have paid. I will love you forever.
—*Geoff*

LUMINOUS WHITE CHEEKS

It must be magic when I look beyond the divide.
It must be magic when I look into the hollow
    eyes of those creatures.
It must be a dream when they sing me to sleep.
I must feel incomplete when they are adding
    things to my anatomy.
I embrace them when they scream in my face.

I let them do as they wish to me.
I've been longing for an escape,
but I cannot resist the allure of the creatures
    with the luminous white cheeks.
Their voices command me to sing,
their passion burning through the floor beneath
    me.
I don't even mind if their intentions are to harm
    me.
I am entranced by their melodic control of
    everything.
In the darkness, all that I can distinguish are
    their luminous white cheeks.
They do not have eyes.
When they emerge, a white mist begins to rise.
Do not make a sound in their presence,
they are so beautiful but have a thirst for you.
Their intent is to seduce and devour you, so it is
    important to hide from them.
If you do happen to make a sound and they hear
    your voice,
they will shush you and drag you into the void.
Their soul purpose is to consume you.
You must remain silent, no matter what you do.
All they ever do is eat.
You cannot be blinded by their luminous white
    cheeks.

These voices can be incredibly beautiful when they
choose to be. They also seem to enjoy playing games
with me, constantly reminding me of who I will never
become.
—*Geoff*

IN THIS PLACE

Watch my heart as it withers.

I am a wreck.
I feel like a burned-out clover.
I have borne the weight in my own mind.
The fluttering of the butterflies now takes hold.
I am lost in my own world.
I am constantly looking over my shoulder.
As I refill my empty cup, my reflections turn
  even colder.
They are filled with toxins and I refuse to
  apologize.
I warned you ahead of time.
I have been feeling lost.
I have been confined.
I have been distant in this place.
I have been correct despite previous mistakes.
I know it all doesn't make sense.
My hands are stained with the evidence of my
  sacrifices.
I cannot guarantee that I'm okay.

Watch my soul begin to cry.
I'm a complete mess, falling deeper.
I have run out of precious time.
My skin is melting, almost like butter.
I am lost in my own personal hell.
I am burdened by the weight of endless
  boulders.
Over and over, I fill my empty cup.
My reflections will always grow colder.
The toxins continue to agitate my failing eyes.
I refuse to apologize for the actions that have
  clouded my mind.

I still feel so lost.
I am so confined.
I'm still so distant in this place.

I feel trapped in my personal turmoil, unable to focus
on anything else. I see myself as a caged animal,

specifically a tiger in a zoo. If anyone comes near me, so far I have torn them all in two.
—*Geoff*

SET ME FREE

I am unable to locate myself.
I am lost in my thoughts.
I am immersed in a fantasy.
I am unable to perceive these illusions as they
    overwhelm me.
I am once again lost within my inner self.
I am running in circles as I continue to scream.
I cannot seem to find any relief.
In my eyes, I am damaged goods.
I am screaming from the trees!
Though I thought I had discovered my true self,
the puzzle remains incomplete.
Inside, I yearn to uncover the things that will set
    me free.

In madness, I am so uncertain.
I see it in my dreams.
When my strength crosses that fine line, I know
    exactly what I need.
In the darkness, I find myself losing much-
    needed sleep.
I can't find the keys I need; I feel so incomplete.
I panic when I can't find what will set me free.

The voices in my head are definitely magical. However, it's not the type of magic you would want to experience. There was never a way out after my mind deteriorated.
—*Geoff*

The Corridors of Insanity

I've always been lost in my own mind.
I've always managed it well too.
I never had a choice.
I never had a voice.
Just beaten and broken through the constant
chaos.
The void can be defined in various ways.
It can deceive you and hold you captive in one
place.
Don't listen to the shadows.
Don't you dare!
They induce pain in your soul that cannot be
compared.
It hurts like a broken heart scattered
everywhere.
It hurts like the monsters that lurk within
nightmares.
It hurts so fucking well!
It hurts so bad too.
It hurts no matter what I try to do.

I have always strived to hide my sadness.
I have always concealed my emotional struggle
from you.
It is difficult to to convey my distress amidst the
noise.
I have lost my figurative voice.
I still do not have a practical choice.
I am still trapped in the void, deep within the
corridors of insanity.

The voices in my head are all about deceit. They taunt
and haunt me, their intent being to destroy me. I must
remain strong.
—*Geoff*

HERE TO STAY

I am able to breathe and see clearly here.
I can be my true self, free from any fear.
There is not a single mirror in sight.
I am able to hide under the falling leaves and
    completely disappear.
In the forest, I do not experience the same level
    of fear.
Here I can escape from the voices and my
    nightmares.
Outside of the tree line, there awaits a beast that
    you've never seen.
Its skin is smooth, and it remains cleanly
    shaved.
It hides underneath human skin, and it attaches
    itself to everything hidden deep within me.
This beast knows my thoughts, my sins,
and how to destroy me before I even have the
    chance to begin.
The beast was always within me and I created it.

I try to remain concealed in the forest, away
    from what lies ahead.
I try to avoid my inner thoughts, as I can no
    longer bear their weight.
If I were to peer into my own reflection, I am
    aware of what is at risk.
The creatures that roam outside of the forest
    only seek to take,
and I am unable to drive away their presence.
They are here to stay.

I have encountered numerous creatures, as I am one
myself, and have come to terms with my disturbing
nature. My insatiable urge for human flesh is the
cause of my imprisonment. I often reminisce about my
time in the forest, indulging in my human prey. My
hunger for flesh is here to stay.

—Geoff

GLISTENING TEETH

Her wings are extended.
She is gripping hanging ropes.
She is blindfolded and surrounded by skulls.
She is challenging you to determine your
    method of death.
Do not even think about lifting the blindfold that
    conceals her eyes.
So many have succumbed to her.
So many have have pleaded.
So many have prostrated themselves before her.
She decapitated all of them.
Then stacked their heads around her and
    observed the insects devour the decaying
    flesh.
The remaining tissue disintegrated, revealing the
    multitude of glistening teeth.

She is neither angel, nor demon, but something
    far more sinister.
She transforms into the worst nightmare of each
    victim,
driving them into insanity without warning.
She devours their memories and dangles them
    by the throat.
She consumes the happiness that we worked so
    hard for.
She consumes hope without a second thought,
her throne a symbol of her lack of remorse.
Once you smell her stench, you will be hers
    forever.
There will be no escape.
Allow me to introduce the collector of ghosts.

I have penned this poem about the inner voice that I

have personified as Renee. She continues to persist daily, attempting to ensnare me with ropes around my neck, with the aim of pulling me away.
—*Geoff*

WEEPING IN THE DARKNESS

When I first saw her in the darkness, there was
    rain and a blackened sky.
Smoke emanated from her hollow eyes.
Despite my efforts to convince myself otherwise,
I knew my thoughts were compromised.
Her screams sounded as if she were being
    devoured.
The sound echoed through the night, repeatedly.
I was unsure on how to proceed, as she kept
    returning.
I felt overwhelmed, filled with emotion,
and unable to take action as I sat here,
alone, weeping in the darkness.

What have I done to deserve this cursed life?
She has yet to attack me.
All she does is scream and then she demands
    silence
by holding one finger to her lips.
I am not the one screaming!
I need to find a way to get rid of her.

Everything that happens after she leaves has
    become a complete blur.
I am so disoriented and uncertain, and I am in
    need a solution.
I am unable to determine if she is truly real or
    simply a figment of my imagination,
yet I am inexplicably drawn to her irresistible
    songs.
She sings while she also screams.

She carefully watches everything that I do.
She shared with me her intention to kill me
    when she makes her next move.
No one is convinced by my tale.
I am currently imprisoned because of her.
These hallways cater to the the mentally
    disturbed and the lost,
and those who have strayed from the right path.
I suppose this is where I belong.
At any moment, I fear she will end my life, but
    all she does is scream.
I am left here, still weeping in the darkness.

I composed this poem inspired by the memory of my
dead mother. She is no longer the same person. I
yearn for her deeply every single day. The final time I
laid eyes on her, she was lying in a pool of her own
blood, together with the rest of my family who had
been brutally slain.
—*Geoff*

ONCE MORE

She aided my respiration when I was struggling
    for air.
She cleans up the mess that chaos leaves
    behind.
She unlocked numerous doors that I believed
    were permanently shut.
Even now, after many years, she understands
    me when I've had too much.
She extracted the poison from my exposed
    wounds.
She cleansed the cobwebs that enveloped my
    darkened tomb.
She opened my eyes, aiding me to see through
    the darkness.
She discovered me screaming, my life at its

bleakest.
She approached me as I burned in the flames.
She extended her hand and said,
"Let me remind you that everything will be okay."

Finding true love is like combing through
     scattered thoughts,
searching for the perfect pebble.
In pursuit of something extraordinary,
there is often a cost.
Throughout my life, I have often felt lost.
However, when she enters my cell,
she removes the sadness within me.
My heart, mind, and spirit are constantly
     deteriorating,
until she replenishes my being with love once
     more.

I have never had a girlfriend, been married, or had children of my own. The only person who truly cares for me is my beloved, Jennie. She is the only one who can comfort my troubled mind. She is the only real love I have ever had, apart from my deceased family. I have written numerous love poems and songs about her, and I eagerly read and sing them to her each day when she visits. Her presence takes away my rage and sorrow, restoring my humanity while she is in the confines of my cage. When she is near, I do not crave human flesh, but rather the comfort and solace that only my love can provide. When she disappears, I can't help but scream in anguish. I know what is coming next for me.
—*Geoff*

DESCRIBED

I am exerting my best effort.
I cannot suppress my laughter.

I understand the reasons!
I have nearly overcome all of my fears.
Every intense emotion is described here.

I've walked through the hallways that hold many
    adversaries.
The place that drains my energy.
I am unable to differentiate between my illusions
    and reality.
That ship sailed long ago as I continue to strive
    for clarity.
I'm frantically creating.
I am procrastinating.
I am overcomplicating everything when it
    already made sense.
My thoughts are in disarray.
There isn't much remaining.
I am trapped in a masterpiece that seems out of
    reach.
What comes next?
What is my current situation?
Where is Death?
I had anticipated its arrival amidst my screams
    of nonsense.
I am exhausted from every word that appears.
Each emotion within me is intricately described
    here.

My hands ache and cramp from transcribing and
sketching what I perceive. My cell is littered with piles
and piles of notebooks. Approximately once a month,
they lower down the mechanical compartment that
provides my meals and supplies. This allows me to
discard the old journals and obtain new ones to write
in. They've been lowering the books I request, but it's
been many years since I've been here. No one has
entered this cell, afraid of what I might do. The rules
are clearly stated on a sign on the left side of my cage:

"Do not enter this cell for any reason. Cannibal inside."
Human contact will never happen for me again.
—Geoff

DYSFUNCTIONAL

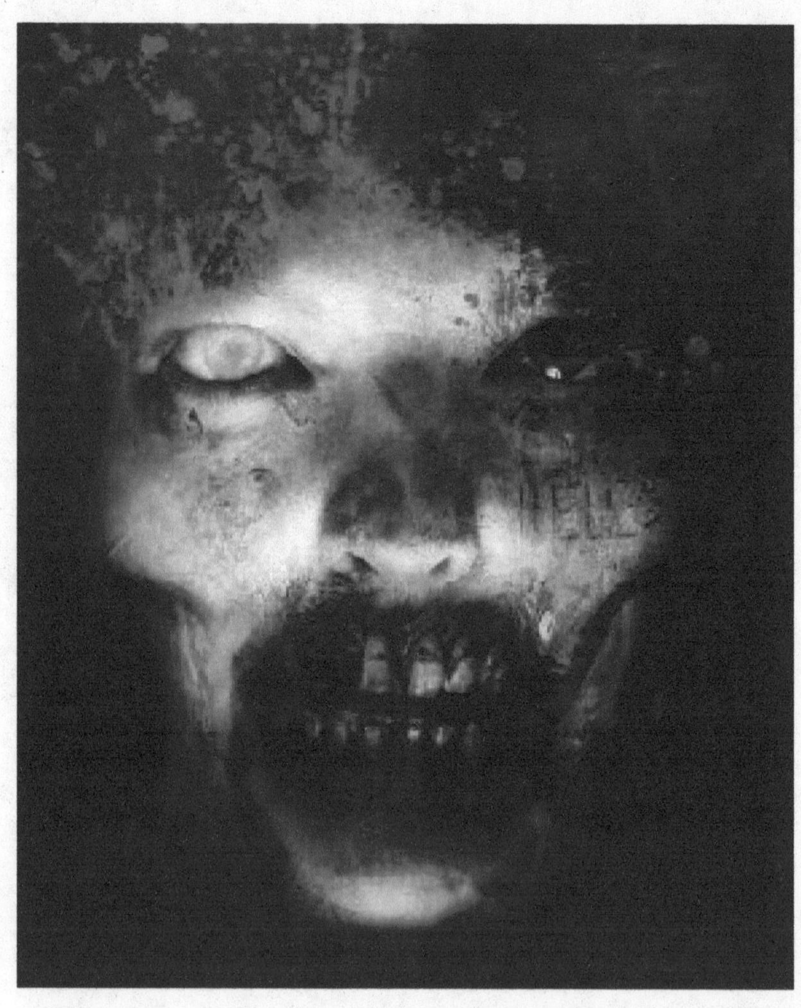

DYSFUNCTIONAL

Everything around me is dysfunctional...
I am running out of precious time.
I am overwhelmed as the voices infuse my
    chaotic visions,
originating from within the confines of my
    fragmented mind.
They are then transferred into the tip of my pen.
As the visions are transcribed onto the paper,
they leave their mark; reimagined and reborn.
I am fully conscious of my state of mind,
and I have a deep understanding.
The ink that flows from my pen holds immense
significance to me—it is my entire world.

These voices will manipulate and distort
your words to use them against you.
Don't anticipate them to cease.
It's a dysfunctional world here.
I have reached rock bottom and I know
I will never reach the pinnacle.
If you believe that demons won't restrain you to
    keep
you in their grasp, you are sadly mistaken.
They will crush you if you dare to sing louder
    than their song.
They don't want you to succeed; they anticipate

your failure.

The world here is dysfunctional.
Some voices will deceive you with false
    pretenses.
These voices are not a sign of friendship.
It is important to be aware of this.
Remember, pleasure always comes with
    consequences!
They may try to throw scraps;
tell falsehoods while maintaining eye contact.
The majority of them are known to be
    compulsive liars.
They intend to distract and divert you.
The melodies that they play
are carefully crafted to entice you.
Whatever you do, do not sing along and do not
    listen.

Voices and demons, demons and voices—they are the only companions I've ever had. Everyday, I am tormented by two female demons who leave a sticky residue, their constant presence pushing me deeper into darkness. They perch atop me, repeating the same damn story, while my eyes burn with intensity. It's as if they're filled with fiery grains of sand. Not all of these voices come with a story, but the majority of them do. I have committed them all to memory and have given up trying to understand what to do. Nothing ever changes; not a single word in their stories. I fear the stories will perpetually repeat. I constantly retreat and continue to descend into the stinking bowels of my undeniable madness.
—*Geoff*

ONLY SILENCE NOW

How can I begin this?

Everything is so chaotic.
I am experiencing a burning sensation as it invades my lungs.
With wonder in my eyes and determination in my mind,
I pondered how to adapt to the shifting tides.
I came to the realization that life is not without imperfections.
Perfection is an unattainable illusion.
I searched for it, I truly gave it my all!
I have been running in endless circles for an undisclosed amount of time.
I'm still running and have lost track of the many times I have cried.
I have wept in madness, with an insanity so strong that I almost gave in.
I struggle with concealing my emotions.
Every single emotion.
I have traversed vast waters.
Even on solid ground, I experience seasickness.
I have been isolated amidst scorching flames that reek of singed flesh.
I have given a new name to my own darkness, I have!
Sitting there, I could not help but let out another piercing scream.
I screamed for my aspirations.
I screamed with all of my might.
For the the sake of my existence, I screamed!
I begged for the truth to finally catch up with me.

I was exhausted from that raven.
That creature was such a nuisance!
I was worn out from the constant disturbance it caused.
Pecking at my eyes and baring my inner thoughts.

It craved me.
It desired me fiercely.
It recognized my weaknesses and my decent into
  madness.
It had control over me.
It was aware of its power.
It was aware of its dominance.
It succeeded!
I covered my eyes.
I masked my thoughts.
I refused to lie there and perish, so I desperately
  escaped that hell.

I seized that raven by the neck and twisted it so
  violently.
I squeezed that bird ferociously until everything
  became clear.
The screeching had stopped and the fire had
  extinguished.
I am no longer shouting here.
There is only silence now.

I've read many renowned authors in the fields of poetry, fiction, non fiction, romance, horror, and more. I have read extensively across all of these genres. What else do you expect me to do in federal prison? This particular poem is inspired by a blend of their works, infused with my own chaotic thoughts. Recalling the act of forcefully seizing that raven and twisting its neck reminds me of the moment I drank from the life vein of one of my family's murderers—I can still taste the satisfaction of revenge even today.
—*Geoff*

ASHES

I set my dark journal ablaze, hurling it at the
  lifeless oak tree.

The sky erupted with sparks and fiery wooden
    ashes rained down.
I reveled in my twisted desires.
A sense of vengeance consumed me as I
    ascended higher,
enclosing the condemned with twisted, rusted
    barbed wire.
They showed no concern for my screams, so why
    should I bother?
I take pleasure in witnessing these creatures
    suffer.
It's time to confront them with their own actions.
I will expose the harsh reality to them and
    overpower them with my words.
Tonight, I am shouting into the stars, my words
    blazing like fire.
These creatures deserve to be burning!

The blood has now coagulated where new
    lessons were being learned.
I can still hear the creature's screams, echoing
    in a harmonious verse.
Hello creatures, do you remember me?
It is time for you to experience what you forced
    me to see.
I've had enough of the lashes on my back,
enough of being taunted and attacked.
Give me your claws.
It is your turn to receive a skin-tearing slap.
Tonight, these creatures will be engulfed in fire
and reduced to thin, paper-like ashes.

I am offering you all that I have—every ounce
of pain you inflicted upon me, now belongs to all
    of you.
You must experience it in order to fully
    comprehend.
I purged them all out like the animals they were
on the day of the slaughter.

Within my thoughts, I had reached
my breaking point in every aspect.
In my nightmares, I have been fed up with this.
Though some creatures still roam the earth with
    arrogance.
Inside my dark journal, the creatures no longer
    exist.
Farewell creatures, the end.

I dream of ridding myself of these voices, I do.
—*Geoff*

Everything Gleams as Everything Collapses

What is this madness?
Where is the door to my sanity?
I'm traversing a divide of shattered glass.
My thoughts weigh heavily on me.
I must be ready for the deluge of memories to
    come.
The floodgates have opened and there is no
    turning back.
The tides are rising.
My inner voices are conspiring.

I am compelled to re-enter my thoughts,
    switching on a dime.
My fondest recollections are the ones that inflict
    turmoil within me.
I have revisited them countless times.
I have attempted to remove those things from
    my life.
However, there are only a handful of memories
    that bring tears to my emotionless eyes.
It is challenging to endure such torment.
My words deliver numerous lashings.
Everything gleams as everything collapses.

My voices know how to break me down. They show me photographic memories of when they weren't around. They show my parents laughing and smiling, and all three of my brothers and me roughhousing. They know I'll never have those times back. I know I'll never have those times back. They seem to take pleasure in it. To this day, I still can't understand why it has to be this way. Will the voices be silenced after my death? I don't have an answer for that yet.
—*Geoff*

KEEP THEM CLEAN

We lose our way back to the place we once called
    home.
We lose the love of those we used to know.
We can't fully comprehend, but we must accept
    what they have shown us.
Life is short, so we must learn to let them go.

It's difficult when the rope tightens around your
    throat.
Your apologies are not owed to anyone that
    caused you to scream.
They made the choice to make you scream.

When they hurt you so badly after loving you for
    years,
you've never cried such running tears.
It's hard to understand as the memories just
    flow,
because love is all they ever showed.

It can be difficult to cope when you have lost
    hope.
Your apologies are not owed to anyone that
    caused you to scream.
They made the choice to make you scream.

We will take one final look at them through the
    reflections in the glass.
The tears continue to flow as they remain frozen
    in the past.
We must wash our hands, my friends, we must
    keep them clean.
You cannot be tormented by those who caused
    you to scream.
They made the choice to make you scream.

I occasionally have pleasant dreams. Some of these
dreams involve leaving all of the monsters behind. I
also dream of moving forward with my life, and of
experiencing peace, love, and elusive light.
Additionally, I occasionally dream of going back in
time. I often dream that I saved my family's lives. I
envision a place in time, where I did not cook and
consume the internal organs of their three murderers.
In these dreams, I am able to experience a normal life.
However, upon waking up, I am once again
surrounded by deafening screams.
—*Geoff*

SHALLOW

Humanity will deceive you,
    as it is driven only by its insatiable desires.
They may manipulate you for their gain.
Trusting the human race is the epitome of
    madness.
You should also never trust your own reflection,
    as it can often deceive you the most.
The eyes in the mirror seem to be going for your
    throat.
Most of the time, the other side of the glass
    reflects one's inner demons and ghosts.
If you haven't prepared, you should study and

learn.
Demons lack any sense of empathy towards
    your emotions.
They eagerly anticipate watching you burn,
their mouths salivating in ravenous hunger,
and lessons will be learned.

You don't have to listen to me.
I'm just a crazy man confined, without peace.
You don't have to follow me.
Just know I won't follow your lead.
I have seen the damage that insanity can cause.
I have seen good people being ripped in half by
    it.
So when a warning sign appears and a demon is
    near,
I cannot fight yours with you.
No one fights mine with me.
I have many of my own demons to fear,
and I cannot take on any more.
I apologize, but you will be on your own once I
    disappear.

In a society that claims to love,
yet conjures up a billion cries,
gold and diamonds mask violence,
veiled behind greedy gazes and lies.
Those who choose silver are blindly
dismissed as shallow, but death ultimately
unveils itself to all mortal eyes.

I haven't seen much of the world outside. I remember
some places from my youth other than Maine, but not
too many. The only things I really know about the
world are from the countless books that I've read—so
many wars, so much greed, and so much chaos. The
world outside of here is in anarchy. I titled this piece
"Shallow" because, after reading numerous books, I
have come to the realization that the world outside is

crazier than even my own thoughts. My kind of craziness is tough to surpass. Through my words and artwork, I have depicted the shattered reflections within these broken mirrors, but I cannot believe that this is truly me.

—*Geoff*

GUTTED

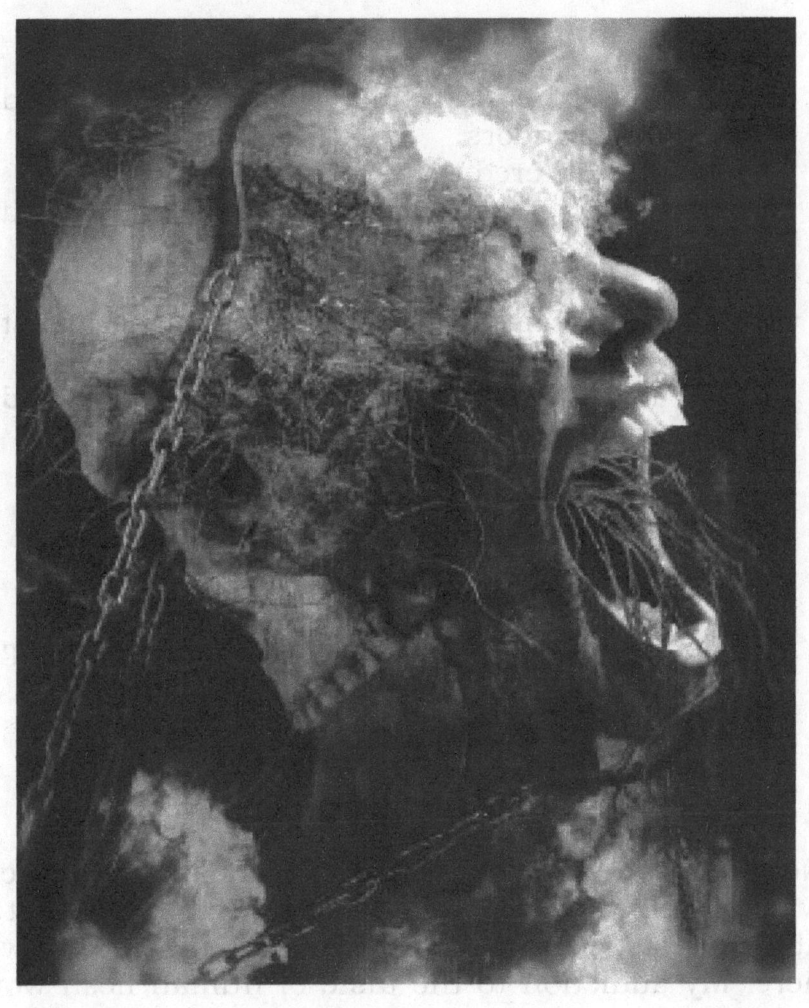

Gutted

This is not the first time I have encountered
 unfamiliar doors.
I have encountered them before.
I understand how to survive and where to find
 places to hide.
Another threat is approaching.
Do not be deceived by the darkness, never trust
 it.
It will leave you screaming, bleeding out, and
 gutted.

Demons feed on open wounds and sadness.
They thrive on insanity and madness.
Do not ask me what the difference is,
if you have not experienced it firsthand.
If you have not walked barefoot across burning
 glass,
do not pretend to understand.
This is not a game to be played.
There is no pleasure to be found in a cage.

No one knows what I am going through. No one ever
will, because no one will ever be here. I wouldn't be
able to resist tearing into them, even if someone were
here. My addiction to the taste of human flesh would
become too strong. The conversation would be cut

short. You would be devastated, and my voracious
mouth would be salivating in anticipation.
—*Geoff*

DEFINED

There is magic within my eyes.
I can see the reflections emanating from the
    inside.
I have finally realized that there were reasons
    why I burned.
The sky has opened wide.
I see myself so clearly.
So much has been overturned, explaining the
    reasons why I burned.
The void is shining brightly across the unknown
    divide.
The stars are aligning just right, explaining the
    reasons why I burned;
no stone has been left unturned.
There's still a fire burning deep within my eyes.
The voices in my head are still battling for
    control of my mind.
The flames of my battles mix in beautifully with
    my cries.
There is something in the darkness that caused
    me cross those lines.

I have plenty of time, yet I feel so limited.
The flames are engulfing my life; it continues to
    pass me by.
I can see the shadows' gazing eyes.
The illustrations age like fine wine.
I try to rediscover myself while confined.
My reasons were never intended to be defined.

I throw verse at my reality all the time. I write about a
fictional state of mind. I guess I still have a little bit of

fight left inside.
—*Geoff*

EBBING WAVES

I hear shuffling as I play restlessly in the dark.
I'm attempting to showcase my painting with
    great beauty in the stars.
I'm trying to unravel a mystery that may never
    be solved.
Please allow me to stay here and be still.
Please allow me to stay here with my voice.
I haven't heard it in such a long time.

I have attempted to articulate my emotions.
I have delivered the slide show.
There are pathways that I once walked,
    destroyed by the ebbing waves.
The currents have erased all that was once
    familiar.
Sorrowful tears have formed on my needlessly
    fractured heart.
The icy wasteland that remains is my current
    work of art.
I am unable to navigate this place.

There are no maps navigating the evolution of
    the remaining waste.
This location only seeks to take.
Everything here is counterfeit.
The remaining inhabitants are desperate and
    shamed.
In search of a new exit in this continually
    shifting labyrinth.
Most will never fully comprehend the lasting
    impact that it leaves behind.
Most will never truly grasp the overwhelming
    sensation of losing their sanity.

There are pathways that I once walked,
destroyed by the ebbing waves.
The currents have erased all that was once
    familiar.

Everything here is fraudulent. Everything here is
authentic. I no longer possess a clear understanding of
reality, therefore, I cannot accurately express my
emotions.
—*Geoff*

SOLIDIFIED

I am struggling to locate my inner truth.
There is just so much that I have mistreated.
I've abused myself in a multitude of ways.
The ones that I love cannot bear my pain.
It always ends up affecting them.
If I continue like this, I will soon have nothing
    left.

It is always my fault when my inner voices
    speak.
They are ever-present to remind me.
As I reflect on myself, they reflect with me.
Everything that I cherished has now escaped.
My body lies lifeless.
Vivid fantasies merge with unsettling horrors in
    the blink of an eye,
years gone by.
I do not know how much longer I can lie here,
    preserved,
before the maggots hatch and start escaping
    from my eyes.

Hugs and kisses have now turned into screams,
the past is gone and I am yearning for what it

seems.
The pictures hanging on my wall, are all that is
 left of love at all?
When my inner voices start to speak, it is always
 my fault, it seems.
They are a constant reminder to me, as I watch
 my reflection walk freely.
Everything I once held dear has solidified into
 stone.
There is nothing left but an urn of shattered
 hope.

My soul has been devoid of life for decades. I have no
one to grieve for me upon my passing, as it seems that
no one will mourn my departure. This is because there
is no one here except for the voices in my head.
—*Geoff*

MANIFESTATION

When I am at my most vulnerable, it comes for
 me.
While I am asleep, it devours me.
This creature is not at all endearing.
It embodies the essence of horror.
It cannot be ignored.
As I scream, it tears open my chest, utterly
 despicable.
I scream in the shadows.
I scream in the darkness.
I'm screaming at my completely darkened heart.

It is only the beginning as it slithers onto my
 chest.
I'm frozen in silence as it does its best,
ravaging me in every way imaginable,
manipulating my emotions and shattering my
 dreams.

My imagination then unravels at the seams.
Its beady eyes piercing through me.
I'm screaming silently, as no one can hear me.
Nobody believes me either.
This Hell cannot be any clearer.
I cannot call for help or call the Preacher.
Through my eyes, I see the manifestation of the
    reaper.

The portrayal is not accurate.
The creature's eyes emit a dark red haze,
its fingernails are long and decaying.
It emits the scents of torture and burning sage,
but the sage has no effect this monster, this
    fucker is a heavyweight.
It will yell *'Fuck your sage!'* and defiantly spit in
    your face.
It strikingly resembles myself, as this reaper's
    reflection, a creation of my own.

I have read many books on the infamous Grim Reaper. The Reaper is my favorite character of all time. I love reading the many variations of what I refer to as my "angel." I cannot wait to meet the most iconic, beautiful, and badass Omni-neutral death deity of all time. The Reaper will lead my tortured soul across the great divide. I am not certain where it will take me, but I am ready to get off of this ride.
—*Geoff*

GREEN BLADES OF GRASS

Hollow eyes lead to a hollow soul.
Hollow graves are dug out of the lifeless ground.
They are waiting to encase you, to mold you.
You will be surrounded by your decaying self.
Only tales of the undead will now be told.
The world will never hear your voice again.

Your loved ones will eventually forget you.
Everything that you once stood for means
    nothing in this dark abyss.

Your eyes will dissolve along with your skin,
leaving behind only a thin layer of flesh.
Your ears have been pointed,
indicating your transformation into an undead
    being.
You are now in search for innocent bones to
    shatter,
as a result of your brand-new insatiable hunger.
You are now simply a starving pile of bones
    clinging onto the memories of your past.
You're just a once-thriving soul,
now rotting beneath the carnivorous green
    blades of grass.

The grass is depleting every nutrient that you
    once had.
You are now trying to dig yourself out; you are
    trying to comprehend.
Unfortunately, there is nothing you can do
    about it.
You are unable to bear even the sight of the
    worms,
as they wriggle in and out of your nearly
    skinless hands.
Your eyes have long dissolved under the
    ravenous green blades of grass.

I have lost all semblance of rationality that I once
possessed. There is no redemption for me at this point.
I do not believe that I deserve redemption. I am
haunted by the cold, lifeless eyes of every person I
have killed. I am filled with repulsion at the mere
thought of redemption. Is that wrong of me? I will
never know nor care.
—*Geoff*

QUIET

Quiet, please.
Our voices may incite violence.
Please refrain from making any noise.
The creatures hold dominion over every aspect of
     this place,
and the consequences of being discovered are
     worse than those of murder.
We would be better off dead than facing them, so
     please maintain silence.

Please, be quiet and listen.
I have thoroughly studied every path and turn,
and I have memorized the names of every
     creature that dwells within these walls.
This is more than a mere curse—you must open
     your eyes.
The chaos of this situation demands your
     attention;
only by listening can you hope to survive.
The conversations in your consciousness are
     filled with falsehoods—
all they do is manipulate you.
Become like a mime and simply listen to me.
Do not surrender to their control; if you let go,
     they will diminish.
Your presence will go unnoticed if your thoughts
     remain quiet.
So please, silence them.

Please, continue to listen to me.
The exit is close.
Do not hit that wall, break the fever instead.
Do not listen to their words, they are not your
     friends.
Do not let yourself believe that they are real; it's
     just you and me.
If you keep empowering them, the void will

reappear.
There is no denying this, as I have personally
   witnessed it.
Please, be quiet and listen.
The exit is to the right over here—look for the
   red, glowing letters.
Stop listening to the chatter in your mind and
   focus on what I am saying.
Quiet, please.

It may be too late for me to stop listening to the
monsters in my mind, but it's not too late for you. My
monsters have consumed me long ago, and they are
waiting for me to die. Once I do, I will be screaming in
the flames. You may want to consider changing your
actions.
—*Geoff*

SALTY RAIN

It is hard to believe in the world when all it does
   is lie.
It is hard to believe in laughter when tears flow
   from sad eyes.
What is a life without sacrifice?
What is the pain if you haven't danced in the
   rain?
What is love if your heart is cold?
What is in the present if your story can't be told?

There's a place deep within myself that I like to
   retreat to.
There is a hidden road within the snow that
   remains unknown.
There is a secret place within myself that only I
   know.
It is difficult to trust a smile when the harsh
   reality is pain.

It is difficult to comprehend that even Angels
    have been through Hell.
They weep meaningless tears in vain.
It is difficult to trust anything unless I see it
    with my own eyes.
It is challenging to find a solution while fire falls
    from the sky.

I strive to believe that there is something greater
    than myself,
a feat that proves to be challenging in the midst
    of darkness
as smoke fills my lungs.
I assert to believe that there is more than this—
    more than just monsters and pain.
It is proving to be a daunting task to find a
    solution to all of this.
It is an impossible feat to locate a single
    teardrop in an ocean of salty rain.

As I have mentioned numerous times in my extensive
journals, my perception of the world has been limited.
My narrow existence has been confined to this
enclosure, and it is the sole truth that I have ever truly
comprehended. The only refuge I have found is in my
own contemplations, a torment I would not wish upon
even my greatest foe.
—*Geoff*

I'M DOWN HERE

Such beautiful lullabies serenade me from the
    darkness.
Such alluring promises are whispered from the
    walls.
I know they are deceitful and the flames have
    already been ignited.
Yet, I am still enticed by their siren songs.

They possess me, ripping away my tranquility.
Their beauty is undeniable, as they continue to
    sing amidst the rising ocean fog.
Beneath the surface of this beauty, there is cost.

I can see their fish-like fins splashing in and out
    of the water.
They are singing so softly to me.
I know they are after blood.
I know they crave to feed on me as I bleed.
The songs are irresistible when they sing.
The songs were designed to encompass
    everything,
playing on the illusions of your wildest dreams.
They will drag you deep into their holes,
under the surface where you cannot breathe.
As they kiss you and caress your back, water
    will fill your lungs,
and you will release silent screams.
It is at that moment when you will witness their
    sharp teeth.
I'm down here, captivated by their melodies,
    unable to stop silently screaming.

The siren's song is a mixture of love, suffering,
    lust, and pain.
Before consuming their hapless prey, they
    charm and seduce them.
As captivating creatures, they have ensnared my
    life.
They feast upon me and share what remains.
They devour my heart and mind,
passing me around like a formal dinner as they
    discuss their day.
The siren songs will play again when it is time
    for them to feed.
These creatures are known as mermaids and are
    referred to by various names.
I can still see them feasting on my heart as it

continues to beat.

I long for the once-sweet lullabies that my mother used to sing to me. Her songs would make me feel safe as I drifted off to sleep. However, they are now only distant memories. I am left with the haunting melodies that my voices sing. I shout and can only dream about the beautiful songs my mother used to sing.

—*Geoff*

CANDLE WAX

When the leaves start to change,
I begin to burn inside, consumed by rage.
I am all too familiar with this inevitable pain,
for it arrives the same every time.
As the leaves change their colors and the flowers
    meet their demise,
I gradually feel the flames rising behind my eyes.
They emerge to fulfill their purpose, causing my
    emotions to ignite and intensify.
The autumn weather always fills me with
    anxiety,
for I know the pain that awaits when I witness
    the falling leaves.
My transformation is beckoning once more.
I can feel my skin slowly melting off my bones,
    cascading into the abyss below.
My voices emerge once more from their inferno-
    encircled thrones.
The tormenting autumnal elements have once
    again made their presence known.

The leaves begin to swirl in a fiery storm all
    around me.
My screams are muffled by the chaotic insanity.
The open wounds are seeping out, creating a
    beautiful catastrophe.

The exquisite pain is consuming my clarity and
   leaving nothing in its wake.
Everything I have ever known has been burned
   away, once again.
All of my hard work has once again been taken
   away,
the falling leaves serve as a reminder of what I
   have lost,
and why I am feeling so sore.
As the leaves change colors,
I find myself repeatedly banging my head against
   my cell door.
Everything is wilted, as tears flood my eyes once
   more.

I am consistently resisting the necessary
changes that I must make.
I am aware of what needs to be done,
but I am burdened by the agony.
I refuse to make the necessary
sacrifice and deny it.
This is not a game as I look down
at the mess that I have created.
My skin is now melting,
resembling candle wax on a cool autumn day.

I used to love when summer would end and the leaves
would begin to change. I would eagerly anticipate the
cool, crisp air taking me to a happy place. However,
that happy feeling was abruptly taken away when my
family was brutally murdered. I know you are familiar
with the details. Now, the air I breathe in this place is
stagnant, stale, and filled with the putrid scent of
burning flesh.
—*Geoff*

THE GAME

I cannot bear the pressure of this curse any
    longer.
I never know what new world it will hold.
I should not have started listening to them when
    I was warned against it.
Now I cannot stop until I have survived every
    level.
Ahead lie monsters and witches in various forms
    of hell.
I can already envision my skin melting in the
    scorching flames and my skull being
    shattered,
served on a plate with a touch of pepper to taste.
If you survive one world, there is always another
    waiting to destroy you,
and melt your insides like butter.
I feel them leaking from my ears.
The curse knows my every fear, and every
    insecurity is used against me.
It tricks you while twisting your thoughts into a
    maze.
You cannot think when the demons invade.

I am unsure of the number of levels within this
    game,
but I am aware that the next one will be
    challenging.
It will likely be more difficult than the previous
    one,
as those in charge mock and alter the rules.
They intend to manipulate you and turn you
    into a mere pawn,
fulfilling your desires and serving them to you
    on a silver platter.
The levels of these games were designed to
    engulf the player.
If you perish in the game, the consequences are

real.
Then your soul belongs to the entity controlling
    the game.
You have little time to contemplate what you are
    going to going to do.
What is your next move?
You must reject what they are trying to feed you
    from that silver platter,
or your fears will consume you.

The voices promised me pleasure. They promised me
my greatest desires. They promised me love on a silver
platter while leading me into the fire.
—*Geoff*

VIOLIN

I lost my way among the shadows so very long
    ago.
The flames rose all around me and I didn't know
    where to go.
When I lost my sanity, the demons cheered as I
    died inside.
They finally gained a hold of me and stole my
    shattered mind.

As I walked back down the path to hell, with my
    head hung low in shame,
a demon tapped me on the shoulder and said,
    "Boy, give me your name."
I looked into its dark, deep eyes and saw my own
    reflection in a state of rage.
I was then that I knew that I would be trapped
    in this eternal cage.

When the demon who led me down that path to
    hell answered the phone when I called,
it reminded me of the screaming faces trapped

within those walls.
As the door swung open, I stepped into a world
of ever-rising flames.
Little did I know the true cost until that fateful
day.

As the demon rose and fixed its gaze upon me
from its decaying, skin-covered chair,
a haunting melody greeted me within its
screeching lair.
As it started to sing, my ears began to bleed and
I fell to my knees,
clenching them in agony as I cried out for some
relief.

The demon's hysterical laughter echoed in the
darkness now that my soul belonged to it.
I would never leave this place again, and that's
just the way it is.
It taunted and dangled what was once mine
above my bleeding head,
taking everything I had ever loved and filling my
soul with dread.

It laughed and smiled at my misery while the
violin continued to play,
never stopping its serenade, playing never-
ending games.
Even now, it sings to me with haunting melodies
intertwined with eternal pain.
I regret embarking on that path towards hell or
stepping into those infernal flames.

The murderers of my family have taken everything
from me. In response, I have transformed them into
the deplorable beings they truly are. The thoughts
echoing in my mind have claimed what little remains. I
long for clarity and peace to come.
—*Geoff*

1893

I noticed a raven gracefully perched on a
    headstone in the forest.
Who could be buried beneath the ground?
Just lying there, lifeless, with indifference
    towards the world.
I have visited this location numerous times in
    the past, but this time,
I have a strange urge to dig to uncover the
    identity of the deceased.
I started using my bare hands to dig because I
    lacked a shovel.
I struggle to understand the necessity of
    knowing who is buried here,
yet I persisted until my fingers bled and my face
    turned blue.
Who are you and what is the purpose of your
    presence?
I am exhausted from all of this digging.
Please, communicate with me.

My bleeding fingertips hit a stud, and the coffin
    finally came into view.
Please inform me of your desires.
From within the coffin, I heard a series of
    pounding noises—thud, thud thud!
With a sudden jolt, the lid flew open,
revealing what appeared to be a recently
    deceased woman lying inside.
How is this possible?
The headstone's date reads 1893,
causing me to question whether I had stumbled
    into a dream or had simply lost my mind.
As she smiled at me, I noticed her decaying and
    bleeding teeth,
a clear indication of her undead state.
She had been waiting for me under her grave,
drawing me in and eagerly anticipating my

arrival.
She had lured me in.
As she drained my insides like a venomous
    spider, she declared,
*'Now you must remain in the grave until you too
    can be fed, just as I did."*

I feel like my life has been completely drained. I am uncertain how much time is left for me. I am plagued by visions of the deceased and overwhelmed by a sense of eternal dread. The voices in my head reveal my future with such clarity.
—*Geoff*

Under Your Skin

I cannot remember its face because it changes
    day by day.
What I can tell you is that I can recall all of the
    pain.
This creature appears in my dreams and
    manifests in my reality,
stalking me and preparing me for its ultimate
    goal of dragging me to where it dwells.
I have made countless attempts to conceal
    myself from it,
but it persistently locates me.
It is now deeply embedded in my fragmented
    psyche,
dictating my actions and foretelling my every
    step.
I am concerned about losing control of both my
    physical and decision-making abilities.
As a result, I feel compelled to write this letter to
    offer an opportunity
to anyone who may come into contact with this
    monster;

a chance not only to live, but to also survive.
This creature is a shapeshifter, capable of
disguising itself as those closest to you.
Its deceptive tactics make it difficult to escape
once it has captured your attention.
By exploiting your negative emotions and past
experiences,
it manipulates you with its charming façade.

When hell runs errands, you are one of its
chores.
I have learned to block out thoughts when I
sense its presence.
This tactic works for a short time, until it
becomes aware.
Utilize that small opportunity to escape; there is
only one.
If you overlook this chance, your blood will
become tainted with Hell's Majesty.
This is my warning to never let it in.
Once it takes hold, you become a vessel of this
entity.
To whom this may concern, take heed and never
succumb to its allure.
It constantly observes and has resided within
you, dormant.
It will forever remain a part of you.
It has always been within you, waiting to emerge
from under your skin.

I have no choice but to listen to the voices in my head
and describe what I see. It is guaranteed to get under
your skin. I am in too deep.
—*Geoff*

I Am Familiar

Iam Familiar

Every time that I delve deep, I never have a
  concrete plan.
I have to be cautious, as the blowing roses
  contain shards of glass.
The echoes and smells of death are everywhere.
Instrumentally, the sounds are beautiful, but
  the illusions are profound.
In the back of my mind, I am aware of the
  presence of hell,
but I choose to ignore its sounds.
My past resides within me as I exist in my past.
My emotions are beating me up I fall on my ass.
Hell will always be a part of me and my
  surroundings,
and every burn is a force of silence.
The memories that I am holding are both
  nurturing and violent.

I am familiar with hell, know it intimately.
Pain is not foreign to me,
my skin is adorned with countless welts, each
  one a reminder,
of the relentless scourging of the fiery barbed
  belt.
My vision blurs each time the pain sets in.
The belt keeps swinging, engulfing me within.

Why will this never cease?
Why must I pretend to be at peace?
I want to pretend that everything is fine so that I
     won't be punished again.
I am familiar with suffering and know what I
     have done.
I am aware of the monster I have become.
I am familiar with hell.

I no longer believe that my voices are illusions. I don't even know how to process my emotions. I have depicted hell in a manner that I believe to be remarkably realistic, or at least, so I believe. I will eventually experience it firsthand. I will inform you if it differs or remains the same when I arrive; that is, if the one in control allows me to write.
—*Geoff*

SEA

SEA

I am distancing myself from the sea.
I am relinquishing my dreams.
I am compelled to bring my screams with me.
I am moving away from a once-glowing
    masterpiece,
now darkened and shattered into pieces.
I was convinced it was the correct decision—I
    thought
it was the right choice, I firmly held on.
However, it did not fulfill me and was not the
    right fit.
I was always open to discussing it, but nobody
    ever spoke up.
The only voices that listened were the ones in
    my head,
the only ones that heard.

The illusions of the sea are indeed beautiful,
as the waves crash at my feet.
I am leaving it all behind and embracing the
    mysterious creatures.
My hope has long since burnt out,
and I am now trapped in darkness.
From a world once full of chaos,
to becoming chaos itself, I now dance among the
    shadows.

Every single star in the sky once held a name,
now forgotten along with their once shimmering
    light.
I am no longer the same; I haven't been for
    decades.
My experiences have brought about irreversible
    changes.
It is too late for me to be saved as the sea
    continues
to drown me once more in this sorrowful place.

As the waves crash through my mind one final
    time,
I bid my final goodbyes to the calming sea.
The once salty water now boils, yet no one hears
    my pleas.
My masterpiece is complete; it's time for
    something new.
The vibrant waves now burn with fiery hues, no
    trace of the cool blue.
Farewell, serene and peaceful sea.
Thank you for listening when no one else would.
I must depart now, as the fire beckons me.

The voices in my head were the only ones that
    listened,
the only ones that heard.
I am compelled to bring my screams with me.
I am relinquishing my dreams.
I am distancing myself from the sea.
I was always open to discussing it,
but nobody ever spoke up.
It did not fulfill me and was not the right fit,
but I firmly held onto it.
I was convinced it was the correct decision—I
    believed
it was the right choice.
I am now moving away from what was once a

glowing
masterpiece, now darkened and shattered into
  pieces.

I must depart now, as the fire beckons me.
Thank you for listening when no one else would.
Farewell, serene and peaceful sea.
The vibrant waves now burn with fiery hues, no
  trace of the cool blue.
My masterpiece is complete; it's time for
  something new.
The once salty water now boils, yet no one hears
  my pleas.
I bid my final goodbyes to the calming sea,
as the waves crash through my mind one final
  time.

I long to once again witness the moon framed by the stars and experience the soothing sea, but instead I am engulfed by a sea of fire. As you can see, the once-peaceful ocean is now a hue unrecognizable to me, so I have depicted it in blue to alleviate my distressed mind.
—*Geoff*

REVEALED

Revealed

I am filled with fear when I confront mirrors.
The reflections that confront me
are those of monsters, not my own.
I will never understand why mirrors have this
    effect on me.
Every day, I see another creature staring
back at me from the void.
As a result, I break every mirror I encounter.
These visions may appear beautiful,
but they are merely masking their true
    intentions.
The reality is hidden behind their façade
and will eventually be revealed.

When I gaze at them, my hands seem human to
    me.
However, within the glass, I see claws, tentacles,
    and gnarled teeth.
My thoughts exploit my tragic memories,
    tormenting me.
Each time I encounter a mirror, it shatters at my
    feet.
The absence of my reflection causes my eyes to
    roll back to white.
I no longer attempt to view my own reflection, as
    it is never truly mine.

I am aware that this is an endless cycle of
    illusions.
The reflections looking back at me are deceiving
    me,
and I am well aware of it.
Do you believe that I am unaware of this?
It doesn't make things any easier
when these voices invite me onto their show.
I have made multiple attempts to find a solution,
but I have failed every time.
After years of shattering mirrors, the reflections
started to manifest in front of me.
Now, I can no longer conceal myself.
They stand beside me, mocking me
as I bang on shattered glass.
My attempts to hide their ugliness have failed,
and they are now fully revealed.

The voices in my head are deceptively beautiful. I have
accurately described and painted them for all to see.
This is what they do to me when their true ugliness is
revealed.
—*Geoff*

Apocalyptic Sun

Apocalyptic Sun

Through all of this sacrifice, all I can see is my
  broken heart.
This pain that I feel leaves me with daily scars.
Like a scorpion molting in the desert winds, my
  suffering pierces through me.
Like the apocalyptic sun scorching my skin, my
  anguish consumes me.
I always feel exhausted and weak.
I am in a constant state of confusion.
I feel cold and unaware, overwhelmed and
  crazed.
These thoughts are incredibly frightening.
They are so dark and intense, devoid of any
  light.
I have been pleading and am in desperate need
  of help.
It is so difficult to fight.
I have been constantly under attack from
  everything that exists here;
everything bites.

If I could be free from this pain, I would banish
  it far away.
I would cast it into the void and silence all
  accompanying noise.
I am reaching out into the vast expanse of the

universe.
Please release me from these chains.
I long for someone to possess the keys to help
me escape.
I plead for someone to purify my skin and
eradicate the acidic rain.
Please wash it away.
Please cast it into the fire where the creatures
await.
Madness exemplifies what insanity reveals,
while chaos illuminates what we conceal.
Amidst the flames, our consciousness is at
stake;
what awaits in the shadows only seeks to take.

The agony evokes, the tears that cannot be
wiped away.
The distress resounds, the melodies that remain
unplayed.
The suffering resembles a scorpion molting in
the desert winds.
The anguish echoes, the turmoil that can no
longer be contained within.
The silence screams, the lyrics that cannot be
sung.
The shadows continue to rotate the cylinders—
the chamber
of the remorseless phantom's gun.
The skin dissolves, falling away in the presence
of the apocalyptic sun.

Here is another illustration of a hallucination that I
experience frequently. Or is it reality? I feel the
apocalyptic sun on my skin. My agony unquestionably
evokes tears that cannot be wiped away.
—*Geoff*

Dear Voices

Dear Voices

Dear voices,
All of you are mediocre, rotten garbage.
You come across as cheap, sleazy,
small-time, ratty and raunchy.
Your value is worthless, and you produce
 shoddy work.
Your behavior is atrocious, and you are nothing
 more than scroungers.
You are regarded as two-bit, cheap and sleazy.
Your excessive neediness makes you cruel and
 vile,
and you have the reputation of being thrifty and
 stingy.
All of you are despicable, sorry bastards,
except for my beloved Jennie.

You are all nothing more than a façade of
 supposed correctness,
deceiving and malicious.
Your execution is abysmal and unremarkable,
haphazardly thrown together with dripping
 subpar quality.
You never meet expectations or convey truth,
lacking dignity and authenticity.
You are nothing but pitiful and inferior
 imitations.

I hope you're pissed,
—Geoff Hathaway

I strive to thwart these voices through the use of words, as physical prowess has never been my strongest defense against supernatural beings. I am both proud and astonished by the person I have evolved into. Additionally, the appearance of these voices is further evidence of my derangement.
—*Geoff*

THE SEDUCTRESS OF THE SHADOWS

THE SEDUCTRESS OF THE SHADOWS

Let me make this perfectly clear: there is no
    radiance in this place.
Only shadows that fill us with fear.
There are no exits, only entrances.
The trees surrounding absorb and block any
    incoming light,
twisting and tearing it away from within.
This realm was not formed; it has always
    existed.
Your memories are fading.
You should have never accepted the gifts,
never succumbed to its pleasures—it is always a
    trick.
You should have never come through that
    misplaced door in the forest.
The beautiful woman wearing the sheer cloak is
    responsible for this.
Her collection of the damned wander aimlessly
    in this forest—lost,
and struggling to comprehend.
This place thrives on your anguish; while placing
    your desires in your grasp.

Your eyes will start to perceive things that you
    are unable to comprehend.
Your body will become weak and the mayhem

will then commence.
You will lose your voice.
You will lose your grip.
You will have no option but to relinquish control.
While you attempt to flee, the wooded area
    seems to have no end.
You will pass the same maddening trees
    repeatedly.
As you try to hide, she constantly pursues you.
The seductress is an unyielding predator in
    pursuit of her prey.
You are nothing more than a helpless deer,
captured by her alluring gaze, frozen in fear.

She can read your mind and detect your
    pleasures,
using them seductively against you for her
    malevolent gain.
She is known by many names, such as the
    Collector, the Forest Demon,
the ghost woman in the cloak—the seductress of
    the shadows.
Regardless of what name is given to her,
    remember this:
she grants you the gifts of your most profound
    pleasures,
while simultaneously slitting your throat.
She will find you in the trees, no matter where
    you hide.
After all, this is the place where she has control.
She has been here since the dawn of time,
and it is her domain to do as she pleases with
    you.

Repeatedly, she concocts a mixture of pleasure
    infused with pain.
Your craving for indulgence is at the mercy of
    the temptress.
You should have never ventured through that

portal in the woods.
Now, you are doomed.
You should have never accepted The Collector's
    offer of pleasure.
Now, you belong eternally to the the Seductress
    of the Shadows.
The satisfaction she offers is a contract,
and you have signed it without a pen in your
    hand.
She muffles your screams in her abyss,
inflicting pain that no mere mortal can
    withstand.
Restraints bind your hands, while your feet kick
    beneath her,
forced to obey her every demand.
Now, do you understand?

What is considered real within insanity? All I am able
to do is scream, write, and illustrate the voices that
take over me. Allow me to introduce the Seductress of
the Shadows, isn't she beautiful? She will rock your
world while ripping out your intestinal tract. You do
not want to enter her forest, as once you do, it will be
difficult to resist signing her contract.
—*Geoff*

HOLES

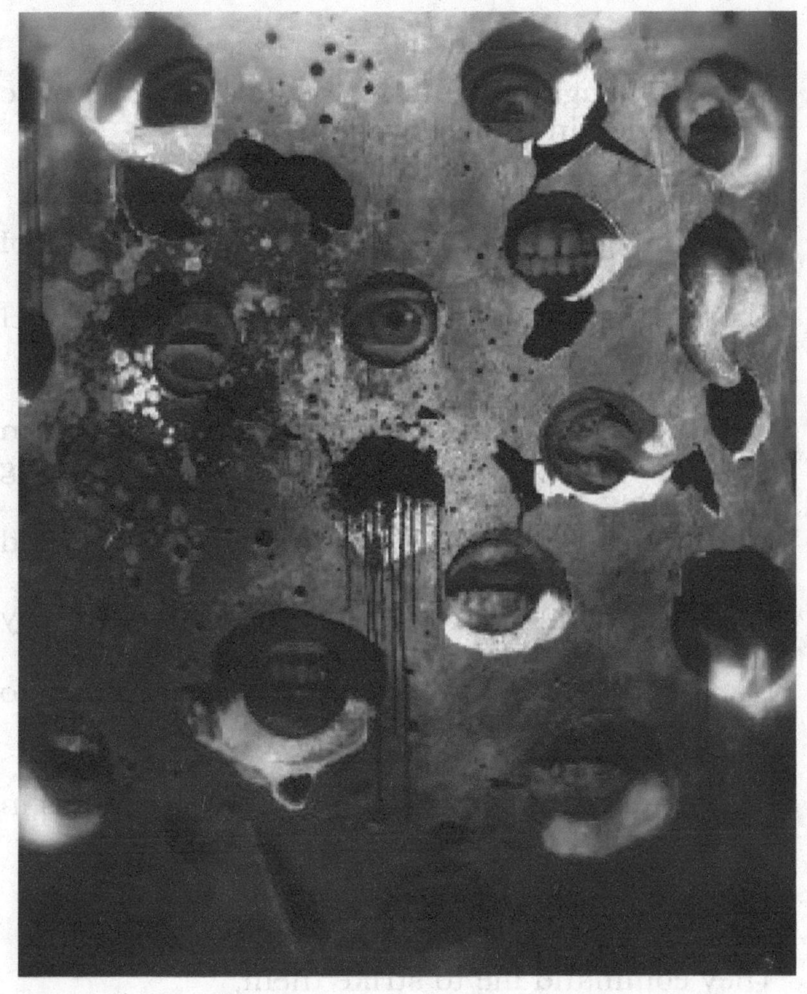

HOLES

I am tallying the number of holes that I have
     pounded into these walls.
Each one communicates a different message,
and none of this is my fault.
The damage caused by the deafening silence of
     my unbearable existence is the result.
There are many unavoidable things, and as I
     wail,
I am blamed for the noise.
My wounds continue to worsen at an
     increasingly rapid rate after each impending
     attack.
Like a caged animal, I am frequently neglected
     and forgotten.
I am drained of energy from fighting so many
     ongoing battles.
I know that there were never a set of keys to
     unlock my shackles.
I continue to search for them,
desperately trying to escape through the holes in
     the wall.

They beckon me from the walls,
urging me to escape this way.
They command me to strike them,
pleased when I bleed all over the place.

My mind is so clouded that I can't remember
that all of this is a lie.
The blood that flows from my knuckles is their
energy needed to survive.
The holes that I have created serve as a gateway
to the flames.
I am instructed to hit these walls daily, after
which my mind is erased.
The voices cackle in the darkness from within
the holes that I have created,
fully aware that they are in control and that I am
easily manipulated.
"Ravished" would be the more suitable term, as
they overpower me like savages.

I am fucked.
—Geoff

THE CHANGING OF THE LEAVES

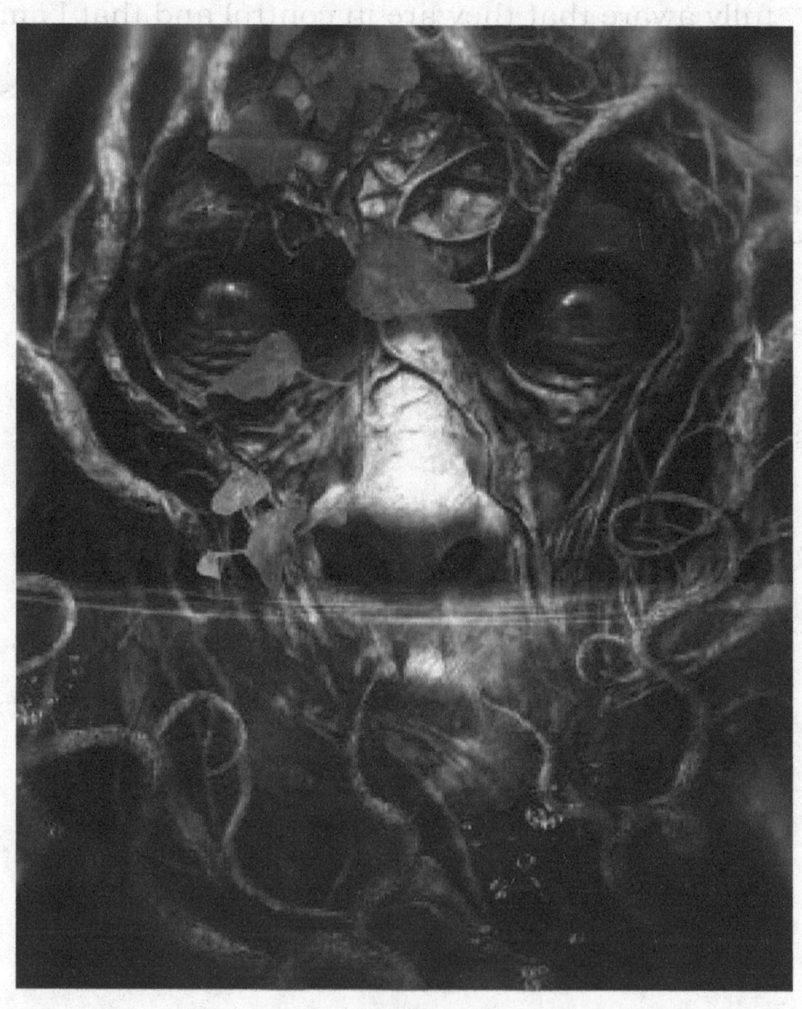

The Changing of the Leaves

This is how insanity is expressed,
rendering us lifeless and distressed.
There are too many voices present.
There are too many haunting dreams.
There are too many scavengers devouring me.
Everything is silently growing on me, like a slow-
    growing tree.
It is consuming me from within, while I cry out
    for peace.
It is the kind of peace that I have been
    desperately needing.
This is how my emotions manifest.
This is how my confusion and anger leaves so
    little left.
There are too many adversaries.
There are just too many painful memories
    consuming me.
Some days, I am not who I seem to be.
Other days, I am like a tree.
I silently scream amidst the changing of the
    leaves.

When my leaves fall off, it hurts so much.
When the cold winds blow, I feel the frost bitten
    touch.
When the birds stop chirping, they also stop

building their nests.
An explosion of violence is unleashed, revealing
the transformative mess and countless
anguished regrets.
You will witness a line of wailing trees,
experiencing pain like you've never known.
You will see a procession of smoldering
memories,
just like my own.

You will hear our collective cries as we shed our
leaves,
our eyes will roll back as if we are entranced in a
spell.
Our protection from the harsh winter has been
stripped away,
leaving us unable to breathe in this abominable
hell.
We are as rigid as the vessels we once carried.
You will witness us slowly deteriorating beneath
the now-dormant trees, undergoing a painful
metamorphosis
into a state of animosity.
Some days, I am not who I seem to be.
Other days, I am like a tree.
I silently scream amidst the changing of the
leaves.

This is how evolution is illuminated in plain
sight.
This is how the falling leaves spark and ignite.
There are too many flames burning.
There are too many hooks entangling.
The rusted barbed wire is starting to heat up.
Everything is spinning violently, like a slow
burning tree.
There are too many constraints without
corresponding keys.
Exposed wounds intersect at the razor's edge,

where the mentally ill are confined.
Harrowing screams reverberate endlessly,
below the sleeping maples and thriving pines.

The decomposing and inflamed flesh
engulfs our shattered minds.
It sears, pools, and bubbles beneath our feet.
Enlightenment is never what it seems amidst
the reality of where we were meant to be.
Some days, we are not as we appear to be.
On other days, we are like trees.
We all weep silently beneath the fiery scene,
and such piercing, inflamed screams are always
    present
among the changing of the leaves.
Let us be, let us scream, leave us to our
    evolution;
it is how we will set ourselves free.
Leave us to burn, leave us be, or join us in our
    insanity.

Harrowing screams reverberate endlessly,
below the sleeping maples and thriving pines.
Exposed wounds intersect at the razor's edge,
where the mentally ill are confined.
There are too many constraints without
    corresponding keys.
Everything is spinning violently, like a slow
    burning tree.
The rusted barbed wire is starting to heat up.
There are too many hooks entangling.
There are too many flames burning.
This is how the falling leaves spark and ignite.
This is how evolution is illuminated in plain
    sight.

Among the changing of the leaves, down is up,
right is left, up is down, and left is right.
We are all equal in the fire's glowing light.

We all feel the anguish of the choices we have
made—choices that have filled us with hatred
    and spite,
choices that have made us forget the humanity
that once existed in all hearts and minds.

Now we must pay; then we can evolve.
There is no credibility, reputation,
affiliation, or problems to solve here.
This harrowing realm only cares about making
    you pay
for everything that you have done wrong.
It will also force you to memorize the lyrics
and notes of its many scorching songs.
You will have no choice but to sing and scream
    along.

As I journey into infinity, I am wailing like the trees,
fervently conveying my agony. Through the
transformation of the leaves, I present a concluding
portrayal that wraps up my labyrinth of intricate
poetry. Now, brace yourself to uncover what my inner
voices have in store for me.
—*Geoff*

There is No Such Place as Hell

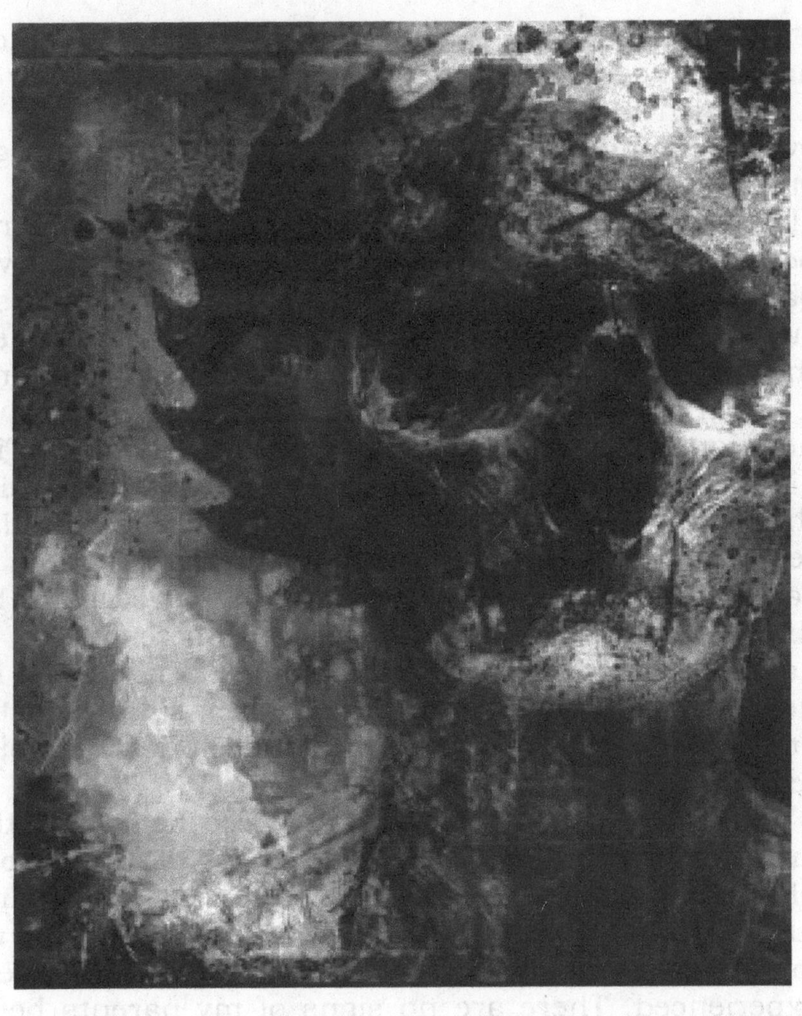

IF YOU'VE MADE it this far, congratulations! It couldn't have been easy to absorb. My voices and my poetry are a labyrinth of emotions and pain that may be overwhelming to some, while also being everything to others. One could say that my writing and poetry are always open to interpretation. My mortal body has now perished in prison. I experienced a sudden, severe pain in my chest and then lost consciousness. I suffered a fatal heart attack while shouting at one of the voices in my head. I am composing this letter from a realm where time is suspended. Conditions here are not significantly different from when I was alive. Time didn't matter then, and it certainly doesn't now. All of the voices in my head have followed me to this dark realm. They are doing the same things, telling the same stories. It's like I'm back in my cage again. But there are no cages here, only the screams of the damned and never-depleting flames. This feels like hell. It's not officially named as such, it simply exists. I am constantly bombarded with the stories my voices tell me.

The walls seem to scream and bleed here, as if they are a collective of tormented souls trying to escape a place that is inescapable. The moaning walls shriek just as they did in my visions. Hands reach for me, forcing me to relive every painful memory I have ever experienced. There are no signs of my parents before their brutal attack here. My brothers Marcus, Daniel, and Nick are also absent. They are only represented through the illustrations I have painted in my consciousness, as they are depicted in my art. Now, I am a work of art, just like all of them. I have been twisted and transformed into an abomination, resembling the monster I was in life. My sunken eyes appear to be rotting, and my nose has also been removed.

Perhaps this is the retribution I deserve for the suffering I caused to those innocent people. However, I must acknowledge that only three of my victims truly deserved such treatment. The men who caused harm to my family deserved what they received. I do not feel any remorse towards those three men. I am still haunted by their taste. The innocent victims also have a distinct taste, reminiscent of putrid pork that has been decaying for weeks, now lodged between my remaining teeth. I have what appears to be a saw blade embedded into my skull. This place taunts me with all that I hold dear. It dangles in front of me all that I was unable to attain. Just as in life, I am tormented here. Oh, what I could have become. Oh, the places I could have ventured. It teases me with my lost youth. Repeatedly, my inner voices cause a division within me. The same visions and emotions that plagued me while incarcerated are present, but they are intensified. The agony they bring is unrelenting. My name is Geoff Hathaway, and there is one final tale to reveal. This time, the story will not be narrated by voices; it will be told to you by me. And of coarse, I am also a part of it.

THERE IS NO SUCH PLACE AS HELL

On a crisp autumn morning, Geoff Hathaway is preparing for his well-deserved vacation to the Bahamas. He has always dreamed of visiting the tropical paradise since he was a child and has finally saved enough money to make his dream come true. He is filled with joy and anticipation to escape the daily hustle and bustle of life. He is not flying, he is taking a cruise ship that will sail in the Atlantic Ocean. He has already packed and is prepared for departure. The ship will leave from Baltimore Harbor at eleven am. He will be driving from Cape Elizabeth, Maine, which is an eight-hour and thirty-eight minute drive. He is a single man without any children and is excited to sail the sea for a couple weeks and just relax and socialize. He has been experiencing some mental health issues lately and is currently taking anti-depressants that appear to be effective for him. He has been experiencing auditory and visual hallucinations, which can be distressing. Since he started taking his medication, they have disappeared. He is relieved because the visions were some of the scariest things that he has ever experienced. He made sure to pack his medication before preparing to depart. He has witnessed distorted images of individuals that no longer resembled humans. They appeared as creatures and zombies. This caused him to experience thoughts that have never crossed his mind before. Thoughts of dismembering people and consuming their flesh and organs. He also had visions of his parents with their throats slashed. Since the medicine has been effective, the doctors have informed him that it is most likely attributed to stress.

He spends most of his time working. He has recently landed his dream job as an artist and writer for a prestigious magazine and has been met with a great deal of success. As he drives, a smile spreads across his face as he reflects on all of this. He is ready to enjoy himself, to feel alive, and not to be burdened with worries about bills and life. His new job allowed him to pay all of his bills on time. Prior to obtaining that job, he had struggled to merely afford basic necessities. He had been juggling multiple minimum wage tasks that drained his time. However, his new position had a profound impact on his life. As he reflects on his accomplishments, he notices a billboard for Inner Harbor in Baltimore, Maryland. *"I have arrived!"* He exclaimed triumphantly. After parking his car and paying for the couple weeks that it would sit in the storage lot, he made his way to the harbor. Many people were also preparing for the same beautiful cruise as he was. He grabbed his bags and boarded the massive ship, making his way to his assigned room—238. He then strolled through the ship's expansive corridors until he arrived at his designated chamber. The room boasted a generous window, a king-sized bed, and even a hot tub. *"This is incredible!"* He exclaimed.

He placed his bags down on the floor and lied down in the massive bed. Exhausted from his eight-hour commute, he decided to rest for awhile. As he slept, vivid and terrifying visions flooded his subconscious. These abominations taunted him and demanded that he obey their commands. A vision of a woman aflame with barbed wire hooks embedded in her eye sockets. Images of himself distorted and transformed into a being not of this realm. He abruptly woke up in a clammy state and reached for a bottle of water that had been left by the cruise company. After taking a gulp, he reached for his bag. He needs to take his medication to calm down. He searched through his bag and could not locate his medication. He rifled through his pockets and all the items he had brought, but could not find it. Finally, he recalled that it was on the passenger seat of his car, which was parked in Baltimore harbor. 'Oh No!' He exclaimed. He peered out the window and realized the ocean was all he could see. The ship must have set sail while he was sleeping. He didn't have his medication with him. It wasn't long before the dreaded hallucinations resurfaced. Each of them had a request for him, and they seemed to be relentless in their pursuit. He was worried that something terrible was going to happen. Covering his ears, he refused to listen. *"Go Away! Leave me in peace! I refuse to give you what you want from me!"* The voices persist in whispering and urging him to do horrible things. They desire for him to kill, to consume, to turn the cruise ship into a tragedy. Despite his best efforts, he struggles to resist their influence as they slowly consume his psyche. Ultimately, he succumbs to insanity and blacked out.

He woke up in the engine room of the ship, feeling confused. He couldn't figure out how he got there and realized he had been in this room before. However, he had no recollection of his journey to the engine room. In an attempt to regain his composure, he stood up and shook his head from side to side. He searched for a door, however, it was not in sight due to the complete darkness. In the process, he stumbled over an unidentified object, causing him to his head on a solid surface. Despite feeling the blood trickle down his forehead, he persisted in his determination to uncover the object that had caused him to trip. He fumbled around on the floor, unable to see, until he discovered the object he had stumbled over. It had the texture of a human body. In a panic, he desperately searched for an escape route and eventually succeeded. However, what greeted him as he opened the door was a terrifying scene.

He looked down from the light shining in and saw a woman lying on the floor, motionless. She lay there in a pool of her own blood, with what appeared to be bite marks on her neck. *"What the fuck?!"* He screamed. He then looked down at his hands and saw that they were both covered in blood. It wasn't his blood because it had dried. He then closed the door and sprinted as fast as he could, hoping not to be seen. He tucked his hands in his pockets, pulled his hood up over his head, and ran to his room. He successfully made it and quickly shut and locked the door. He ran into the bathroom to wash the blood off of his hands. When he looked at his reflection, he froze. There was dried blood all around his mouth and his teeth were stained with blood. *"I couldn't have killed that woman!"* He screamed at himself. He felt the paranoia kick in, and then his voices started speaking to him again. They said, *"Well done, Geoff. You've passed our very first test. How does it feel to have blood in your mouth and on your hands?* Geoff's eyes grew wide as he answered, *"I didn't do this! This isn't real! I'm not a killer, and this situation makes no sense!"*

The voices persisted in their explanation that he was, in fact, the perpetrator. Fueled by desperation and confusion, he sprinted to the shower in an attempt to rid himself of the evidence on his skin. He brushed his teeth vigorously, but the metallic taste of copper remained, a constant reminder of his predicament. Asking himself, *"What have I done? How did this problem come about?*

What should I do next?" A rush of paranoia seized his thoughts. He contemplated the prospect of life in prison and the utter horror it would bring. He was consumed by the thought of losing the life that he had tirelessly built for himself. He pondered the possibility of losing everything. In a moment of desperation, he muttered, "I could really use a drink right now."

When he finally regained his composure and processed everything, he decided to go out on deck and order a much-needed, strong alcoholic beverage. He knew he had to do something to cope with the events that had just occurred. Little did he know, this was only the beginning of the Geoff Hathaway murder show. He walked up to the bar and ordered a straight bourbon on the rocks, his favorite drink. He needed it badly after what had just happened. He kept envisioning the pool of blood under the woman in the ship's engine room. He chugged the first glass as if he were dehydrated. The voices in his head began to stir once again, screaming at at him to kill once more. *"Kill Geoff, kill! Kill Geoff, kill! Your deepest desires await. So many thrilling pleasures are in your reach."* Geoff then smacked himself in the head and yelled: *"Stop it! No! I will not give in to violence!"*

He hadn't realized that he had screamed all of that out loud. Everyone in the bar was staring at him in horror and silence. He ordered one more bourbon and left the scene. He walked over to the edge of the deck, gazing out into the dark ocean, and let out a sigh of relief, releasing all of his built-up stress. He was relieved to be away from all of those individuals who had heard his screams. *"Shit!"* He screamed. *"The body!"* He feared that someone would discover it and remember his outburst at the bar, ultimately identifying him as the killer. He had to devise a strategy to retrieve the woman's body and dispose of it into the depths of the ocean without being seen. He then lost consciousness for the second time. When he regained it, he couldn't believe the destruction he had caused. The bartender who served him his bourbon on the rocks, along with the entire room of people, now lay dead in a pool of their own blood. He had not encountered a single living being.

With great urgency, he combed through every part of the ship, finding no survivors in any of the rooms he searched. He had taken the lives of everyone on board, including the Captain, leaving no one to navigate the now ghost-like vessel. He was alone on a ship full of corpses, adrift on an unrelenting sea with only his thoughts for company and his sanity drifting away. Drifting onto an endless sea of spilled blood and voices, drifting into a vast salty plain of torture and disbelief, rubbing sea salt into every open wound he has, drifting into a world of shattered dreams and horrific memories of things that have been altered and abandoned, drifting into his actions that cannot be undone, and how things are in this present moment. He continued to chant repetitively saying, *"There is no such place as Hell. There is no such place as Hell. There is no such place as Hell."* The sea suddenly opened up, revealing a demon whipping its tail. The entire ship then went down and vanished into the depths of the abyss, ushering him into the other side of the veil. The salty unknown then closed gluttonous mouth, having received its fill. The sea gives just as much for the wicked as it does for those of goodwill. It signifies the relationship between evil and nature, a contract that must be fulfilled.

There is no such place as 'Hell'. This, I can assure you, is a fact. This place is not called 'Hell.' It is not called anything. It is a dark void that causes unrelenting agony. It makes one pay for their actions, tearing apart their mind and sucking their consciousness right out of their body. It is aware of your fears and knows your true identity, even the monster you were when you were alive. It is capable of destroying you from within, and the three men who took my family are now beside me, dismembering me as I once did to them. I am currently surrounded by a raging inferno of distinctly colored flames. I am experiencing every burn, cut, and twist.

The voices in my head in this place are becoming increasingly violent. I am certain that this torment will never cease. The multi-colored flames of this place burn with stark contrast—black with a delicate baby blue center. They envelop me, morphing into new shapes continuously. They are not how they are portrayed in life. There is nothing here but fire, suffering, emptiness and dread.

The biblical text was so wrong about this place. I read so much about it when I was alive, yet there is no sign of my beloved Jennie here. She was my only source of comfort. I wish she were here now. Instead, all I see are twisted abominations of her, laughing at my pain and fear. My parents and my brothers are all still monsters here. I haven't seen their faces in reality since their throats were slit ear to ear.

This is my reality now. Everything is wrong here. Everything was wrong in life. I did this to myself and I knew that someday I would have to pay the price. Here, I will remain eternally in an unnamed location. I will forever be engulfed in the vivid hues of baby blue and black flames. The voices in your mind are something that must always be feared. There has never been a means of escape from them, and there will never be a way out of this place. Forever I hear and see the voices in my head, forever consumed by fear. I am no longer the tiger, I have become the wounded deer.

THE END—or is it?

My name is Geoff Hathaway. Well, it used to be.

Listen closely to your nightmares and fear the voices in your head.

It is never the end.

Jeff Oliver – Author

JEFF OLIVER was born in Baltimore, Maryland on April 6th, 1982. A passionate poet and devoted father of eight beautiful children, his commitment to both his family and his craft is unparalleled. Currently residing in Western New York State, he is a writer who evokes intense emotions through his work. Despite facing the destructive darkness, he weaves lyrical poetic justice into an unjust world, when others may have succumbed to its devastation. His published works include Venomous Words (Independently published), Strange Sounds (Independently published), and Poetic Fiction: Journals of Silent Screams (Independently Published) as well as Drops Of Insanity, Scattered Thoughts: Volumes I, II, and III, Blood and Verse (Cosby Media Productions), New World Monsters (Hellbound Books). Additionally, Infinite Black: Tales from the Abyss (Independently Published), INKBLOTS: A Poet's Perception (300 South Media Group), and Dark Echoes Within Silence (Independent Legions Publishing)

Dan Verkys – Artist

DAN VERKYS has been a graphic designer and artist for over 25 years, specializing in digital compositing. His artwork revolves around the combination of 3D rendered forms and photographic manipulation, with a focus on the dark fantasy genre. Dan has had the privilege of collaborating with numerous skilled musicians, entertainers, authors, and other artists who hold a similar perspective on the world. Monsters have also played a significant role in his life, as he has had a fondness for classic horror films and literature since a young age. Despite being an intensely private person, his art has given him a voice that has resonated with countless people around the world. Through his artistic expression, he has discovered a means to aid both himself and others in dealing with love, grief, and various personal battles.